THE BLUE ROOM

Borgo Press Books by S. Fowler Wright

Arresting Delia: An Inspector Cleveland Classic Crime Novel
The Attic Murder: An Inspector Combridge & Mr. Jellipot Classic Crime Novel
The Bell Street Murders: An Inspector Combridge & Mr. Jellipot Classic Crime Novel
Beyond the Rim: A Lost Race Fantasy
Black Widow: A Classic Crime Novel
The Blue Room: A Novel of an Alternate Future
The British Colonies: No Surrender to Nazi Germany!
The Capone Caper: Mr. Jellipot vs. the King of Crime: A Classic Crime Novel
Crime & Co.: An Inspector Cleveland Classic Crime Novel
Dawn: A Novel of Global Warming
Dead by Saturday: An Inspector Cleveland Classic Crime Novel
Dream; or, The Simian Maid: A Fantasy of Prehistory (Marguerite Cranleigh #1)
Elfwin: An Historical Novel of Anglo-Saxon Times
The End of the Mildew Gang: An Inspector Cauldron Classic Crime Novel (Mildew #3)
Four Callers in Razor Street: An Inspector Combridge & Mr. Jellipot Classic Crime Novel
Four Days' War: The Alternate World War II, Book Two
The Hanging of Constance Hillier: An Inspector Cleveland Classic Crime Novel
The Hidden Tribe: A Lost Race Fantasy
The Jordans Murder: An Inspector Combridge & Mr. Jellipot Classic Crime Novel
The King Against Anne Bickerton: A Classic Crime Novel
Megiddo's Ridge: The Alternate World War II, Book Three
The Mildew Gang: An Inspector Cauldron Classic Crime Novel (Mildew #1)
Murder in Bethnal Square: An Inspector Combridge & Mr. Jellipot Classic Crime Novel
The Police and the Public: Some Thoughts on the British System of Justice
Post-Mortem Evidence: An Inspector Combridge & Mr. Jellipot Classic Crime Novel
Prelude in Prague: The Alternate World War II, Book One
Red Ike: A Novel of Cumberland (with J. M. Denwood)
The Return of the Mildew Gang: An Inspector Cauldron Classic Crime Novel (Mildew #2)
The Rissole Mystery: An Inspector Combridge & Mr. Jellipot Classic Crime Novel
The Screaming Lake: A Lost Race Fantasy
The Secret of the Screen: An Inspector Combridge & Mr. Jellipot Classic Crime Novel
The Song of Songs and Other Poems
Spiders' War: A Novel of the Far Future (Marguerite Cranleigh #3)
Three Witnesses: A Classic Crime Novel
Too Much for Mr. Jellipot: An Inspector Combridge & Mr. Jellipot Classic Crime Novel
The Vengeance of Gwa: A Fantasy of Prehistory (Marguerite Cranleigh #2)
Was Murder Done? A Classic Crime Novel
Who Murdered Reynard? A Classic Crime Novel
The Wills of Jane Kanwhistle: An Inspector Combridge & Mr. Jellipot Classic Crime Novel
With Cause Enough?: An Inspector Combridge & Mr. Jellipot Classic Crime Novel

THE BLUE ROOM

A NOVEL OF AN ALTERNATE FUTURE

by

S. FOWLER WRIGHT

WRITING AS "SYDNEY FOWLER"

THE BORGO PRESS

An Imprint of Wildside Press LLC

MMIX

I. SOMETHING ABOUT CATTLE

"GOD FORGIVE ME," Édouard Richter said to himself, as he left the white, straight-windowed building in the Quai d'Orsay where the Committee of Public Safety met, and entered his waiting car—"God forgive me, but it will be the best way in the end."

The expression was no more than an atavism of speech, for it was a June evening of 1990, and Édouard Richter, youngest and most brilliant member of the Committee on which the security, if not the existence, of Europe depended, was not likely to have his mind encumbered by any superstition of the existence of a personal deity.

But the clear light of science had not yet proved sufficient to overcome the weaknesses of human emotion, or the instabilities of the human will, and the decision from which he had come might well effect the serenity of the man who was primarily responsible for it, though those who knew him best would not have understood the particular mental disturbance which his exclamation disclosed, for it arose from a knowledge that was still private to his own mind.

Yet the decision to which he had listened less than half an hour before was one which might make his name famous as a world-conqueror for long ages to come. It might leave whatever should remain of a victorious Europe offering gifts at his feet. That was, if it should succeed, about which he had no doubt whatever. And for itself—what was it but an affair of cattle?

So greatly, in half a century, had the humanity of science mitigated the old ferocities of war!

There had been—it is only fair to recognize that—an intervening episode. There had been the Great War. That is the name which is given to every widespread conflict, till the next one obliterates it from the minds of men. This—the war of 1979—had not been barren of horror. But it had been barren of victory. It had left no post-war problems for the embarrassment of the exhausted belligerents, for those belligerents had ceased to be. When the war ended, two-thirds of Asia was a poisonous waste from which human life had disappeared completely. Ten years after, it was empty still. For the

Great Powers that remained—the United States of Europe, the Commonwealth of English-Speaking Nations, and the Latin-American Union—had seen the folly of destroying themselves in a new struggle for its possession, and any suitable agreement had still been beyond the resources of the statesmanship of the world, when this new war had suddenly broken out.

But this one was to be without the horrors of the older and more barbarous conflicts. With the warning before their eyes of the desolated Asian plains, where a hundred million human corpses had rotted, and where tigers and cobras bred among the ruins of their empty homes, the remaining Great Powers had faced the fact that scientific civilization could not endure such another war.

The idea of a League of Nations had still survived, though it had moved its locality, reconstructed its constitution, and changed its name.

The formation of the United States of Europe having rendered Geneva a situation for its deliberations unsatisfactory to the English Commonwealth, it had been decided that Latin-America, as being somewhat weaker than the three other world-Federations (one of which had now disintegrated and disappeared), would be a more suitable location. It had been established at Quetta. There it was to be serene, above the contentions of a fretful world. It was the Council of the Clouds.

It had faced this problem of conflict, on which the existence of its civilization—it called it the existence of humanity, which was rhetoric rather than a statement of logical consequence—depended. It had been decided that it would be impracticable to eradicate the instinct for war, or to avert the possibility, however remote, that it would break out again. It had sought therefore to arrive at such rules of conflict as would be generally accepted, and would be likely to be honourably observed. After several years of argument and negotiation, it had formulated a method and rules of strife to which the Three Great Federations (which the destruction of Asia had left in entire possession of the earth's surface) had affixed their solemn signatures, and which their peoples had approved and acclaimed as providing a sufficient severity of conflict, while removing the probability that a future war would be of an inevitable and universal fatality.

It was generally recognized that the next war, as had been that which had made a desert of Asia, would be one not of steel or muscle, or of the primitive violence of high explosive, or the crude clumsiness of poison gases which the wind might turn, but of the quiet deadliness of the test-tube, the secret processes of the laboratory.

Each of the three great powers had its research workers whose discoveries were reported, in vague whisperings which their own governments may have encouraged, to be of new and very dreadful kinds. If the folly of war should yet again threaten the foundations of scientific civilization, let it be contested in orderly scientific ways. Let the complainant Group have the first right to let loose any aggressive weapon which did not directly menace the lives of its opponents, and let the scientists of the assaulted lands show their skill in neutralizing its effects. Should they succeed, so that the attack had failed to bring them to the point of submission within three months, then the challenging nation should let loose a counterattack which should be limited only by the same rule. So in turn might each assail the other, till one should admit defeat.

If these rules were broken, then the neutrality of the third power should be cast aside, and all the weight of its own strength be put forth against the delinquent, in whatever form, for it would be loosed against those who would have outlawed themselves from the comity of civilization.

So it had been agreed among the three powers, who had resolved with equal solemnity that nothing would lead them to the folly of further warfare, even though it were restricted by such rules as these. And then, sudden and fierce, the cause of conflict came, and the temper of conflict rose.

The trouble was that the English Commonwealth had warmed a sea. That, in itself, was no crime. It was near no lands but their own, being that which lay between their peopled territories and the Antarctic continent, which was also theirs. By this act they had enormously increased the supply of certain fish which had become of a high commercial value since the last whale had died. That was all to their own, and the world's, gain.

But the United States of Europe looked at it in a different way. They complained of a change of wind. To change a wind was a breach of international law. There could be no dispute about that. The Warsaw Convention of 1959 had laid it down in words which were beyond disputation. That had followed the successful experiment by which the genius of Lebrun had brought rain-clouds to the Sahara, and presented the United States of Europe with an enormous fertile plain in Northern Africa, which was now occupied by seven million European colonists. No one had complained about that. It had had no sinister consequence on a large scale, though there had been some unforeseen disturbance to navigation, and a liner had gone down with the loss of a thousand lives.

But the experiment had raised questions, which the Convention had faced, for the future peace of the world. If to change one wind could bring rain to your own, to change another might bring drought to a neighbouring land. It had been solemnly resolved that no nation in future should change a wind without the common consent.

But the English Federation said that they had not changed a wind. They had done nothing but warm a sea. If a change of air-currents had followed (which they did not admit), who could blame them for that? If such a principle were allowed, where would it stop? Almost every human activity had some effect on the winds. There were the crops that draw moisture from the air. The dryness of air influenced the direction in which it moved. Must they ask their neighbours' permission before deciding what crops they would sow? It was a self-evident absurdity. They repeated that they had not changed a wind. They had no desire to do so. The air-currents had been well enough as they were. All they had done was to warm a sea.

The United States of Europe replied that that difference had made a profound disturbance in the great winds of the world. It threatened the climate of Europe in unendurable ways. This was a natural consequence of their action, which the scientists of the Rhodesian Institute should have been able to calculate in advance. Indeed, if their first object had been to change a wind, what more natural method could they have adopted than that of warming a sea?

The issue had not been one which could be lightly decided, nor on which unemotional logic could be expected from either side. The stake was too great. The change of wind which had been evident for one season, and might be of a constant recurrence, threatened to reduce the fertility of Europe to a precariously low level. On the other hand, the prosperity of the southern portion of the eastern hemisphere was vitally staked upon the new temperature of its Antarctic waters.

What government could ask its citizens to accept privation that another race might enjoy prosperity in larger measure? The English Federation temporized. Could not the combined scientific resources of the world find some method of dealing with the difficulty which would be satisfactory to all? It proposed a conference. The United States of Europe consulted its Committee of Public Safety. Confident in the assurances it received, it rejected the proposal, and declared war.

By the new laws, the aggressive party had the first right of attack. It must give fourteen days' notice of the injury which it proposed to inflict upon its opponent, who could use that period for the making of peace if the threat were one which it was not prepared to endure, or which its own scientists were not prepared to resist.

Now the Committee of Public Safety of the European Federation, which had succeeded the War Offices of the old barbarous times, had met and decided, amongst a selected number of the methods of attack which had been prepared by its members against such an emergency, to adopt that of Herr Édouard Richter in the first instance, for it seemed an exceptional improbability that any antidote to it ravages should be discovered; and, should it fail, they could still try the more terrible expedient of M. Labord. For they had no dread of the intervening attack of the English Federation which they must be prepared to sustain, they having purchased, as they believed, at an enormous and yet trivial price, both the secret plans of their opponents, and the methods which would be sufficient to reduce them to nullity.

So, in due form, they arranged to notify their opponents of the date and nature of the first assault which would be delivered against them.

II. THE ADVANTAGES OF A GOOD MEMORY

PARIS HAD CHANGED little in the last century. The war that had commenced in 1939 and continued during the larger part of the following decade, having been fought by the crude methods of high explosive, had done much to alter the face of Europe, and to prepare its cities' for the architecture of the following period; but Paris, having escaped damage by the treason or cowardice of those who should have been the inspiration of its resistance, had been subsequently selected by the Council of the new European Federation to be preserved as an example of old-world architecture, furnishing, and social customs.

It was a decision which French opinion had received with discord, some maintaining that it was an exceptional honour, the Council of Europe having suitably recognized the pre-eminence of its most beautiful city, so preserving an excellence which would become more evident as it would be increasingly contrasted with the utilitarian building of succeeding years; and others regarding it as a more dubious distinction, such as would emphasize forever the craven policy which had preserved it from the destructions of siege and storm.

Where some are doubtful and others resolved, the issue will be to those of a settled mind. Paris stood as it was: not merely excused the mania for reconstruction which entailed so much destruction of ancient, lovely, and precious things throughout the rest of the continent, but deliberately preserved in its archaic form. Its crooked streets remained unstraightened, its narrow boulevards unwidened, its hills were not blasted flat. Even the obvious convenience of a central airport was prohibited. Its distinction had become greater in contrast with the utilitarian architecture of a time which had made comfort and security its ignoble gods. It had been left deliberately without land or air protection, having been declared by a charter, to which every government of the whole world had subscribed, to be outside the sphere of any future hostilities. It may have been owing to this fact, though they had other plausible pretexts, that the European Committee of Public Safety had held this secret decisive meeting in its neutral area.

Now Édouard Richter returned to his unobtrusive but most exclusive hotel in the Boulevard des Italiens, and prepared to make a prompt removal to the Stuttgart Laboratory, which he owned and controlled, and the secrets of which made him one of the crownless kings of his day. One of the crownless kings? By the spring of the next year he meant to be more than that. He meant to do, with cold efficiency, that which the blundering Hitler had attempted fifty years before. He might become far more generally feared. He might become more universally hated. He had no occasion to care. For he knew that there would be the vital difference that every man would desire to guard the health of Édouard Richter as sedulously as his own.

Amelie was alone when he entered. She was stretched on an old-style couch, and was dressed to match the ancient atmosphere of the room. But she was one who would have been beautiful by any standards, at any time, and to whatever period she might have been dressed and groomed.

"Settled it?" she asked lazily, without raising her eyes to his.

"Yes. They will try my formula first. The ultimatum will go tonight."

"Poor beasts!" she said lightly. And then: "I expect we shall be going back?"

"We'll think about dinner now."

"I never think about dinner without being glad that I wasn't born until after 1952."

"It must have been a good deal later than that."

"A fair bit…I expect you know."

"Not at all. I never burden my mind with any nonessential fact. I know everything about you that is necessary to me."

"Well, that's something!" she said lightly. There was no real intimacy between them, but there was a bond of mutual interest and dependence which may give an even stronger security than the loyalties of friendship or love. He had given her everything that she had. He promised her more, to the limit of all desires. And they both knew that she had become irreplaceably necessary to him.

He had searched the world to find her. He was assured that she had the best memory in the world. That memory was now the depository of the results of many secret experiments, of innumerable formulæ as potent as the magic spells of the fairy tales of an older time: things far too dangerous to be committed to the hazards of paper, things which must be stored without other record in his memory and hers. Some which—though he guarded this secret well—had become too numerous and complicated for retention in his own mind, so that, should he require them, he would be entirely dependent upon her.

Her allusion to 1952 had, of course, been to the great Food Riots which, during that year, had deluged Europe with blood. The trouble had its origin in the rationing system which had been copied from the British Food Office, and had been continued long after it had been abandoned by the land of its conception.

The British Food Office had entrenched itself strongly during the war which had given it birth. At its conclusion it had urged, with some force of reason, that rationing must be continued in a world which was hungry, and in which shipping was inadequate for all requirements.

It had then produced elaborate formulæ for what it called "scientifically balanced" diets for all ages and all manners of life. It promised its disciples (who, at first, had been numerous and enthusiastic) that, as the food situation eased, the danger of monotony should be avoided by alternative diets, for any of which people of suitable categories could register on giving the three months' notice which difficulties of supply and distribution required. It called this latitude the "theory of equivalence," and advanced it as evidence of its desire to leave individual freedom undisturbed, so far as might be compatible with the paramount necessity of maintaining national health.

It required, and obtained, parliamentary sanction for controlling agricultural production, so that no farmer could sow turnips, no market-gardener grow a field of peas, without its licence. It argued, reasonably, that, without this authority, it could not undertake to feed the nation with the rational diet which it considered their health required.

It was given the right to prosecute people who were so lawlessly indifferent to the requirements of their own health, as defined by the Ministry's expert advisers, that they would exchange items of their rations with people in other categories, so that both would suffer from the unsuitability of what they ate. The difficulties of preventing this pernicious form of health sabotage, especially among members of a family, were recognized to be too great for any but the most drastic penalties to suppress it; and when a young woman, being convicted of bartering the whole of her meat and bacon rations for a month for the family's chocolate, was sentenced to two years' imprisonment, the Press described it as a too lenient sentence, while finding satisfaction in the thought that she would be scientifically fed for some time to come—a reflection which raised the doubt of whether it could be properly described as a punishment at all.

The climax came when it was disclosed that the Ministry had ordered that the growth of spinach should be increased by 140,000 acres, from which it was readily deduced that the population was to be fed on larger quantities of this reputable herbage during the following year.

Appreciation of spinach is not universal, and those who dislike it usually do so with emphasis. They proved to be an unexpectedly large, and annoyingly vocal, minority. Liberty of action in Britain had, at this time, been almost entirely eliminated, but considerable freedom of speech remained. In the height of this controversy, an enterprising journalist secured, and photographed, the menu-card which had been issued for a Food Ministry banquet, and then, amid a roar of execration, the Food Ministry went down to its belated grave. The Minister became a viscount, his staff were distributed to other ministries, and a number of wholesale firms recognized that they were likely to pay less income-tax than had become their annual habit.

But in Europe, where food scarcity had been more acute, and distributional difficulties greater, the plague continued until 1952, by which time it had become an established organization, with vested interests which appeared too strong to be overset. And then, even more suddenly than in England, the storm had broken, and over the same worthy but unpopular vegetable.

At that time a large proportion of the inhabitants of Europe had become so used to hearing of the imposition of brutal penalties for slight offences, particularly if they were of a political character, that it had been found impossible to maintain public order, especially in Germany, by inflicting sentences of normal leniency, so that it had become a humanitarian custom to deal with most convicts by imposing suspended sentences of gradually diminishing brutality. It had been calculated during the previous year that there were actually over three hundred thousand people in Western Europe who had been sentenced to death, and who were legally liable to be called up for judgment at any time.

It followed that when a child of ten absolutely refused to eat her ration of spinach, it excited no indignation and little notice when she was sentenced to death, it being added that the sentence would be suspended for six months, and then indefinitely, if it should be reported by the inspecting officer that she had become docile to the orders which she received, as it was assumed that she would.

But the unexpected happened. The increasingly apprehensive parents lied vainly in assertion that she ate the provided vegetable. The inspector made many calls. He was persuasive. He was patient. He tried threatening. But all was vain. The child, tearlessly stubborn, said, and appeared literally to mean: "I would rather die."

So a small matter became great. A state cannot afford to be persistently defied by a child of ten. And this child, if its resistance should succeed, would have shown a way by which all the children, at least, if not the adult members of the community, might bring scientific feeding to utter wreck.

It is useless to impose fines on a child which it cannot pay. It may have no goods which can be seized. You may imprison it, but what if that should have no effect? You cannot imprison all the children of the nation without much resulting disorder, with consequences more disastrous than the overcrowding of cinemas by parents who are having an easy time. The question became serious: should the sentence be executed? As time passed, it became imminent. Suddenly, riot flamed. The premises of a Food Office in Ghent were mobbed. There was an attempt to set them on fire. The international military force (scrupulously called police in the post-war Europe of the mid-century) fired on the mob. But while it was overawed, and the dead and wounded were being cleared from the street, and vans were being filled with arrested men, a warehouse in another part of the city was entered (it was said by some that it had been thrown open to the crowd by the treachery of its own staff), and was looted of so many tons of dates and sugar that it had become a physical impossibility for the Ministry to provide a properly balanced diet over a wide area for the following fortnight—the position being made worse by the fact that distribution had become exactly organized, and large reserves were not held.

Within forty-eight hours, the example of Ghent had been followed in almost every city of Western Europe. The plundering of food warehouses produced such confusion that law-abiding citizens could no longer be properly fed. Even during the first week of these disorders there was a case in Berlin where slaters, doing open-air work, were issued food containing precisely the same vitamins as was supplied to decorators, whose requirements, as they were engaged upon interior work, could not be identical. Naturally, the decorators struck work and went to lie on the roof.

For nearly three weeks the Federal Government of Europe struggled against the storm, fortified by the assurance of the food experts that the energy of the rebels must decline rapidly as the confusion of vitamins would increase within them. But if this were so, its operation was not swift enough to be decisive. There came a time when even the troops were beyond control, declining to throw bombs at those who threw food at them. Amid a general howl of triumph the Food Ministries were swept away. The lives of some thousands of their more prominent or zealous officials were saved by sending them to an Imbeciles' Home, which was prepared for their exclusive reception. It was named Insanity House, as the whole world knew; but the kind President of Europe had given authority to the sign-painter to leave a short space between the second and third letters of the first word, so that it became an assurance to its inmates that they were the sane exceptions to a lunatic world.

In the disorderly days that followed, the prices of food, after some extreme fluctuations, fell permanently as they had done in England under similar conditions) from the high levels at which the Food Ministry had maintained them; and the people lived or died as their muddled vitamins might allow. Édouard Richter understood very easily when Amelie said that she was glad that she had been born after 1952.

"Have much trouble?" she asked in the same drawling, detached voice as before, which maintained conversation pleasantly enough, but as though she had no personal concern in the matter of which she spoke. Perhaps it was natural—a correct attitude in one who was his hired secretary, in constant companionship only because she was the depository of his mind, into which, at any moment, he might have something further to enter.

"Not much," he replied. "Betz wanted them to try his contraction formula. Fatal enough, of course. But I told them I knew three ways in which they could settle that, and it would be odd if they couldn't discover one of the three. I told them I would stake my life that they'd find no answer to mine."

"Yes, I suppose we do."

"Yes. But they didn't mean that."

"No. Of course not. It would be awkward if we should both happen to die."

"Awkward for the rest of the world. But that wouldn't matter to us then."

"No. I don't see that it would."

For a moment her dark eyes were lifted to look speculatively at the great scientist whom she was so highly privileged to serve, and to whom she rendered a service few others, if any, could. It was strange how easily most people forgot. Why should they? When you heard something, or read it, the natural thing was to remember. The difficulty—perhaps the impossibility—would have been to forget.

But she wasn't thinking of that now, as she looked at a man who was not looking at her. Her thought was: "Suppose he should die, and I live. What would he expect me to do then?"

She had the kind of wisdom that knows when silence is best. It was not an eventuality which he would be likely to care to discuss. He might even detect disloyalty in the thought. And he was one whom it would be easy to dread. Especially knowing all of him, and his plans, that had been necessarily confided to her. Perhaps he was to be dreaded all the more because he was, as she well knew, a weak man. But she looked at him, and whatever discretion she might exercise, she was not conscious of any fear. She was too absolutely necessary to him. And when had she been less than loyal at any time, either in word or act?

Indeed, she might have asked the opposite question: What would he do if she were to die? But, again, silence was best.

She said: "I've been thinking—"

"Yes. About what?" There was surprise in his voice. He did not credit her with capacity for thought. It was something which he did not require her to do. And he considered it to be a scientific certainty that, with her abnormal capacity for remembering, capacity for thought would be proportionately subnormal. And when anyone of his training and traditions applied the adjective "scientific" to any conclusion, it became a closed issue, concerning which there was nothing more to be thought or said.

"I've been thinking you'll have to keep quite a lot alive if there's to be much comfort left in the world."

He answered her seriously, for it was a question which had become the constant preoccupation of his own mind: "It is the most important matter I have to decide now; and it is one which I should have been glad to have more time to consider. I hoped that war wouldn't have come for at least a couple of years yet, and by that time I should have been ready, war or not, to go ahead in my own way."

"Yes. You don't need a war at all. It's just forcing your hand."

So it was. Without war, at his own time, he could have brought the civilization of man to an end, or under his control, in his own way. But now that war had come, he must be first to act, lest he should be himself the victim of some incalculable enemy action, different, but as deadly, as that he himself designed for his fellow men.... A waiter bowed at the door. "Madame, Monsieur," he said, "dinner is served."

III. THE DIFFICULTIES OF A GREAT PLAN

THE MAN WHO had little doubt that he would soon be the unquestioned lord of a world reduced to his own measure, and controlled to his own ends, found that he had no power to induce sleep, which declined to come.

He had sufficient knowledge of his own nature, and that of narcotics, to avoid drug-taking, and, as a rule, being one who worked hard, he slept well.

But in his mind there was a coward's doubt, which he could not still. Was he great enough to bring this stupendous dream to a good end? By a good end, he meant one which would be for his own comfort and well-being, and would give him supreme power.

When he had first discovered the virus which would sweep away all mammalian life—unless it should be inoculated with the antidote of which only he and his secretary would know—he had thought of destroying the whole human race, with the exception of a small number of women, thinking vaguely that all the riches of earth would then be his.

But further thought had shown him the fallacy of this plan. Excepting such forms of wealth as would be already accumulated, and of durable kinds, he saw that a single man, surrounded by all the riches of earth, would be condemned to a life of toil. After a time, even means of transit would not be maintained without much menial work, and then only in primitive or diminishing forms. Should he save a few horses? He knew little of what service they would require, but he saw easily that they would not feed or water themselves in the winter days. He had once seen a man clip a horse's coat in the spring. He had no desire to do that.

He was not sufficiently modest, or sufficiently self-analytic, to observe that this desire for the elimination of his fellow men was evidence of subconscious recognition of his own limitations. The necessity for a pattern—for an orderly form—so repugnant to Nature, is felt by all finite minds. And, however monstrous his dream, the pattern to which he would naturally work would be very small. A man may have a profound knowledge of physics, and yet be unfit either to govern or guide.

He did not observe this, but he wished that he had had longer time to ponder, and to resolve. He felt a sense of irritation, as of one who was being unfairly rushed. He would have so little time to decide who should be kept alive, and how their security was to be arranged without their knowledge; or how, if they should be told, it should be made certain that they would not act in ways which would be disastrous to him. Self-interest—the kindred motives of hope and fear—would be sufficient to silence most. But there are some of whom you can never be quite sure.

He hesitated, as he had done more than once before, over the idea of destroying only the English-Speaking Commonwealth and the Latin-American Federation, leaving the Federation of Europe to occupy an empty world. The jealousies which had left the vast barrenness of Asia unoccupied would be swept away. Europe would be the heir of the world. But it would not be easy to arrange, nor sure in its results for himself. He might be blamed, rather than praised, for doing so great a thing without the authority of the Council of Europe. And to do it—to take the precautions which would save the inhabitants of Europe—without premature knowledge of their fate coming to the outside world, would be difficult in several ways. Even as he had planned it to be, there must be a period of danger, when desperation might strike back blindly in ways hard to foresee or avoid.

He determined that he would commence at once to make a selection of those which it would be politic to preserve, not, at first, resolving on any total figure, but making individual selections, which he would communicate to the safe and secret depository of Amelie's memory as they would come to his own mind.

On the relief of this resolution, he should have slept, but he had a tumult of thought which he could not still, so that he was glad when the dawn came.

Delayed by the archaic necessity of driving by car to an airport which was ten miles from the centre of Paris, he yet caught a plane which landed him at Stuttgart during the morning hours, and before noon he was in the laboratories in which he had done work of recognized brilliance during previous years, and in which he reigned in unquestioned supremacy.

Here he had much to do, much to direct, so that action must hinder thought. At three in the afternoon he was on the telephone to the European Ambassador at Havana, giving him precise information as to the threatened action which he was to announce to the Premier of the English-Speaking Federation before returning to Europe. It might yet be that the threat would be sufficient to secure a last-moment peace; and he was conscious that such a solution, postponing the occasion for decisive action, would have brought him a great relief.

IV. ULTIMATUM

WHEN THE GENIUS of King David united, for a brief period, the alien races of Israel and Judea, he observed the impossibility of inducing either of them to accept a capital city in the opposite territory, and so, leaving Hebron and Shechem to equal obscurity, he took Jerusalem from the Jebusites and established a royal city which ad been foreign to both nations before. The United States and the British Dominions had resolved contending jealousies in a similar, though less violent, manner, by building a new capital city upon land which was neutralized for that purpose.

When the Commonwealth of the English-Speaking Nations was formed, it became evident that the greatest difficulty would not be the English royal family, which the majority of Americans were rather keen to accept, but the selection of a city in which the Council of the Federation would deliberate, and which would have the prestige and prosperity which must belong to the centre of so vast a power.

It was clear that Washington and London would be equally impossible. The suggestion of Capetown had a partial popularity, which was not sufficient to sustain it.

In the end, three places were selected, none of which was upon the territory of a major member of the proposed union, and the final choice was made by a solemn lottery, safeguarded by many ingenuities against the possibility of fraud.

By this means, Havana became the capital city of one of the Four Powers of the world, and that which was, by many standards of judgement, even after the defection of India (so fatal to its own prosperity and independence), held to be the first of the four.

The island of Cuba, which might have hesitated as to whether it would have allied itself to the Latin American Union, to which it had affinities of race and language which warred against its economic relations with the United States, swallowed the glittering bait, and became the official centre of the English-Speaking world. The Capitol of Havana, a magnificent building which had been erected at the beginning of the century during Machado's presidency, became the headquarters of the new government, until an even more imposing edifice could be built upon higher ground in a fold of the wooded hills.

By the period with which we are now dealing, the population had become so numerous, and its prosperity so great, that the whole island was thought of throughout the world as a huge Havana, and the name of Cuba was seldom heard.

The old Capitol was now occupied by the Interfederal Ministry, which was in charge of Lord Seeley Whitcombe, a New Zealander by birth, whose immaculate dress and somewhat Etonian manner of speech concealed the fact that he was an anxious and worried man.

He had spoken against the sea-warming project with eloquent earnestness less than a year before in the House of Lords, which now met in the West Indian island, and of which he was a distinguished member (the retention and reconstitution of that House had been due, oddly though, almost entirely to feeling in the American States); and he was still striving, with some temporary loss of popularity, to avert the consequences of the policy which he had been unable to change.

It was a full hour before noon when he gave audience to the European ambassador, but he had already received the plenipotentiary of the Latin-American Union, and had a long conference with his own Premier, Mr. Silver Long.

Mr. Long came from Oregon, where he had shown conspicuous ability as a lumberjack in his early days. But his dexterity with an axe had been far less than that with which he had felled his way through political thickets to the eminence which he now held. There was, and would be, no lordly title for him. He was fond of saying that he was a plain man; and his native land, which now contributed numerous titled members to the House of Lords, had, with a pleasant inconsistency, idolized him for this contemptuous attitude.

Lord Whitcombe had found some welcome encouragement in Mr. Long's shrewd and sturdy optimism.

"It doesn't much matter what you say" had been his parting remark, "so long as you make that dirty skunk understand that we don't care a hoot for anything they can do, and hell, it's our turn we shall give them hell."

He might have spoken differently to different man, but his confidence in Lord Whitcombe was not great. He thought that he lacked the backbone that the occasion required, in which he did less than justice to a man whose tenacity was no less than his, though it might be demonstrated in different ways.

Now the "dirty skunk" was announced, and Seeley Whitcombe rose to receive the representative of the United States of Europe.

Herr Bocker was a small neat man, not typical in appearance of the Hanover from which he came. He could be genial in manner during hours of relaxation, but it is improbable that he ever failed in watchfulness over the words which left his mouth with such careful economy. His official manner was precise, formal, reserved.

An invisible onlooker might have thought that neither of the two men who now confronted one another was great enough for the stupendous drama in which they had been cast for such leading parts. But is that not an observation of almost universal application? It is seldom indeed that the cross-chances of human destiny combine the great moment with the great man, who is unlikely to emerge with punctuality of time and place from the million mediocrities among whom it is most probable that he will have been obscurely born. And this improbability of emergence had been increased by the standardization of life which had been the social characteristic of a century which had abolished freedom of action and discouraged individuality. It was a condition of life in which it had become harder to sink, and therefore harder to rise.

With no consciousness of either absolute or relative inferiority, Herr Bocker said: "My instructions are to make what must, I regret to say, be a final enquiry as to whether your Government will secure the peace of the world by ceasing to warm the eastern currents of the Antarctic Ocean."

"We would do much," Lord Whitcombe replied, "for the world's peace, which we have no purpose to break, but the eastern part of the Antarctic Ocean is our domestic concern, over which even the Latin-American Union makes no claim, and still less can the United States of Europe assert a right of control. I cannot think that your Government will convulse the world, to its own ruin, in such a cause."

"My Government," Herr Bocker replied, "has no such intention. It is your own ruin which it would mercifully avert, if you would listen to either reason or right. But unless you will do so now, I must give you the notice which our treaty requires, for it is our intention to proceed in every way (as it may be needless to mention) in accordance with international law.

"The treaty you mention," Lord Whitcombe—who would not have trusted either Herr Bocker or his Government with a nickel coin—replied smoothly, "requires not only that you shall give fourteen days' notice before commencing any operation of war, but that you shall disclose the nature and intended consequences of that operation, from which you shall not deviate, and which you shall in no way exceed."

"I have a written memorandum here by which those conditions will be covered, and it is one which may incline you to the more conciliatory attitude which the position requires."

As Herr Bocker said this, he handed over a folded paper, which Lord Whitcombe opened, and at which he glanced, while endeavouring, with a politician's long-practised ease, to control his expression to that which he considered appropriate to the event.

He laid it down with a gesture of the hand which seemed to wave it contemptuously away. "We can easily deal with that," he said casually.

"You will find that that will be wholly beyond your power…. I need not remind you that, under the terms of the treaty, you must endure the consequences of your own obduracy for a period of three months, during which you will make no reprisal at all."

"We shall have no occasion for haste," Lord Whitcombe replied, with the same complacency as before. "But there is a warning which I must ask you to convey to your own Government, which it will be well for them to consider before they commence that which they may find themselves unable to stay.

"They must not rashly conclude that, if they should fail in this attack upon us (which you can assure them that they most certainly will), they will then be able to retire from a conflict which they have been sole to provoke. We may decline to consider peace until we have given them such chastisement as the world will not forget for a million years."

"I must take exception," Herr Bocker replied, with characteristic precision, "to the implication your words convey. The provocation was yours, and we are being forced to engage in defensive war. But, beyond that, I must add that it is a war which we should not begin, even under the provocation we have received, if we were not entirely sure of what its issue will be."

"Then," Lord Whitcombe said, with more of dignity than he would often show, "there is no more which it will be useful to say."

"There is nothing except to urge upon you the wisdom of giving way while there is yet time; and to state that I will wait upon you at the same hour on the fourteenth day for your final reply."

Lord Whitcombe made no further comment. He walked with the ambassador to the door, which he opened for him, without shaking hands, and in a manner which left Herr Bocker in some doubt of whether he had been shown an exceptional courtesy or kicked into the street.

But it was a point upon which he was not greatly concerned. He was convinced that his Government would not have issued such an ultimatum had they not been confident that they had the game in their own hands. He thought it would not be long before he would be interviewing Seeley Whitcombe to find him in a less ambiguous mood. It might even be that the threat which he had conveyed would be sufficient to bring submission. He dined alone with his staff, who found his spirits, his dry occasional jests, and the dinner, to be equally good.

V. THE COURAGE OF SILVER LONG

AFTER closing the door upon the European ambassador, Lord Whitcombe proceeded at once to wait upon Mr. Long, and these two gentlemen were joined in conference almost immediately by Sir Leslie Monk, the Minister of Agriculture and Fisheries (a quaint-sounding combination of offices inherited from the traditions of British Governments), who, in his Fisheries capacity, may be held to have had a special responsibility for the trouble which had arisen, and, as Minister for Agriculture, a particular interest in the threatened reprisal.

This threat was set out with menacing exactitude in the document which Herr Bocker had delivered, and which now lay before them.

It said that, on the morning of the fifteenth day, unless terms of peace should have been previously concluded, a wasting sickness would be observed among the cattle of Canada, such as would end in speedy and certain death, and that the plague spreading downward from the Arctic regions, would, within six days, have reached the northern border of Mexico. (That country, being a member of the Latin-American Union, would not, of course, be affected.) It would then spread through the West Indian Islands, cross the Atlantic to extend its blight throughout central and southern Africa, and then, through Madagascar, by way of the great East Indian Islands (which had remained outside the destruction which had desolated the Asian mainland, and were populated and prosperous members of the English-Speaking Commonwealth) to Australia and New Zealand, which would be reached before the end of the same month.

Within a week of its appearance in any locality, the blight would spread to other forms of mammalian life, which would be subject, though in some cases more slowly, to equally certain destruction. Only the human race (as the treaty required), together with birds, reptiles, and insects, would remain immune.

There was a concluding warning that the curse would not be temporary but continuous. To import fresh stock at any subsequent period would be wasted effort. It would be geographical in its operation, and permanent in its results.

The three who were considering this sinister proposition had a common aspect, though Mr. Silver Long had not lost his pugnacity. They looked perturbed and puzzled.

The Premier said: "It sounds cock-eyed to me. How could you set a geographical limit to such a plague? I shouldn't be surprised if they think they can catch us out with a good bluff. They think, if they threaten some impossible thing, our scientists won't be able to say that they know how to deal with it, and then we shall just give way. It's as likely as not that they mean to give way themselves at the last moment, if they can't bounce us into lying flat."

He looked at Sir Leslie Monk as he spoke, for it was a matter on which his opinion would have exceptional weight. Sir Leslie was an elderly, rotund man whose health was not good. He had held office in succeeding governments as an expert rather than a politician. He had begun life as a veterinary surgeon. He was reputed not only for brilliance in his own profession, but as the first authority in the world on climates, soils, and manures. Now his hand on the table was trembling weakly, and he breathed heavily as he gave an inconclusive reply: "I don't know what to think about that. They've got some clever men in Berlin. And there's that Stuttgart fellow—it'll be his idea, more likely than not. We ought to get Murchison's opinion before we decide anything."

"We can't go to him direct," the Premier said. "Conroy'd have a fit. We'll have to do it through the Institute in the usual way."

"That oughtn't to mean any real block," Seeley suggested. "They'll all be sitting up taking notice now. I suppose we've got to let this loose to the Press?"

It was a point on which the Premier's decision was already made. "I've called the Cabinet," he said, "for one-thirty, and the House meets at two. You know that. The Cabinet's got to see it first. But it's not a thing we can hold back. And if we shouldn't make it public at once, Berlin probably would."

"You won't go into secret session?"

"No. Just the contrary. We'll have the proceedings in the House broadcast direct. That'll make Linkwater toe the line, if anything will."

He added, seeing the doubt in Seeley Whitcombe's eyes, which provoked him to his more truculent manner:

"I'll start by reading this dirty screed to the House, and then everyone'll know where we are."

He spoke with a contagious confidence, and the doubt receded from Seeley's eyes. "I dare say," he agreed, "it'll be the best way."

It was a characteristic decision, showing the quality of audacious courage which the opponents of Silver Long had had past occasions to dread. If anything would produce the bold parliamentary front, and the unity of national spirit which he considered that the moment required, it would be the knowledge that every spoken word would be heard, not only through their own worldwide Commonwealth, but in enemy and neutral lands. And it would be a procedure of additional significance because it was not the common practice to allow a direct broadcast of parliamentary debates, except on opening and other formal occasions, the rule being for reports for broadcasting to be submitted to the Speaker, and subjected to what might be no more than the formality of his approval, before they would reach the ears of the outer world. "And," the Premier thought, with a satisfaction which, even at that moment, brought a smile to his lips, "it sure will make Linkwater mad."

His thought was interrupted by Sir Leslie's: "Well, we've got fourteen days. We've got to think out what we can do "

"We've got fourteen days and three months," he answered sharply. "And then we've got to do something that'll make them wish they'd never been born."

"You feel sure," Whitcombe asked, "that they'll keep the rules of the game?"

"I'm not sure of anything. But if they don't they'll have to be darned quick at any monkey business they think they'll try. They'll have Mendoza watching them like a cat, and he won't lose a second in using every card he's got in a nasty pack. And if they don't wipe us out about as soon as a clock's tick, they'll be smelling brimstone from us."

Mendoza was the President of the Latin-American Union. As the neutral member of the three Great Powers, it had the treaty obligation to attack, without an instant's delay, and with every possible weapon, either of the belligerents who should fail to wage the conflict under the restrictive covenants to which they had all subscribed. The knowledge that the whole world was acquainted with disintegrating agencies of a potency before which the existing civilization of the human race, if not its existence, must be swept away, with the object lesson of the silent desolation of the oldest and greatest continent, the inhabitants of which had settled their internal differences in the peace of mutual destruction, might well be sufficient to restrain the rulers of the United States of Europe from a course of action which would bring instant and annihilating retribution upon itself.

It made it particularly unlikely that it would engage in any limited violation or excess of the agreed conditions of war. If it should deviate from them at all, it must be in the hope that it could bring both its opponents and the neutral power to such swift destruction as would allow them no time for retaliation.

It was not wonderful, in these circumstances, that the Latin-American Union wars regarding the threatened conflict with wary anxiety, or that its preparations for intervention were fully made. Yet its ambassador, when Lord Whitcombe had received him during the earlier morning, had spoken words of encouragement rather than counselled restraint to one who, he knew, had he controlled the decision, would have been disposed to a peaceful settlement of the dispute; and this attitude may have done something to harden that of Lord Whitcombe, when he had confronted Herr Bocker as representative of the British race.

"It is not," Del Littori had said—in his pleasant, temperate manner, which would have given a sound of plausibility to extreme opinions (such as he would be unlikely to utter)—"it is not that we welcome what you have done, which may even be of some disadvantage to us, of which it is too soon to say, but we have so deep a distrust of those who now rule from Berlin that we feel that there may be some relief in having the issue determined as to what, within the limits of law, they may be able to do, and whether they may have the will to go beyond that which we have some confidence that we could counter in a way which would be their end."

"Which," Lord Whitcombe had answered boldly, being both encouraged by Del Littori's friendly confidence, and led into unusual freedom of speech by the excitement the crisis brought, "you might not be unwilling to see?"

The ambassador had hesitated, and then, judgment supporting inclination, had replied with the frankness which he felt that the position allowed.

"Our relations with Europe are of normal friendliness, and we wish no ill to the inhabitants of that continent and its adjoining settlements. We desire peace—peace for all, and security for ourselves.

"But our President has had long-standing doubts of whether such a sense of security can ever be felt while the European Federation endures, and is so largely controlled by men of Germanic blood.

"At the conclusion of the first war of this century, the conquerors of Germany drew its claws, but allowed them to grow again, with consequences at which no one could reasonably be surprised.

"After the second, they took precautions of a less transient nature, but they allowed the Germanic tribes to remain in their own territories, and without even the elementary precaution of settling others of different dispositions among them in numerical majority, so that succeeding generations might have been modified in type. For the time, their powers of evil were checked, but the stock and its instincts remained.

"It is in direct consequence of that policy that, half a century later, we are confronted with this difference, that, while we have taken no side in the dispute, and while our interests are rather with them than you, we have no fear that you will do anything contrary to the pledges which you have given, or treacherously hostile to us, but we have no such confidence in them.

"I confess that while, unless our own existence were directly at stake, we would do nothing to bring about so great a calamity, if we should see Europe an uninhabited desert, from the Urals to the North Sea, we should feel a confidence in the future of the human race which is lacking now."

It was with this assurance of the friendly attitude, or even the potential support, of the Latin-American Federation—a relatively more powerful combination than it would have been in the earlier part of the century, owing to an enormous growth of population and development of natural resources throughout Central and South America (which had included the draining of the huge Amazonian swamps, and the discovery of mineral deposits which they had covered from the days when the Andes had been lapped by Atlantic tides), and with the knowledge that he had the support of a very resolute Premier, that Lord Whitcombe had met the European ambassador at the interview which was described in a previous chapter.

VI. THE OPINIONS OF THE EXPERTS

IT was shortly before noon on the following day when Mr. Silver Long summoned his ministers of Agriculture and of Interfederal Affairs, to consider with them the reports of the scientific experts on whose abilities, replacing the obsolete activities of aerial, naval, or military forces, the Commonwealth must now rely, if not for its existence, at least that it should not suffer a devastating calamity at the hands of its truculent foe.

So far, he had had the satisfaction of being able to feel that he had handled the situation well.

He had found that his policy of parliamentary publicity had been justified by its results. He could recall with an inward chuckle the angry look and the muttered curse with which the Leader of the Opposition had heard his decision that the debate should be broadcast to a listening world, after which Mr. Linkwater had risen, and given, in his silkiest tone, assurance of his approval of this procedure, of his unequivocal support of the Government in an hour of national crisis, and of his impregnable confidence in the ability of the technical departments concerned to nullify whatever evils might be intended against the welfare of the Commonwealth.

Mr. Long had then read the ultimatum, and had added, with the brevity which distinguished him among verboser colleagues: "Such is the threat which has been made against us. It would be obviously inappropriate at this stage for me to make any comment upon it, or to give any indication, either of the measures which we may take to resist it, or of the far deadlier counterattack which, in due season, we shall announce to our anxious foes." He had quoted the text: "Let not him who putteth on his armour boast himself as he who taketh it off," in a manner which had made it no less a challenge to their enemies than a word of warning against overconfidence to themselves; and he had ended the short speech amidst delirious cheers by declaring: "It will be a war which the European Federation has begun, but which it will be our part to end."

Neither the speech nor its reception could have given encouragement to Berlin, especially if (as he was disposed to hope, if not to believe) there had been the intention there of frightening the Commonwealth to submission with a threat which might be beyond possibility of execution; and its support front the House, and afterwards from the Press, had shown that the whole Commonwealth was united and resolute in his support.

A natural result of the prompt publication of the ultimatum had been that several sacks of radiograms had already been received, proposing measures or devices to combat the threatened scourge. But these would take time to examine. They must go to the Institute of Research. He was not yet concerned with them.

It was the reports of Professors Conroy and Murchison, which he had requested the institute to let him have before noon, which he had asked his colleagues to join him in considering. Apart from Sir Leslie, these two professors were the leading experts on mammalian infections on whom he must now rely. They had had nearly twenty-four hours in which to consider the possibility of the threat being genuine, and the means of resisting it successfully. It was of the first importance to learn what their conclusions were, and to have Sir Leslie Monk's opinions thereon.

When the three ministers met, these reports had not arrived, and it was during the brief interval of waiting that Seeley Whitcombe said:

"By the way, did you notice that the ultimatum didn't mention Great Britain or Ireland?"

"Yes. Do you attach any importance to that?"

"It seemed queer to me."

"So it was. But it may have been no more than a recognition, unintentional or spiteful, of their geographical insignificance. Berlin may mean us to understand that they'll just take them *en passant* on the first day."

"You don't think Blake could possibly have double-crossed us in any way?"

"No. How could he? Besides, it's incredible. We know Blake. It may be that they're leaving Great Britain out because it's so near to Europe, and its omission saves them from some danger, or preventive measures which would be more trouble than its inclusion would be worth while to them. Anyhow, so it is. We shall soon know. Thank you, Anderson. Yes, you d better stay. I may want you to take something down."

The last words were to his private secretary, who had entered with the expected reports.

Mr. Long opened one of them. His eyes glanced down it rapidly. He could hardly be said to have read it. He passed it over to Sir Leslie with the remark: "Convoy's a washout. I hope Murchison's done better than that."

His inspection of the second report was rather longer, but it appeared to give him no greater satisfaction. He laughed shortly: "Murchison seems to think that it will end in us and the insects getting on quite nicely together. If these are the best men we've got, we'd better put our muzzle between our paws and flap our tail on the ground. I expect that's about how it looks to you?"

He spoke to Sir Leslie Monk, who answered reasonably: "I'd better see the report first, but I don't see how we can do much till we've got more to go on than we have now."

"Then you're the third, if you think that. To my mind it makes the whole thing look more like a bluff than it did before."

"I doubt whether it's that. Richter's known to have been working on cattle infections for many years. And he's a clever devil. It was he, you'll remember, who wiped out foot-and-mouth disease, like sponging a slate. That must have been seven years ago, and if he's been on the same track ever since—"

"Well, we've still got six days to find out whether there are any brains on our side."

While they spoke thus, Seeley Whitcombe was quietly reading the reports, from which he saw that there was little comfort to come. Professor Conroy said that there was no known virus, or other infective agency, which had the potency or other qualities indicated by the terms of the ultimatum and he could not profess to identify it.

But he pointed out that, if Professor Richter had made such a discovery, its consequences could not have been the subject of extensive experiment or observation, which it would have been impossible to conceal, and he deduced that these effects must be matters of logical induction rather than demonstrated certainty, and there had been several instances during the past half-century when the danger of relying upon such inductions had been demonstrated.

He dwelt on the obvious fact that the proposed geographical limitation of so potent a plague, and the assurance that the human race, alone among mammals, would remain unaffected, indicated confidence in an extraordinary measure of control over the mysterious agency; but he felt that there must be less than absolute reliance upon the ability of those who would put it into operation to secure these limitations, both because of the absence of adequate experimental research already mentioned, and (especially as regarding the immunity of mankind) because the comparative slowness with which animals other than cattle were to be infected indicated a virus which could gradually adapt itself to overcome variations of resistance.

He concluded by suggesting that preparations should be made in districts where the plague was first threatened to combat it by all known means of anti-virus treatment, from the comparative results of which much might be learned; and he proposed to include some which had fallen into disuse, owing to the elimination of the diseases which they had been designed to combat...

The first paragraphs of Professor Murchison's report were very similar to those which completed that of Professor Conroy. He advocated identical measures, while appearing to have little confidence in their adequacy. He expressed a somewhat bolder doubt as to whether the threats which had been made did not go far beyond the possibilities of accomplishment. And then, having dealt with these aspects of the subject in easy brevity, he went on, at much greater length, to discuss and depreciate the adverse effects which would follow the elimination of the mammalian population of the English-Speaking world.

He had a persuasive style, and as he developed his arguments it might well have appeared to a receptive, non-analytical reader that the threatened destruction was of no more than minor importance, even if it might not be found to have some compensating advantages.

Comparatively, if not absolutely, the learned professor certainly regarded it with something approaching equanimity. For suppose it had been insects which were to perish? Or even earthworms? He quoted from that ancient record of scientific experiment, *Vegetable Mould* (Darwin), to suggest how incalculably serious such an elimination might be.

He showed that a general destruction of insects must result in profound natural disturbances, such as might leave the earth (or such parts of it as should experience the plague) unfit for the sustaining of human life. There would be few forms of vegetable or arboreal life which would continue to propagate. Only plants which were independent of insect intervention would continue. Many—almost all—forms of bird life would disappear for lack of essential foods. There would be further consequences, sinister in their implications, and bewildering in their complexity. The elimination of malaria, and a few other insect-borne diseases, would be a comparative triviality. He concluded that the destruction of insect life would be a calamity which only that of bacteria could exceed.

Even the destruction of birds might have proved to be a much greater disaster, for many forms of insect life would be left thereby to such unchecked increases as must lead to a variety of desolations and plagues, the full horrors of which imagination might fail to forecast.

But the disappearance of mammals threatened no such disasters, except for their insect parasites. It might involve nothing adverse to the prosperity, and little to the convenience of men. There would be loss of meat, and—which was more serious—milk. But large quantities of meat might be imported, and a larger and perhaps healthier population may be supported on a granivorous, or graminivorous, than upon a carnivorous diet.

It was also to be observed that some domestic mammals, such as dogs and cats, are parasitic upon mankind, and the community would be relieved of the burden of their support.

Seeley laid down the reports. He said: "Well, if Murchison's right, we ought to give Richter a vote of thanks."

Silver Long said sharply: "Murchison's just an ass. If he'd got a stable like mine—"

Sir Leslie Monk, who was himself fond of racing, though his income did not enable him to emulate the Premier's ownership ventures, said sympathetically: "You might get Fire-Eater, and one or two others, sent into Mexico, as a precaution, during the week."

"Nonsense. What effect do you think it would have if I set such an example as that?"

"I am afraid," Seeley interposed, "the question is of no practical importance. I heard, just as I was leaving my office, that the Mexican borders have been closed to all transits of livestock, following a protest from Europe. They say that about half a million of livestock of various kinds had gone over before the barriers were put down."

"Then, if they can't be moved into the Latin lands, that leaves nowhere but European territory, and they're not likely to go in that direction."

"On the contrary, I have reports that the movements from Central into European African territories have been going on all across the continent for the last twenty-four hours, with prices falling all the time, till they're scarcely worth taking now."

"So they summed up what the Institute can do at about the right figure," Silver Long commented grimly. "Well, if it isn't a bluff, we've just got to face it out."

VII. THE COURAGE OF SEELEY WHITCOMBE

"BORISWOOD'S OPINION IS that we might cease to trade with them entirely without violation of the treaty conditions, so long as it should result entirely from private inaction, without Government influence; but if we were to pass adverse legislation of any kind, or even to advise that orders should be diverted to the L.A.F., it might be a breach of our undertaking which would be a technical justification for total war."

Silver Long looked up from the Attorney-General's report as he said this, and Seeley Whitcombe answered: "That's about how it looked to me. But it leaves it a hell of a headache, all the same. Should we have to keep putting the empty cargo-liners into the air?"

"I expect we should. Unless they were stopped by consent. We mustn't forget that diplomatic relations will go on as before."

"It seems a nightmare to me. There are a hundred things about which we shan't know where we are. I'm not sure that it wouldn't be better to have total war from the first. We should know what to expect, and it would be over a lot quicker."

"Boriswood seems to be of much the same opinion. He thinks that's how it's bound to end; and the way we're placed they'll be the first to begin."

"It's lucky that the L.A.F.'s friendly to us. That'll make them go slow, if anything will."

"Yes. But it may only mean that they'll attack both at once if they think they've got anything sufficiently infernal to lay us out."

"We can't do more than avoid anything that might give them an excuse, and keep wide awake, so that if they do start anything unexpected we shan't be many seconds later than they."

"Yes," the Premier answered, in the tone of a man whose thoughts are on other things. "I wish we could find some way to scotch it before it starts."

"You're not thinking of knuckling under?"

"No. If we should do that, we should have the same trouble over something else, before long. I don't say they haven't got a case against us, of a sort, though I think they're wrong. But there's something deeper than that. Look at the trouble they made over the Asian question! As though we ought to agree that it's to be taken over by Europe alone, just because the lands join, and we have a dividing ocean! There's no give and take about them. There's no goodwill. That's the trouble. There's no goodwill. They'd see the rest of the world dead tomorrow if they could manage it without risk to themselves. I believe that the time's sure to come when it will have to be us or them. And I'm not sure that it's far off now." He added, in the same preoccupied tone as before: "I only wish I could see a way of stopping it now."

His eyes fell again upon the report he had received from the Attorney-General, which dealt with a score of dubious juridical questions which had been raised by various Government departments affecting the relations which would exist between the belligerent federations if a state of war should exist in a week's time. They were bewildered by lack of precedents, and the anomalies which must be occasioned by a condition of limited war.

"You can't stop them, unless you give way."

"No? How about letting them know in advance—know *for certain*—that we can nullify what they'll be trying to do?"

"Well, of course, if you could do that—"

"I was talking to Brewster yesterday evening. I can't blame him. He's done wonders. If it had been any of Betz's devices, he says he knows them, and the answers, by heart. He got a copy of Betz's private diary complete for several weeks, two months ago, and the things it contains just show you what fiends they are. But Richter's a different matter. He says he goes about everywhere with a woman secretary, and he repeats everything confidential to her, and trusts it to her memory, to be written down somewhere, he supposes at the end of the day. She must have a wonderful memory if they keep to that plan, and avoid any previous notes. But, if there be such a record, or if he keep a private diary, it can't be found.

"He says that when Richter cured the foot-and-mouth disease, he was so secretive that even the men in his own laboratories didn't know how it was done. No one dealt with the thing completely, and there were some things he wouldn't let out of his own hands. Even about that it was understood that there were no written records. Richter is reported to have said that if they didn't like his methods, he could easily start the disease again, and they could handle it their own way."

"All this may let Brewster out, but it doesn't seem very helpful to us."

"I guess it isn't. But you can't do much about putting a thing right till you know what the trouble is. What I was thinking was, mightn't it be worth while to slip over there and see what I could find out for myself?"

Seeley looked his astonishment. "If you were to do that," he said, "everyone'd think we were throwing our hand in. And, anyway, what could you expect to find out? You'd be watched everywhere, day and night."

"I didn't mean to go openly."

"I don't mean to be rude; but it sounds a crazy idea to me."

"Of course it does. And that's just what makes it so good. Just think, Seeley. Brewster's watched. So's everyone who goes within half a mile of him, more likely than not. He doesn't know but what his phone's tapped. No one can. He told me that he's got one spy in Berlin who he found out was taking money from Betz; and the man admitted it, but said he wasn't selling him anything worth knowing.

So he paid him extra to go on being paid by Betz, and to fool him; and he isn't sure that Betz isn't paying Rodd—that's the beauty's name—extra to double-cross us over again. There's such a slough of cross-bribery that no one knows whom to trust, or even whom to distrust, which is a lot worse.

"But one thing's sure. Brewster couldn't start any man off to Berlin or Stuttgart tomorrow—or Paris, for that matter—and be *sure* that he wouldn't be known and watched, however secret and round-about the procedure might be. The chances are all on the other side. But if I were to start off on my own, with no one knowing but you, and you were to put it about that I should be so much engaged in investigating methods of fighting this coming plague that I couldn't see anyone, or attend to anything else—I'd give you and Simms authorities to deputize for me—I might have beginner's luck, and blue the whole show."

"I don't see how you'd do anything. I don't see how you'd go about it at all."

"Well, there might be ways. I might get Richter himself in a quiet spot, and put the fear of God into him—or the fear of death. He's not the sort of man who'd believe in anything but himself, but he'd value life, as we all do. And one thing's certain—no one'll be watching me to see that I don't go over to Europe to spy there. The idea'd never enter into their heads. And that's where I shall get a clear start."

Seeley Whitcombe saw that the proposal, however fantastic it might sound, was seriously meant, and could not be put aside by a word of protest. He answered: "I doubt whether it would be as simple as that. But say it would. Say you could get there without being watched or anyone guessing. How much further on would you be? Men go to Europe every day without the police taking much interest in them. They don't merely know nothing about them. They know enough to be sure that they are harmless men, occupied on their own business affairs. But even if one of them should suddenly get wild enough to make up his mind that he'd try to find out what this secret is, would he have the remotest chance of success? If he should find that he could get within a hundred yards of Richter or his secretary without rousing suspicion, let alone getting solitary interviews with them, I'd say he'd be a most lucky man."

"That's sense, Seeley. That's what I expected to hear you say. It's long odds. And I'm not kidding myself that it's less than that. But think what a stake it's for!"

Seeley saw that. For the first time the idea lost its grotesqueness, and became reasonable. So small a chance—but for so much!

And with the vision came the idea. It was scarcely a thought. A feeling rather. An abstract recognition of fact. He was hardly aware of being personally concerned as he said: "That's true enough. But you're not the one. I don't want to be rude—I said that before—but it's a thing I could do far better than you, and I shouldn't be missed in the same way."

It was Silver Long's turn to look surprised. He had not regarded his own proposal as of heroic quality. But he had been accustomed to take risks, to gamble with Fate, from his childhood days. It was that readiness which had brought him to the high position he held: that quality which had fitted him to meet the prevent crisis with a bold, almost jaunty, front. But he had thought Lord Whitcombe to be of another order. Had he been obliged to give truthful evidence, he might have said that he did not regard him as a man of much courage, and even argued that this opinion was supported by Seeley's attitude to the dispute they were facing now. But you never know!

"I wouldn't think of your doing that," he answered. "It's my idea, and, besides, the whole trouble is of my making rather than yours."

"I don't think you ought to let that weigh with you at all. The sole question is which would be the better man. You'd be missed here more than I should. And you'd be more liable to be recognized there. I don't suppose you've ever disguised yourself in your life."

Silver Long recognized that he had heard an argument which he could not meet. Among Lord Whitcombe's versatile abilities, that of amateur acting was not least, though it had only been shown on occasions of private festivities since his college days. Silver Long had regarded it with some unspoken contempt, as an undignified, even unmanly occupation. But he saw that it might now be of essential use. He gave way, with a reluctance which first told him that inclination, as well as judgment, had urged his resolution. He had wanted to go!

The conversation which followed was too lengthy to be recorded here. Plans were made to prevent suspicion of Seeley's absence being aroused. Many ideas were discussed, and theories exchanged as to how an unprecedented position might develop.

At present the two great World powers were at peace. The English-Speaking Commonwealth was simply under fourteen days' notice of coming war. There was no irregularity in travelling from one country to the other, and such movements as were taking place were not only of those who had been in their neighbour's land going back to their own. Many were taking advantage of the interval before war should commence to visit the territories of their future enemy for commercial or private reasons. The airliners were packed with traffic.

Even after war should commence, it was not clear that such intercourse might not continue, grotesque though it might appear to be. Here, as in a hundred different ways, there was absence of precedent, and it is only when this support to fallible human thought fails that men will realize how essential it is.

Up to a century ago the habit of war had been general through the world, but its horrors and hardships had been mitigated by many slowly-established conventions, in the nature and extent of which, since the Middle Ages, there had been a gradual, sinister, little-noticed change.

During the first millennium of the Christian era the ferocities of war had been slightly but progressively mitigated, so far as they were exercised in inter-Christian conflict. The influence of the Church had even, at one time, become sufficient to enforce short periods during which all swords must be sheathed—"Truces of God"—even though conflicts might be at their most critical points.

The development of professional armies had increased this tendency. Men who were paid moderately did not expect to risk their lives every few days. Horses were liable to get knocked about in a battle. A mounted man-at-arms who hired himself for a period to a captain of *condottieri* would want to know what risks his horse would be likely to run, and to have his agreement clear as to who should pay for it, if it should get killed. The captain's reputation for caution and moderation of methods would affect the price at which such hirings could be made, and therefore his own profits. If the result of a threatened battle should appear dubious, there would be a common disposition to avoid it in favour of more manœuvres, and so save expense and waste of life on both sides. If there were plain advantage on either side, both captains would probably see the matter in the same light, and make reasonable agreement on the basis of fact, without putting to bloody test what, as professional soldiers, was evident to their own eyes. It was not a matter of courage but common sense.

There had been great European wars in which armies at no great distances apart had threatened and feinted for whole years without either commander thinking that actual fighting were worth its cost.

But then—slightly, gradually, but on a tide which did not turn—first, the conventions of Christian chivalry had declined, and its restrictions had been ignored, and then the conservative customs of professional warfare had fallen into discredit until there had come a logical conclusion in the horrors and havoc of total war. And now they were trying to go back to humaner methods. But it is always hard to return from a downward way. And they had chosen to make the attempt on a strange road, where there was an absence of guiding signs, and they must go forward in darkness and doubt.

"Well," Seeley said at last, "we might go on talking forever, and get no further. We can ask each other a hundred questions, and the answer's the same to each—that we don't know. It's too much like a kitten chasing a tail it can never catch. And I've got a good deal to do." He rang up his dentist.

Next morning, he moved his offices into the Premier's official residence, after a public announcement had been made that he would be too fully occupied upon the business of his department during the next week to appear in public. His secretary remained available on the telephone; and, if he did not consult his chief before replying to important enquiries, he appeared to do so.

The man who left the Premier's residence, and entered a waiting car in the dusk of the next evening, was curiously like the Minister of Interfederal Affairs. At a first casual glance anyone might almost have thought it were he. But a second look would have shown the absurdity of the idea. He had more prominent teeth. His hair was darker and parted differently. He was well enough dressed, but not with Lord Whitcombe's extreme precision. There were other differences which a close observer would see. If a thought of Lord Whitcombe should rise at the first glance, a second would correct the error.

The man was probably aware of the resemblance, and tried to ape one who was so much greater than he. But the attempt failed, perhaps because he was—well, hardly a gentleman. And, of course, his teeth would always give him away.

VIII. Rex Bulldozer Reaches Europe

REX Bulldozer didn't behave quite like a gentleman. He talked rather too loudly, letting everyone know of his profession—he was a schoolmaster—and of the purpose of his journey to Europe, which was to bring back two ex-pupils who had been studying there.

He made himself uselessly objectionable in opposition to the general desire to change the radio programme. A talk had come on which dealt with the possible consequences, and feasibility, of covering certain parts of the oceans with permanent coatings of oil. The general feeling was that it was impolite, at such a time, and in so mixed a company, to have their minds directed to any question of changing seas. They had preferred—and had—an instructional programme which was intended, by a process of reiterated reason, to eliminate the atavistic instinct for floral growths or decorations.

It appeared that there was no colour and no scent known to the flora of the whole earth which could not be produced in wholesale quantities, and more economically, from coal-tar.

Being overruled on this point, Mr. Bulldozer incurred the rebuke of the head-steward by having the bad manners to hum very loudly the refrain of a silly sentimental song which had been popular twenty years before:

"For Percy lived a life of crime,
And so was hanged in lilac-time."

The indication might be obscure, but his fellow-travellers, who all held intelligence certificates (or they would not have been there), felt that, in however obscurely indirect a manner, he was being disrespectful to the instructional broadcast, if not to coal-tar itself, which was a god on whom they had learnt to lean. If Rex Bulldozer had any resemblance to the Minister of Interfederal Affairs, it was a matter on which Lord Winchcombe deserved any sympathy which might be going about.

The liner glided down smoothly, obeying the attraction of magnetic rails; the sides of the passenger-cabins opened, appearing for a moment to be a rose-red butterfly's half-lifted wings, and then sank outward to form soft-carpeted, gently-sloping platforms of descent; and Rex Bulldozer, bustling obtrusively, stepped down to the soil of France

He appeared to be casual in his approach to the line of attendants, to one of which he must give instructions concerning the destination of his baggage; but it was actually the first critical test of his fitness for the mission on which he came.

There were four of these men, each of whom had been minutely described to him, who were trusted agents of his own government, and whom it would be well to avoid. There were others whose secret allegiances, if any, were unknown or suspect. There was one, a man of military figure and bearing with a lean, hard face, who was known to be at the head of the Paris espionage service, so far as it related to airport traffic. Mr. Bulldozer must not appear to seek this man, but if it could casually and naturally happen that he should come to his charge, it was how he would prefer it to be.

Fortune favoured him at this point to a degree which might seem ominous of coming good to a sanguine mind. But that might be a founded hope, for morning sunshine is no guarantee of a rainless day.

He recognized the man as he approached a line that was beginning to bustle and break; and as Herr Bikker's hard keen eyes swept the descending travellers, they met his own, so that their contact became natural thing.

Herr Bikker took the baggage-ticket with the unmeaning obsequiousness of routine. His practised eye read, at one glance, the name and description of the owner which were endorsed upon it. His secret office did not alter the fact that he was the servant of those who tipped, in a world where, amid many changes, that custom had continued to flourish. His espionage value would, indeed, have been much reduced had he been less the typical steward than he had successfully studied to become.

"To what address," he asked, "will you wish them sent? And for yourself? Or you have a conveyance here?"

"No. I have not been here—I have not been to Europe—before. You will tell me where I should put up. It will be for one night only. I must go on to Stuttgart tomorrow."

"If monsieur will tell me the expense—the grade—"

Mr. Bulldozer became explicit and confidential. He wanted the most expensive place he could get. The gentleman for whom he was acting was paying him an agreed fee, with expenses extra. He meant those expenses to be a substantial sum.

Herr Bikker was quick to understand the position. It was doubtless how he would have acted himself. He said he would have recommended— But now, perhaps— *Mais non!* He knew exactly. There was a little place in the Rue des Italiens, of the most exclusive, and its comforts were of incomparable quality. It was most expensive, but if there were no obstacle in that—

Mr. Bulldozer said that he had no doubt that that was the place for him.

Herr Bikker put him into a car. He spoke a few low-voiced words to the driver. He said that the baggage should follow so promptly that it would arrive almost as soon as its owner. He accepted a most liberal tip, which he would more than double by his commission on the hotel bill, it being as dear and exclusive a place as he had said, and one which would have been unlikely to admit that it had accommodation for the loud-voiced American, had he not been sent, by Bikker, which would be a guarantee of the discretion of what they did.

THE BLUE ROOM, BY S. FOWLER WRIGHT * 39

He might, of course, have been directed there to be kept under observation, though, for that purpose, it would have been a most unlikely selection; but the fact was that Rex Bulldozer had won the trick, though he was still very far from winning the game. Herr Bikker, for all his shrewdness, had taken him for the transparent ass he affected to be, and as one from whom a profit might well be made without detriment to his more important activities; and such profits, large or small, were not neglected as their occasions came.

Curiously supported in his mood by the buoyancy of the character which he had chosen to act, Seeley drove through a green suburban Paris which had changed far less in the last half-century than would normally have been the case had it been an equal part of a less changing world.

He had seen it more than once before, his denial to Bikker having been no more than a diplomatic lie, but the sense of its attractive quaintness had not diminished. Only, when the car turned at last into the narrower streets, he had a feeling of claustrophobia difficult to subdue. The Rue des Italiens was so narrow that he felt an instinctive impulse to stretch out his hands to either side to push back the encroaching walls, though its shortness somewhat diminished the sensation of being held in a closing trap.

He thought: "How much our architecture has changed, in how short a time!" And then: "Has the change been good?"

His mind went back to the solid, oak-beamed English building of the sixteenth century. Men had been sure of themselves then, sure of their faith, sure of a lasting world. But it had been followed by the colder, prouder, less human architecture of the later Stuarts, and the succeeding Georgian era, whose loftier ceilings had seemed to be farther from the warmth of earth without being nearer the light of Heaven. And after that there had been the Victorian degeneration, during which beauty, dignity, and solidity had alike declined, until, as the twentieth century had opened, it would have been hard to show that his own country had had any style of architecture at all. Its coat of arms might have been a plank of unseasoned pine, as that of the Elizabethan period might have been one of well-seasoned oak. But now all that was gone, bad and good alike, except in this quaint backwater of forgotten things; and no one could say that the new architecture was without character or durability. Its concrete walls, high and smooth and white, were made to endure. They were of substance so hard that the explosives of the Second World War would have left them standing unmoved in contemptuous strength; their surfaces were such that they would have been left unmarked by the futile fumes. Certainly it was not an architecture without character. But was that character one which it was easy to love?

Very firmly it stood. But those who built it were less secure.

The change had been as great in the country as in the town, both in kind and degree; and it had not been in continental Europe alone. It had been in England, in the whole world. He remembered (though he had been young at the time) the fierce, futile English agitation there had been against the legislation which had obliged farmers to destroy their hedges within three years, or incur forfeitures or crippling fines. Yet it had been plain sense. A wire fence will take no nourishment from the ground. A windscreen, if it be needed, may be better made of metal sheets, which may be erected, shifted, or removed, as is impossible with a living hedge.

As he would fly to Stuttgart tomorrow, he would look down on land that the tractor could plough, mile after mile, without turn or halt, land where no tree or herb had been allowed to survive unless for a certain use, land where there would be aviaries every half-mile for the regulation number of birds of the approved species to feed on such insect pests as other methods had not eliminated—birds which would themselves be eliminated as soon as they could be replaced by more efficient agencies. He would see gigantic works not yet completed, which were removing hills and straightening rivers, and generally bringing reason and order into the confusion which is the best which can be expected from blind, wasteful, unintelligent evolutionary forces.

Seeley had an absurd doubt as to whether the Earth's Creator (he was inclined to indulge the possibility, or even probability, of conscious design, having been impressed by the implications of the fundamental law that thought precedes action, construction follows purpose and plan) would be entirely pleased by these human efforts to improve upon the methods which He so plainly preferred There was something comic in created beings showing their Maker how the work could have been more admirably done. Perhaps He would learn from them in time, and arrange the stars in a more orderly pattern. Yet their experimental changes might be part of His own design. Might it not all be an entertainment, millennium-long, at which the Gods sat watching what the creatures They had projected would try to do?

Thought is swift, yet it is not surprising that while Seeley Whitcombe had allowed his mind to wander in this erratic manner, he had been deposited at his destination, and was recalled to his environment by the fact that he was at the reception desk, and was not behaving quite as Rex Bulldozer would be likely to do.

It was a danger he must be alert to avoid.

VIII. BULLDOZER SLEEPS ALONE

REX BULLDOZER WAS a talkative man. He made no secret of the errand on which he came. He had to find two ex-pupils who were wandering about and had been last heard of at Stuttgart. He could not say that they had been staying there. But it was from that city that their last radiogram had been despatched. They might have been just passing through. Why did he not seek them through the usual publicity channels? Because he had been explicitly directed not to do so. It was, he believed, something to do with their mother's health. She did not know that they were abroad. Anyhow, it was nothing to him. Their father was an erratic man. It was enough that the instructions were clear and the money good.

There was a flavour of improbability in the tale which made it additionally plausible. It was not such as anyone would be likely to invent. Nor was it probable that anyone coming to Europe for an illicit purpose would make himself as conspicuous as Mr. Bulldozer certainly did. Nor, most clearly, was he such as others would entrust with a mission of secrecy, or where discretion would be required. As a boys' tutor he might be well enough. It was a matter of opinion. Beyond that—

Talking through a dinner which he chose to eat at the public table (such was the general preference at that period, it being considered a sign of dullness, or an affectation, to eat in a private room, though some, such as Herr Richter, would maintain the exclusive habit), it was natural that others, though less boisterously, talked to him; and he was alert to hear conversations he did not share.

He learned some things of interest, including the surprising fact that Édouard Richter had stayed there a few days before. It was a fact that had an important sound, though it was difficult to see what its importance could be.

The other guests were of different sorts and races, both women and men, but they all belonged to the clearly-defined plutocracy of the time—a plutocracy which was no less real because it had no technical possession of real estate, or control of individual capital. Most of those who shared the luxurious living upon which Mr. Bulldozer had so inharmoniously intruded were free of Federal taxation, and had incomes, government-allotted, which they were not only permitted, but required, to spend, under penalty of forfeiture, the notes in which it was paid to them becoming valueless if they were not returned, through collecting bankers, to the Federal Treasury before the close of the year.

Mr. Bulldozer's fellow-guests were entirely European. They spoke of the prospect of war and its probable course without appearing to be restrained by his presence. The prevailing opinion was that the English-Speaking Commonwealth would give way. There was great confidence in Édouard Richter. A man to fear. And the English-Speaking Commonwealth was not normally of a warlike temper. As to the Latin-American Union, its unfriendliness would not be forgotten, but there was little doubt that it would have the discretion to stand aside.

As to the social and economic consequences of limited war, there was lively curiosity but little evidence of concern. The first aggression was to be theirs, and would be for their foes to endure. They did not appear to look beyond that. Nor did they appear to be apprehensive of the coming of total war. They may have appreciated the character of the English-Speaking Commonwealth well enough to know that they had no such danger to fear. If it should be commenced, it would be by them.

Rex Bulldozer went up to the quiet of a room where he could relax, it being certain that he would be subjected to no human interference, unless at his own summons.

The room was large by the standards of the time in which it was built, though it seemed quaintly small and ill-proportioned to him. Quainter far were the number of the things which it contained, for the aim of its arrangers had been to retain, as entirely as possible, the old atmosphere and the old contents, while adding, as unobtrusively as their nature would allow, such appliances as civilization requires.

Rex Bulldozer could be forgotten at last, and Seeley Whitcombe could take what might be his last night of secure rest, and think of something which was in his mind, but was too vague to be called a plan.

He could not forget Rex entirely, as he sat thinking for a time before resorting to darkness and seeking sleep, because the dressing-gown which Rex had brought—and he must now wear—was of a pattern which Seeley could not approve; and his thoughts of Seeley were marred by a contemptuous reference to himself which he had heard at dinner.

He was not ignorant of the fact that Silly Whitcombe was a variation of his name which came easily to the minds, and doubtless too frequently to the lips of men; but he had not supposed that it would be in familiar use by those who spoke in a foreign tongue.

And their allusions to himself had been otherwise lacking (as was natural enough) in appreciation or respect.

There was the discreet, musical *Pip-Pip-Pip* which told him that attention was asked, and he pressed the button which he knew would be under the arm of his chair.

A voice, suitably toned to solicitude for his comfort, enquired whether he desired companionship for the night. If that were so, there would be a choice of blondes and brunettes, besides a redhead of a vivacity few could match.

Should he wish it, pictures of the competitors, with an economy or absence of attire which Dr. Dalton, of a previous generation, would have entirely approved, would be shown upon the television screen which was the centre of the pattern of the opposite wall.

Historical veracity compels the record that Seeley—or was it Rex?—was hesitant in his reply. Questions of inclination and expediency were alike involved. But one thing was clear. Any of these candidates for his companionship would tend to keep him awake; and he needed a good night's sleep before leaving for Stuttgart, which he had planned to do at an early hour. He said: "No." He would prefer not to be further disturbed.

But after that he had doubts. Had he replied as Bulldozer would be likely to do? Might he not have selected a companion who would have told him things possibly about Édouard Richter which it would have been useful to know? Might he not, at least, have permitted the gallery of accessible beauty to be paraded before him?

He did not fail to observe that there would be a particular rudeness about asking to see them, and then saying that none of them would be required. But was not that just a kind of thing that Rex would be likely to do?

The reply was so evident that he rang to say that he would like to see the procession upon the screen. He was told, in a voice of carefully modulated politeness, that, should he do this, and then decline a selection, a substantial charge must be made; to which Rex replied, in a hearty voice: "Oh, damn that! I don't mind the expense," and felt that he had run true to form.

He could not complain that he received grudging value for whatever he might be destined to pay. The moving, speaking pictures explained themselves, one by one, with great frankness, and there was no lack of a similar candour in the captions which set out their qualities, and sometimes their defects, so that there should be no danger of dissatisfaction resulting from inappropriate choice.

Finally, lest memory should be confused, the whole gallery of complaisant pulchritude was comprehensively shown at a single view. A dozen pairs of eyes were turned seductively in his direction. Soft voices from smiling lips wooed his choice, with some attractive variations of accent, in. the Anglo-American tongue.

As the lights brightened, and the screen became blank again, Rex rang up the management.

"Tell those dames," he said, "they're a fine lot. But you haven't got quite the baby for me."

Would he like any further refreshment before retiring? Yes—a glass of grape juice and two peaches—peeled. The delusion that the peach is an exceptionally fine fruit still endured in a changing world.

The automatic waiter brought up the desired refreshment, and Seeley Whitcombe found forgetfulness in a silk-soft bed.

X. RICHTER REQUIRES HELP

THE STUTTGART OF 1990 was no larger in population than had been the bomb-battered city of forty years earlier. It would be a misleading statement to say that it was larger itself. It was not larger, but different.

Being one of the five licensed Cities of Research within the European Federation, it had a static population of 60,000 workpeople, whose families were allowed to reside within a five-mile radius, though they were barred from access to the huge, square-walled *werke*—a city within a city—from which so great a variety of chemicals, synthetic foods, drugs, dyes, cosmetics, and manures were loaded into the trucks that were being backed continually into its marshalling yards, or run up the light electric railway on to the airport platforms, to be distributed to a grateful world.

By that airport the Palace Square, with its surrounding buildings and parks, had been overwhelmed many years before, in which respect Stuttgart had only experienced a destruction which had fallen upon the ancient glories of a hundred cities of the Old World, and the less venerable excellencies of those of the New; the mania which had sacrificed uncalculated material wealth during the earlier part of the century, and a million lives, to the pleasure of whirling that and those which remained, having developed in the anticipated directions, and almost to the anticipated degree.

Onto the passenger platform of this airport Rex Bulldozer was discharged in the usual manner, under a bright sun and a sky of cloud-flecked blue (for sun and rain and cloud still continued, with but little interference from the lords of physical science, though it was not intended that this neglect should continue), at the same time that Édouard Richter, with the constant Amelie at his side, sat in the steel-walled garden of his own residence with Baron Gluck, the European Minister of Education.

They sat in the midst of a wide lawn, an open space at this period being the only possible security against not merely the overhearing, but the permanent recording of what was said, and even that security being far from absolute, particularly unless those who engaged in the conversation submitted to a preliminary examination of a thorough character. But it was the best condition possible for privacy, at a time when most privacies had taken the way that liberties went before.

The lawn was smooth and green, being almost entirely independent of the changes the seasons bring. It was heated from beneath, from which direction its soil was also injected with potent foods, and, for other reasons, it was not soil in which the boldest wireworm would choose to live. Part of this lawn was now covered by movable ceiling, which would protect those who used it from rain or sun, as occasion came. The wind must be boisterous indeed which would overreach the barrier of the high, straight, steel-sheet walls to disturb those who should be sitting below.

Baron Gluck had sat there for two hours, sipping his favourite beverage, saying little, and hearing much. At times his pudgy fingers had moved uneasily round his neck, as though the rolls of reddish skin lay uneasily round his silken collar. But these movements had ceased, and now there came a gleam of anticipation in the small pig's-eyes as he listened to the proposals that the great scientist made.

Herr Richter had selected him as confidant and colleague in the realization of a dream which he could not resolve to leave, and which yet confronted him with problems of appalling magnitude, because the Baron's reputation was for a genius of organization which, rather than any pre-eminence of erudition, had brought him to where he was.

It was that executive quality which now led him to think: "It is our own fault that we let them live to make sleek-fed slaves of their fellow men, who have bartered liberty and all noble things for the mess of pottage which is all that science can ever give, and which it can be so potent to take away." He did not think in these words, for nobility of any kind would be unlikely to enter his mind, but he saw facts. He thought again: "They of the Middle Ages were wiser than we. They would have made a bonfire to cleanse the world."

So reason told him, but he was not concerned for the world's welfare: he considered himself, and, subordinately, a daughter, unattractive to others, but whom he loved as much as men of his kind are able to do. He saw that Richter might have some plan to eliminate him as soon as his usefulness should be done, but he did not think that there was a great danger of that.

Otherwise, his only peril was disclosed by his host's frank declaration that he did not intend that any man's life should continue for a season beyond his own.

"I propose," he had said, "that we shall keep as many alive at this time as will conduce to our own comfort, and enable us to use the earth in the best way for ourselves, and that they shall be such as are of an ignorance that will render them harmless to us. It is your help I ask, for decision and selection of how many and who these survivors shall be. You will see that it is a matter of great complexity, and must be decided in a haste which I had not meant, owing to the outbreak of this cursed war. But I cannot risk what may happen if I allow it to take a precedent course. Mendoza has powers which he might be tempted to use, such as would be fatal to all—even to me. I might still have time to give brimstone to him, but there would be little comfort in that, for I should know that I might have been quicker to make an end. He is a man not to be lightly esteemed, as I have reason to know. Neither are Conroy or Murchison without some knowledge, such as it is useful to have, but they would have scruples to hold them back. They are still slaves of the superstitions that shackle action, though they may allow thought.

"But we will act at once, which will put such dangers aside. We will make the earth an orange for us to suck. I will tell you this: I do not know how I can continue to live beyond the natural duration of man, though I may find that even that can be done, when I can think of it with a free mind. If I should solve that problem, it may be well for others as well as me.

"For I have never intended that the human race shall continue beyond the length of my own life. What could be the purpose in that? I had always meant, and for several years it has been most surely arranged, that, when I die, an infection shall take the world which none will avoid or cure. So it will be at the end. But you must not look as though that may be bad tidings for you, for I am the younger man, and all my organs are good."

Baron Gluck had seen that. It was a most uncomfortable knowledge to have, but it held no immediate menace and, if its threat could be permanently averted, it was a matter of which to think at another time.

And then, as though this thought were known or suspected by him, Richter went on: "I will tell you this also. I have an invention approaching the stage at which it can be put to practical use, by which I shall be able to secure the degree of safety for myself and those whom I am able to call my friends which comfort requires. It is a method of reading the thoughts of men."

"Do you mean under all circumstances?" the baron asked. "Without the consent—or perhaps the knowledge—of those who will be liable to that exploration?"

"It is a question," Richter answered, with an aspect of frankness, "to which it is not yet possible to give a final reply. It has been known for many years that every thought makes a physical registration upon the brain. That being so, and in the light of what has been done for the transference of sound from air to ether, and again from ether to air, it has been evident that it could only be a matter of time before the conditions of successful telepathy would be understood.

"But I need not tell you that there is often a wide gulf between the discovery of a fact or process in physical science and its practical application. I have known for several months of a method by which a thought may be registered on a mind other than that with which it originates, by which I mean that there will be precisely the same registration—the same physical change—in both brains; but the utilization of this knowledge remains a matter very difficult to contrive. There is, among other things, an obstacle of contending or simultaneous thoughts, very curious in its consequences, and beyond brief explanation; and there is a further question of whether the identical registration will be identical in interpretation, which only extended experiment can finally resolve. And even then the means of putting the discovery to practical use must, in several respects, be a matter of further research."

"If it could be fully controlled, it would give its possessors a great power."

"Yes. It would render many forms of deception difficult, if not impossible. As I have said already, I did not wish that this crisis should come upon us before I had this discovery, among others, in practical use. It would have enabled elimination to be made with a discrimination which we cannot apply. It is a matter which I have mentioned to you because its full development—if it should still be of importance in a subdued world—might require the use of a larger number of men (or children, to speak with exactness, for they would be preferable in an important respect), who might not be available afterwards for other uses, and a sufficient number should therefore be preserved, with whatever attendants they may require.

"I should add that I have already made a list of such of my own family and attendants, including those at the laboratories and other activities of this city, as will be likely to be profitable to keep, so that you need not concern yourself about them. And you should know that your own and your daughter's names were among the first to be there."

"That will relieve me," the baron answered, "of what would have been the most difficult part of a matter which is still of extreme perplexity and must be resolved at extreme speed. It would be a safeguard against omission or duplication if you would let me have a copy of that list, for—need I say?—my most private use."

"It is what I should be glad to do, but it is an impossible thing; for it is not a matter of written record but is contrived in another way."

The Baron made no answer to this. It confirmed the opinion, generally held, that Herr Richter had a secret method of recording, though it left him to guess what it might be. He saw that he was being treated with exceptional confidence, or the information would not have been given to him, even in this cryptic manner; but he did not fail to remember that he was in the power of the man with the harassed look and the restless eyes, and that an excessive curiosity might draw upon him a deferred sentence of death, which he would have no means to avoid.

He would have liked to take Herr Richter's rather scrawny throat in his two hands and press his thumbs into it on either side until a limp body could be safely dropped to the ground. But he remembered the warning that Richter had given that he did not intend that the human race should outlast himself. It might be an empty boast. But it might not. Herr Richter's record made it quite probably true.

He said: "I will go back to Berlin at once. If you have a complete plan in a week's time, it will be soon enough?"

"I should have preferred it earlier than that. It might be one that I should not entirely approve. For important modifications, the remaining time would not be long."

"But you will appreciate that it will require thought, and there may be enquiries to ascertain the names of the most suitable selections to make among specialists of particular kinds. At present, I have no clear decision of mind, even as to whether it will be scores or millions who must survive. And you will agree that it must all be very secretly done. If I promise—"

"I would have you promise nothing that you do not perform. The stake is too high for any thought of failure to be allowed. It is to have the world at our feet!"

"Yes…and to save it from a prolonged and, perhaps, most worrying war!"

The baron smiled sardonically as he said this, but there was no response on the face of his host. Herr Richter knew that men jested, though he was unable to understand why. He passed such remarks as though they had not reached his ears, as they scarcely did.

When the Baron had left, Herr Richter summoned the head of the Stuttgart police, who took his orders from him.

"Colonel," he said, "I want a subject for experiments which have become urgent. A child would, in some ways, be best; but it would not be suitable for subsequent return, which might occasion enquiry, such as I prefer to avoid."

"It would occasion remark."

"So it would, though it might not he much. There must be children whom their parents would spare with no great regret. But if you can find a stranger in the town who could be invited here with a plausible word, and whose disappearance would concern no one at a near place, or a near time, it would be a service I should esteem."

Colonel Wagram said that this should be done.

XI. COLONEL WAGRAM INVITES

REX BULLDOZER, HAVING enquired for the best accommodation in Stuttgart, was directed to the Hotel Central, which was on the south side of the town, and so placed in a fold of the wooded hills that it experienced little of the fumes from the *werke*, which, although so treated that they would probably have been unnoticed by an earlier generation, were considered intolerable by the plutocracy of this period.

He was the better satisfied with this choice because the hotel was at no great distance from the high-walled residence of the King of Stuttgart (as Herr Richter was in fact, if not precisely in name), and it would be appropriate to a plan which was now taking shape in his mind—a plan which was of considerable subtlety in its intended development of the blustering clumsiness of his assumed character, but one to which it is needless to give detailed record, as it was not destined to be put to any practical test, unpredictable chance, at this stage, taking the game into its capricious control.

For Rex Bulldozer, having secured the most expensive suite in the hotel not already in occupation, had scarcely settled himself therein when he was both annoyed and alarmed by the information that Colonel Wagram desired to see him.

The name meant nothing to him, the colonel's status not having penetrated to the Interfederal office at Havana, but he was not aware of anyone who was likely to have business with him, unless it should be of a hostile sort.

He answered the polite announcing voice which gave him this information with the query: "Did the gentleman say what his business is?" and received the reply, more polite of tone than substance: "He will doubtless explain that himself. He is on the way up to you."

"Well," Seeley Whitcombe though, "it looks as though the game may be over before it can properly he said to have begun. But, whatever my intentions may have been, I have done nothing yet to which objection can be legally taken, beyond coming here in an assumed name, and even that would not be simple to prove."

Yet it might mean detention, if nothing worse, which would be nuisance enough, and an ignominious ending to an adventure which could only be made to have an aspect of sanity if it should succeed. Or this might be a harmless call, such as only that which was privy to his own mind caused him to fear. But he saw that to be a poor guess. Anyway, he must not forget that he was Rex Bulldozer, and that he must sustain the part as realistically as though it were unshakable fact. His enigmatic visitor was knocking upon the door.

Colonel Wagram entered alone. There was a slight preliminary relief in that. He was, at least, not the head of an arresting posse. Neither was his manner aggressive, though it was too formal, his appearance too official, to encourage hope that it was a friendly or casual call.

"I must introduce myself, Mr. Bulldozer," he said. "I am Colonel Wagram, and I am the representative of Herr Richter, of whom I will not suppose that you do not know. May I sit?"

"Sure you may," Rex replied heartily. "Sit over here.... May I order you something up?"

Definitely, though politely, the Colonel declined the offered hospitality.

You are," he asked, "a North American citizen? You are visiting us at a time of interfederal tension, and it is natural that we should ask what your business is."

"Sure you can. I'm here to find two young guys who are wandering round when their dad thinks they should be a bit nearer home."

"He could have radioed for their return."

"I'd say he could. It'd have been better sense than me coming here. But their ma wasn't to know they've been left out in the rain. And, anyhow, it suits me down to the ground. Dollars talk."

The colonel appeared to understand Mr. Bulldozer's meaning without difficulty. He replied, in his careful English, that he had no doubt that it was a profitable mission, such as a business man would not wish to refuse. If Mr. Bulldozer would be good enough to accompany him, he would introduce him to Herr Richter, who would doubtless be satisfied with the explanation, and all would be well.

Colonel Wagram had accepted his statements so readily, and showed so little inclination to probe them further, that Seeley had a momentary doubt as to whether his mission might not be as simple in its purpose as he would have him believe. If that were so, it would seem that he was to be taken to the man whom it had appeared almost vain to hope that he would be able to reach, with no more risk to himself than was involved in the plausible assertion of that which no one was of a disposition to doubt. But was this reasonable to believe?

It could not be habitual to one in Herr Richter's position to give personal interviews to wandering strangers whose credentials were open to question. That would obviously be a matter for the local police. It was one with which the man before him should be competent to deal. It appeared certain to him that he must not merely be suspect, but suspect in some particularly important way. They could not know the intention with which he had come. That was private to Silver Long and himself, and was too wild an audacity to be made a probable guess. But they might—it seemed that they almost certainly must—have made a correct guess—or have actual knowledge—of who he was.

He was mistaken in this conclusion, but it was reasonable from what he knew, the truth being of an unguessable kind. It was on the assumption that he was betrayed (was there a traitor even in the inmost circles of the premier's household?) that he must decide what it would be best to do. And, as he thought this, and looked at Colonel Wagram, sitting opposite him in polite expectation of his reply, an idea came.

It was a wild idea. But the whole thing was wild! There was no escaping from that. And the uniform—at least to a point—should make it possible. Only, he must know more than he did now. Delay was imperative. Some excuse must be found for that.

"Colonel Wagram," he said, "you have reminded me that there is a prospect of war between our Federation and yours, though it is not a present fact. I hope that it may never be, and, in any event, that there may be no bitterness in what may be done. I am not an owner of livestock, and I confess that the fate of such creatures would not cause me a loss of sleep. Of course I will comply with your request to wait upon Herr Richter's pleasure. I regard it as a command, and also as an honour for me. But it is a fact that I need a meal. Will it strain your kindness too far if I ask you to join me in some refreshment, which I am sure that this excellent hotel will be quick to serve?"

Seeing the look that came to his visitor's face as he heard this proposition, Seeley anticipated curt refusal, but the Colonel remained silent for a long moment. He was doubly puzzled, both as to what he should do, and—for the first time—as to what sort of man Rex Bulldozer might really be, and on what errand he had come. For it had not been Rex but Seeley who had addressed him on this last occasion, and the difference, even to one to whom English was not a native tongue, was too great to be overlooked. But there was one final consideration. Herr Richter had instructed him that there was to be the minimum of publicity in what he did.

It was to comply with that instruction that he had chosen a stranger who had arrived in Stuttgart only a few hours before; and who, he had ascertained, had come straight to the Hotel Central, and had made no contacts in the city.

It was for the same reason that he had come himself on an errand which he would normally have given to a subordinate. Herr Richter would prefer that he should expend an extra hour, rather than that it should be necessary to secure his victim by violent arrest. He said: "If you are really needing a meal—it should not mean a long delay."

Thinking that it might be the last that one—or perhaps both?—of them would be likely to have, Rex gave the order, and it was no more than a few minutes before the automatic waiter slid a well-laid table into the room.

XII. FIRST CASUALTY

THE MEAL WAS good. So was the Moselle wine, of which Rex had ordered two bottles, though the second remained unopened.

The Colonel, who felt that that for which he had come was already done, relaxed somewhat, and gave ready answers to questions which did not seem to be of a dangerous kind. Would it be Herr Richter's pleasure to receive Mr. Bulldozer at his own residence? Yes, surely. No stranger—*no one* not in employment there—ever entered the *werke*. Herr Richter's residence was not far? No. From this window, looking up the valley, its turrets could be seen through the trees. The Colonel politely followed his host to the window to point it out. He also pointed out his car, which stood waiting in the gravelled circus before the hotel. No. He had no chauffeur with him. Except on long journeys, he drove himself. (The cars of 1990 were very easy to drive.) Yes. It was an Aurora. Discussion followed concerning the differences between European and American cars, with particular reference to the special features Auroras had. Would Mr. Bulldozer be able to see Herr Richter at once? That was hard to say. There was an annexe to the main structure of the residence, into which casual visitors were allowed to enter, and it was there that they would have to await the pleasure of the great man.

Other details of probable procedure followed. It was mere perfunctory time-occupying talk to the colonel, the combination of shrewdness and brutality which fitted him for the position he held failing to warn him of any possible peril in informing this self-sure American—Seeley, after that one lapse of forgetfulness, had become Bulldozer again—of the innocent details of his entrance into a trap into which he was to be led without suspicion. Coming out would be a more difficult matter. Indeed, there may have been cunning in the readiness of his replies, as being calculated to increase the confidence of one who was to be brought in that willing way.

Mr. Bulldozer prolonged the conversation to the limit that he felt able to do, but the time came when he must rise from a finished meal. Looking for a moment which would not come, he lingered over his final preparations for departure, while inwardly cursing a wall mirror which he knew he must be careful not to ignore. It was when hope of executing his plan had almost failed that opportunity came. The colonel, preceding him in their intended departure, turned toward the door. In that instant, Rex seized the bottle of wine which was still full, and brought it down with his utmost force on the close-cropped head.

It was a form of attack in which he lacked the judgment that experience gives. A blow half as hard, with a less murderous weapon, might have been sufficient to crack the skull of the unfortunate man. He showed the quickness of mind that the occasion required when he threw a rug over the sprawling body in such a way as to cover its clothes from the pulsing blood.

He looked round at a room which it would have been hopeless to attempt to cleanse. There would not only have been the body of a dead man of which to dispose. There was the mess of the spilt white wine, and the broken glass; and the far-spreading blood which soaked into the close, white, soft-textured carpet. But he had no such thought. He knew that he had started on a road where he could not turn.

He was favoured by the change of custom which had substituted mechanical for manual service. The perfectly-run hotel, by the standards of 1990, was that in which the only sign of living service was the voice which would always answer a call.

Now he touched a bell and said that the table could be withdrawn. He added a request that cigars should be supplied, and mentioned that he was retaining some glasses and one bottle of wine.

He checked himself from adding that it would he another half-hour before Colonel Wagram would leave, realizing that there had been more than sufficient gaucherie in what he had said already. But they might attribute that to the fact that he came from a foreign land! He had wished to make the length of time that his visitor would have been with him seem a natural thing. But the ordering of the cigars should have been sufficient for that!

If anyone should wish to dress himself in clothes worn by another man, who is not a consenting party to the transaction, it has some advantages for the wearer to be unconscious or dead. But it would be in excess of the fact to say that it makes it easy to do.

Seeley approved thoroughness, but he soon abandoned the idea of making a complete change. It would cost trouble—and time—enough to make the change of outer appearance complete.

It was considerably more than half an hour later when the mirror told him that, sartorially at least, he had become a colonel of European police. He blessed the fate that had made him of about the same height as his victim, though the waistband was rather loose, the boots rather large. Neither of these differences was likely to attract the notice of others, though they might occasion some slight discomfort for him.

When he had opened his trunk and got out Seeley's denture (brought with some hesitation, but with a sound judgment that, if he should be subject to such probing investigation as would disclose the fact that he had it, the disclosure would have become unimportant), and aided by a few deft touches of the actor's craft, he was not Colonel Wagram, or anything which, to one who knew him, could be mistaken for him, but he had ceased to be Rex Bulldozer, and might pass readily for the colonel to casual disregardant eyes. A uniform can do much.

Also, he had the colonel's papers, the colonel's passes, which might or might not be of use in the programme to which he had set his mind, but which it was a comfort to him to have; and the colonel's excellent automatic, as to the advantage of which there could be no doubt at all. It was a minor nuisance that, there being so many of his victim's effects that he wished to retain, and so many of his own with which he was reluctant to part, his pockets were inclined to bulge.

It might have been a higher artistry which would have kept nothing to identify him with the late Rex Bulldozer, but he judged that his new personality would never be built up to sustain more than a superficial view.

Locking the door of his room, he went down the automatic lift, out through the hotel hall, down the wide white marble steps that led to the gravelled circus, and crossed to the Aurora car that the deceased had so obligingly pointed out as his, without coming into near contact with either woman or man, or observing any evidence that his movements were of interest to anyone but himself. Remembering the instructions he had received, he unlocked the car with the colonel's key, and sinking into the cushioned comfort of the driver's seat, concentrated his attention upon the mirrors by the aid of which he guided the car.

He knew that the body of Colonel Wagram might be discovered at any time, though there was a probability that this would not occur until the absence of any orders coming from his room, or response to enquiries therefrom, had excited remark. When that should happen, the uniform which he wore would be no longer a protection, but would become a damning clue. He knew that his time of safety was short, though he could not tell how long it would be. And for that short time—was safety exactly the word to use, with the purpose he had in view?

XIII. SEELEY MAY COME IN

AMELIE LATOUR HAD no abnormal faculty: she had a normal faculty developed to an abnormal degree. The world's population through which, with minute enquiry, Herr Richter had searched to find her, had been declining steadily for the previous half-century, but was still, even after the Asian disaster, more than 500,000,000; and among this considerable number her memory was the most perfect that could be found, and had naturally been further improved by specialization and the absence of any distracting occupations or cares.

It is a plausible theory that one cannot forget anything which has once been sensuously experienced, whether by sight or hearing, by scent or touch. That which has not been recalled for half a century, and which no effort of will could revive, may be remembered, even to trivial detail, by some chance association of sight or sound.

It must have been stored in the mind, though beyond reach, all those dormant years.

Amelie had the faculty which could recall at will. In early years it had been remarked and praised, and she had been encouraged by that recognition to deliberate cultivation of a natural aptitude. That which she resolved at the time of its occurrence to remember accurately became a certainty of recollection, and if she used any tricks of association (which is beyond either denial or proof), she was secret in what she did.

Living with what may be described as a passive vividness, abnormally conscious of her surroundings (and of herself as their conscious centre), she was too aware of circumscribing conduct and convention to be likely to do anything which would be discreditable to those standards, unless under temptation far stronger than she had yet experienced. Negatively, her character, when discovered by Herr Richter's exhaustive enquiries, had been impeccable, and so, in the easy conditions of life beneath the great scientist's luxurious roof, it had continued to be.

There were those who, observing the closeness of their association, assumed her to be the mistress of her employer, but (leaving aside the fact that it would have been condoned by the social code of Central Europe at that time) they would have been utterly wrong.

Herr Richter was not one who would be likely to confound business with pleasure. He had a pleasant, ordinary, ineffectual wife. He had mistresses also, commercially selected, and of a casual kind, in which respect he did nothing to outrage the ethics of the decadent, materialistic plutocracy which he served, and aspired to overcome or destroy. Amelie was engaged with a purpose too explicit and important to be confused with such occasional relaxations, and the probability of anything more compelling than physical attraction arising between them would be too slight for regard. The only romance he could ever know (if we may degrade the word to such a use) was in the control of physical and biological forces, and in the dreams of malignant power which they gave to a mind too mean for nobler conceptions to take root within it.

Nor, on her side, was Amelie one of the kind whom propinquity rules, or who can lack emotional experience only at the cost of restlessness and disease. Many such women there doubtless are, but there are others in whom passion appears to remain as potentiality rather than power until it is roused by some ulterior impulse, the impact of which is upon both body and mind.

Amelie, far from unconscious of, or indifferent to, her own sensuous beauties of face and form, or insensitive to the material comforts her employment earned, was undisturbed by the physical and mental isolation in which she lived.

Herr Richter was right in regarding her as one who was abnormally aware of surrounding things: who felt rather than thought. But her feeling had a receptive, impersonal quality which accepted but did not give. Emotionally, if she were not lifeless, she had a life which had not yet come to its waking hour.

Intellectually, she had complete confidence in Herr Richter, whether in his ability to defend Europe from the rest of the world, or to do anything else to which he should turn his thoughts. She had never considered the possibility of thwarting, or the propriety of questioning, anything he might direct or desire. Had she done so, it would have been with a great and reasonable fear of what the consequences to herself would be. But occasion for such a fear would be unlikely to come.

Now she lay, stretched at ease as her habit was, taking record of a series of names which she was to add to others stored in her mind during the last few days. There were already more than three hundred of these, and it was the most difficult feat of memory which had ever been required from her, for she was told nothing (whatever she might surmise) of the purpose for which the list was being made, and it had no apparent unity of its own. Besides that, it was being changed from hour to hour, not only by additions but by deletions, some of which were restored and then might be deleted again.

"I shan't want you to remember these names for more than about ten days," Herr Richter said. "After that, I shall want you to give them to me in written form. Can yon do that?"

"How many more are there likely to be?"

"Not many. Perhaps fifty. Probably less. There'll be another list in a week's time. It may be a lot longer. I don't know. But that will come to us written down. Who's that wanting me now?"

Amelie reached out a hand and made the desired connection. The voice that answered her said that Colonel Wagram was waiting to make his report.

"Wagram speaking?" Herr Richter asked.

Amelie frowned over this query. "No. I don't think—" She checked herself to ask: "Is that Colonel Wagram speaking? He says: Yes."

"Then I will speak to him."

If there were anything strange in the voice, it was imperceptible to Herr Richter's less sensitive ear.

"Have you found what I want?" he asked. "Yes? And he's with you now? Can you say who he is without giving anything away to him?"

The voice answered: "Mr. Rex Bulldozer is here to see you as you required."

"American name? Someone just landed here? Made any local contacts? Well, I'll see him. You needn't wait."

He cut off, and turned to Amelie to say: "There's someone Wagram's brought, whom I shall keep here. But I'm not going to see him now. I want you to do that first. See him in one of the blue rooms. He'll talk freely there. Find out all you can about him, and remember it carefully. You needn't tell him he won't be allowed to go. He's an American, and you'd better make out we want to understand what he's doing here. Let him think we suspect he's a spy, but are quite prepared to believe he's not, if he's open with us."

Amelie stretched out her hand to make another connection. She said: "There's a visitor in the annexe. Let him in. Guide him to one of the blue rooms. Yes, number four will do."

She rose with the easy laziness that was her usual motion when unhurried and unperturbed. She had instructions this time which should be more interesting than the memorizing of several hundred names, which even she had not been finding it easy to do.

XIV. INTERVIEW IN A BLUE ROOM

IT HAS BEEN said that there was little privacy of word or deed for those who lived as the twentieth century its close. That was certainly true, and had been forecast by the tendencies of earlier years. But it oversimplifies the comparison, and may seem to be contradicted by the absence of human attendance which had enabled Lord Whitcombe to leave an unsuspected corpse in his room at the Hotel Central, with some reasonable hope that it would not be discovered for a day or two after he had left.

It is true that the development of mechanical service had reduced human contacts, particularly in the more luxurious hotels and private residences which were organized in the same plutocratic manner; and when Seeley entered the reception room in the annexe to Herr Richter's residence, he had encountered no one to make ocular observation of his identity. But as he stood there, and pressed the button which would announce his presence, he knew that every sound he made was being recorded, and that he was being photographed continually from various angles, and with a thoroughness which would record every item his pockets held.

He knew this, not as presumption but certainty, by a faint rose-colour which distinguished the lighting of the room, and which no scientific ingenuity had been able to eliminate from the projection which such photography required. To neutralize it was to reduce the records to a faint blur.

Of all colours, blue was the most antipathetic to this form of photography, and it was for this reason that it had become a routine of courtesy to receive a guest in a blue-lit room. It was in such a lighting that all private occupations were carried on, and all intimate personal contacts made.

As he pressed the button which would announce his presence, he thought grimly: "Well, in the next five minutes I shall know whether I've been a bigger fool than I normally am."

It was a reasonable doubt. Knowing what the fact was, we may question whether matters would have gone worse, or substantially differently, had he allowed the unfortunate colonel to live, and to bring him where he had thought it better to come alone.

But it was a fact which he would not guess. On the knowledge he had, it was natural to doubt, though it might be premature to condemn the discretion of the course he had chosen to take. If it should lead to meeting Herr Richter alone, it might be much better than to have done so with Colonel Wagram at his side. But was that a probable anticipation? It was hard to say. There was nothing probable in the whole event. It was certainly better to have the colonel's automatic in his own pocket than for it to be a few feet away in that of its late owner. It was less satisfactory to know that if he should be detained here, it would not be as a visitor against whom much might be suspected but nothing proved, but as one who had murdered a high officer of the law.

But all such matters were of minor importance. The one paramount question was: had he, by however little, improved the prospect of carrying out the wild purpose for which he came?

To announce himself as Colonel Wagram seemed to be the obvious, and might be the only, way of obtaining entrance without preliminary altercation: to say that Rex Bulldozer was with him appeared to give the best prospect of reaching the presence of the man he sought.

The reply which this statement met was enigmatic, but not entirely disconcerting. It showed that Richter had really expected the colonel to bring someone, though with some doubt of who it was to be. It was explicit that he would see him. Would it be alone? That could be no more than a doubtful hope.

The next moment, the heavy metal door slid open, showing a long, narrow, steel-walled passage. A voice said: 'Follow the ceiling light, and enter room number four."

As he went forward, the door closed behind him. A line of light in the ceiling lengthened ahead, like a pointing finger of fire. Following it, he came to another door of shining metal which opened and closed in the same way, and then the light guided him through turning passages and past several doors, until it paused above one which had the number upon it which he had been told to seek.

He heard the click of an opening lock. The door moved noiselessly. He entered an empty room.

He was reassured by the blue light, and the thought came to him with a shock, which showed how wild and frail had been his previous hope: "Am I really going to succeed?"

It was all so utterly, incredibly different from anything he had thought or planned. Was it not still almost certain that Herr Richter had discovered his identity, and was using this method to get him quietly and securely into his power? Suppose Colonel Wagram had not been in his complete confidence? That would explain the way in which he had spoken.

Yet, even so, he might possibly have decided to see this most unexpected visitor alone. He might even welcome a talk with the Interfederal Minister of the opposing power such as would be informal and unrecorded. The blue room suggested that. He might be acting in such a way on the instructions of his own government, or without its knowledge. They were suppositions about equally probable to one familiar with the politics of that day.

Perhaps he hoped that his visitor had come secretly and treacherously to sell the secrets of his own land? If so, need he be quick to deny?

Anyway, it would not be expected that he would have arrived in the colonel's clothes. What would be Herr Richter's reaction to that? What could his own explanation be? Nor would he expect him to have the colonel's automatic in his jacket pocket.

Would it be wisest to shoot at sight? Herr Richter's death would certainly be a great loss to the United States of Europe. But what would the ultimate consequences of the assassination be? Especially if his own identity should be disclosed? Could it be considered a breach of the treaty governing conditions of war? As a private action, surely no. But if it should be set up that he had been sent for such a purpose by Silver Long?

As these thoughts crowded upon him during the short moment of waiting, if an act of will could have returned him to his own land, or if he could have brought Colonel Wagram to life again, it is hard to guess what he would have done. And then, not Herr Richter, but a girl, young, smiling, self-possessed, and very beautiful, entered the room

She greeted him with easy courtesy in the German tongue, which had become the universal language of Europe (except in the antique Parisian atmosphere) since the victors of the mid-century war had elaborately federated its various states, with a most contrite and docile Germany inevitably in their geographical centre, and with the largest single population, after it had destroyed the more virile half of those by which it had been surrounded.

But next moment she changed to an English that was as perfect as his: "But is it not the English Commonwealth from which you come? I was misled for a moment—" She looked at his uniform with puzzled eyes.

"Colonel Wagram," he answered boldly, "lent it to me, so that I might come unobserved."

"Yes?" she said. And then, as though supplying sufficient explanation for improbable fact: "Doubtless it was what Herr Richter wished him to do."

"He was—he is not one, I should say, to question any order from that direction."

"No. No one does. Did he say why Herr Richter wished you to come here?"

"I was invited, as I understood, because I was a visitor from overseas."

"Yes. He would like to talk to you himself. But meanwhile you can tell me. He may not be able to see you at once. We shall provide for you in comfort until he does."

"I shall be pleased to stay until I can have the honour of seeing Herr Richter, though I hope it may not be long."

"You will have your baggage at an hotel?"

"At the Hotel Central. We need not trouble for that."

"But it will be none! I will give them instructions to send it here."

"It might be a mistake to do that. I understood that my visit was not to be generally known."

"But they will say nothing. They are discreet."

"I can go back for anything I require."

"That would be the more public way! But I will not urge that which you do not wish. We can provide all you will require."

"I am sure of that." Seeley changed the subject with relief: "What is it you wish to know?"

"Herr Richter would ask: why you are here?"

"I have no objection to telling that."

Yet, having said that, he hesitated how to continue. It was a simple presumption that the girl had been sent to trap him—to persuade him to some damning admission, such as cruder methods might fail to do. Yet he felt instinctively that she was not of that sort, though he was unsure of what sort she was. Her voice, her manner, her attitude—he could not define that which he clearly felt—were of one who was neither hostile nor critical, who was prepared to listen and to believe.

He must tell her the tale of the missing youths—for what else was it possible for him to say?—but he had a curious reluctance to act the part of Rex Bulldozer, as he had conceived it before. It was as though it had gone with the over-prominent denture which he had left in the hotel room.

Told in his own person, it became a new tale, and one of which he was ashamed in a new way. An errand suitable for Rex Bulldozer was one of which one of the most important of world politicians had no cause to be proud. Why must he be himself to the girl, rather than play the part he had chosen to act? He turned from fictitious narrative, as far as her questions allowed, to broader and truer facts concerning the lands and peoples of his own world, which he found her equally ready to hear

The whole interview was puzzling, inexplicable, to him, he having no clue to the evil purpose which had been the occasion for inviting, and was to be the reason for detaining him there. On her side, Amelie, while almost equally ignorant, though not entirely unsuspicious, of Herr Richter's intentions, had had no reason to doubt the innocence of his own conduct, or that he would hesitate to tell her the true object of his visit to Europe.

She had been instructed to obtain information from him. There had been no warning that such information might not be true.

"I suppose," she said at last, "that you have told me all that Herr Richter can wish to know. But he has said that he will see you himself. I cannot say how soon it may be. But I will let you know in the next hour. If he should wish you to stay here for the night, you will be given a better room, and, in the meantime, you can order anything you desire. You will find a push under the chair-arm, where you would expect it to be."

"Yes," he said. "All the world is alike in that." He meant all the world of wealth, for the social order had not changed so far that there were not many who lived in a different way.

She gave him a friendly glance, for he was one whom she thought it would be easy to like, and went back to Herr Richter, with whom she shared the solitude of the evening meal. His wife bored him, as he did not scruple to say, and Amelie had noticed, with some wonder, but less surprise, that her name had not been among those which she had been told to memorize, for what purpose she could guess, though she did not know.

Herr Richter said she must be with him, either to hear anything he wished to commit to her, or to supply any information he might require. There were times when he would talk to her of the affairs which filled his own thoughts, and she would respond with such intelligence as he would expect her to show, but with no opposition or difference of outlook to vex his mind; but, for the most part, he would be silent, occupied with his own thoughts, when she would be silent too, which, in fact, she preferred.

But now he waited for her report.

"He is an American," she said, "who arrived in Stuttgart this morning. His name is Rex Bulldozer."

"It is such a name as Americans have. Of what age is he?"

"Not old."

"Older than you?"

"Oh, yes! Perhaps twenty years—or fifteen."

"In good health?"

"Yes. So he looks."

"Intelligent?"

"Yes. Exceptionally so, I should think."

"Why is he here?"

"He has come to find some boys, on their father's behalf. He was their tutor not long ago."

"Tutor? It is a poor trade. He will be a man of no importance. That is well. Was his coming here known?"

"He has a room at the Central. He has no acquaintance here. So he said."

"It is well again. We want no disturbance before the storm."

She went on to report what she had learned, which she did clearly and accurately, and he accepted it without doubt. The criminality of his own purpose dispossessed his mind of any inclination to doubt the good faith of the stranger whom he had trapped. Only when Amelie said that Colonel Wagram had lent him his own clothes, he exclaimed: "He did *what*? Nonsense. That is absurd."

For a moment his eyes held doubt of he knew not what, and then cleared as he said "Wagram would not lend him his own clothes. But he may have brought him here in a uniform of the police that his identity should not be observed. Wagram is a good man. He is thorough in all he does."

Amelie said nothing to this. She knew that she had been right. It was Colonel Wagram's uniform—that which he had had on that morning—that Mr. Bulldozer had worn. But it was not her part to dispute. She had reported the fact. If Herr Richter did not believe, she would be as contented as though he did

She turned the subject: "I passed Greta as I came here."

"Greta?" he answered absently. "What of her?" His thoughts were on other things, and he did not welcome her opening conversational topics, which she would rarely do.

"It reminded me that her name is not on the list."

"On the list?" There was irritation, if not anger, in his voice now. What was the list to her? Had she ever before given thought to, or made comment on, what he did? Vaguely, he felt as though the world were falling around him before the hour of his own choice.

She knew that it would be vain to urge affection for one who had done her many personal services. She said: "She is useful to me."

Well, it was a small thing! He had nothing against the girl, of whom he scarcely knew. Amelie deserved more from him than that. He asked: "She waits on Freda also?" (Freda was his wife.)

Amelie's wits were abnormally alert. She was fighting for something as, in the course of her easy life, she had seldom had occasion to do. She saw what was in his mind, which it would have been easy to guess wrong.

"No," she said. "She does nothing for her." It was the first time she had lied to him.

"Put her on the list," he said. Telling her by that word what its purpose was, which she had guessed, but not certainly known before.

But a moment later he said: "No, it will not do. I told Gluck I would leave menial service entirely to him. It would be unscientific to have such names on my list after I have said that."

Amelie made no reply. She knew that it would be vain. It would not be scientific to do! She knew that there was no folly, no cruelty, and no crime, that he would hesitate to commit in that sacred name. He saw the discontent on her face, and added irritably: "When he is here with his list, you can mention the girl again.'

After that there was silence. Richter may have been right in his theory that memory nourished in her at the expense of thought. But she was beginning to think now. There was Aline's baby—but it would be clearly useless to ask him for either mother or child. She had, inarticulately, a more heterodox thought, or perhaps feeling would be the more accurate word. She had a doubt whether he were proving equal to that which he was attempting to do. She did not doubt his genius, which was proved. He was a marvellous man. Only, he was trying to be marvellous now in a direction which he had not attempted before. But he was one whom there was no less occasion to fear for any limitation which might be his. He might not only omit Aline's baby from the list. He might omit her. At any shadow of dissatisfaction, any hint of disloyalty, it would be a very probable thing. Suppose that, as the new order should come, she would be no longer required?

Herr Richter had seen the probability that her abnormal memory might imply a deficiency of competing faculties. It had not occurred to him that his own abnormal insight into the operations of bacteria and chemical substances might be accompanied by equally abnormal deficiencies, moral or intellectual, in himself.

As they were rising, he spoke again: "You will give instructions for Bulldozer to be put in the room which adjoins that in which the Zweiter apparatus is set up."

"In—but that room is—"

"Is not furnished? It must be done suitably in the next hour. You will tell Stefan and Yung to be ready during the night, in case they may be required."

He left her as he spoke, his instructions to her rarely requiring explanation, or receiving reply, and she did that which she had been told with more disquiet of mind than she had felt since she had come to his service four years before.

She did not understand the potentialities of the Zweiter apparatus, but she had vague ideas, of which it was uncomfortable to think. She had been attracted to the man with the strange American name in a way which was new to her, and she had a doubt of what would happen during the night.

She knew that, in the pursuit of knowledge, there was no horror, no cruelty, which would cause Herr Richter a moment of hesitation, or of after-regret. He could explain convincingly that such feelings were inhibitions, born of the childish superstitions of more primitive days. And meanwhile, Seeley, having eaten a solitary meal, asked himself: "Am I mad! There may be a report against me at any moment that I have caused the death of the man whose clothes I am wearing: I should be planning what I should do or say if I should be called to meet Herr Richter, as at any moment I may, and with consequences, in literal truth, on which not my life alone—which is, in comparison, a trivial thing—but the fate of the whole world may actually depend—and I cannot turn my thoughts from the face of a girl whom I have only met in the last hour, and who is probably my own, and surely my country's foe."

XV. After a Baffling Night

SEELEY WAS GUIDED to a room which contained every comfort he might require. He was asked what he would like to drink, and chose coffee, of the quality of which he also felt that there was no cause to complain.

After that he slept like a drugged man, of which he was not aware, for when he waked he felt well.

He was roused by a voice which told him that Herr Richter desired his presence at breakfast in an hour's time. That was good to hear, for it would give him the contact for which he came without further delay, and implied that there had not yet been discovery of the body of the man whose uniform he must put on.

He was ready at the time which had been announced, and was guided to a room, small in size, but luxurious in its appointments, where Herr Richter and Amelie were already seated, and had been engaged in a conversation which he would have been interested to hear.

"The American," Herr Richter had said, "will join us in ten minutes from now. There are some further things which I should be glad for you to tell me in the meantime."

She was conscious of a sudden sense of relief, the sharpness of which surprised herself, for it was something different from what she had feared to hear; but she had a perception at the same time that Herr Richter was a puzzled and dissatisfied man. Certainly, whatever haven of safety, power, and material comforts he might be about to win by the most colossal crime that the world had known, he was finding that it was to be approached in no easy way.

"When you talked to this man yesterday," he asked, "he appeared to be telling you about himself without deception—without reserve?"

"Yes," she answered, after a moment of hesitation and frowning brows. "I did not doubt it. He spoke freely of many things."

"Of which you told me all?"

"So I meant to do. I should say I did. Was there something of importance I overlooked?"

"You must tell me that. Did he mention Havana in any way?"

"No. Not at all."

"Did he talk of Silver Long as a man he knew?"

"No. I should suppose it to be unlikely. Of course, he would know of him. Everyone does."

"It is there that the trouble lies. I will tell you this. While he was unconscious during the night, we explored his brain. It was not a thousandth part of the whole, nor could we choose what we would know. But the result was confusing to a fundamental degree, such as to shake the value of half that Zweiter has done during the last three years."

"Yes?" she said, with an interest in her eyes such as they would rarely show, and which may have tempted him to say more than he might otherwise have done.

"So it is," he went on. "We have succeeded beyond our hopes— and are brought to doubt of the value—of the reliability—of what we obtain. We are confused between fact and dream. We know that dreams are compiled of that which has been known or felt, though they may have no basis of fact, and are without the form which waking judgment would give. But we had not supposed that they are recorded, as factual memories certainly are. But it is a possible thing, and if that be so—because dreams can be swifter than fact, and there is a probability that they do not cease during the hours of sleep— they may be more numerous than waking memories by many thousands of times.

"When we took photographic records from Bulldozer's brain, and developed as much as our time allowed, they were of such a nature that I was first led to think that he had told you a lying tale.

"But I considered that that was not a probable thing; and on making analysis in a sound, scientific manner of the records which we have transcribed, I was led to observe that the confusion was not with some other who would be unknown to him unless he were he, but with Lord Whitcombe, a man known to the whole world by repute, and particularly to those of his own land, and of whom he might dream, or even whom, in the confusion of dreams, he might imagine himself to be.

"Havana also was in his mind, and Silver Long, but, here again, they are public to all, and in all men's thoughts.

"You will see where the doubt lies, and of what essential importance it is. For if we are to be lost in a sea of dreams, we may find it vain to attempt to recover the true records which are stored in a living brain, though there would remain a method by which we could capture present thought. At the best, we may have to do much more preliminary work, for it may prove that there are locations of the brain where these confusions do not occur.

"You will understand of how great importance it has become to question this man from an angle you had not got, which is why I have asked him to take breakfast here, as I should otherwise have been most unlikely to do." He added: "I have already suggested to Zweigler a channel of approach by which the difficulty (if it exist, which is not easy to doubt) may be overcome. But it will take time. You must add his name to the list."

He uttered the last words reluctantly, for Zweigler was one whom he had not intended to save. He was a brilliant man, of no better character than his own, and he knew that one such was as many as could be alive in a certain peace.

As he said this Seeley entered the room, and Herr Richter, without rising or offering his hand (for his manners to those around him, for several years, had been, not those of a king, but of the boorish sort that he supposed that a king would have), motioned to indicate the seat that he should take, opposite to Amelie, who was at Herr Richter's right. He said: "I trust, Mr. Bulldozer, that you slept well."

He spoke in English, for the three great languages of the remaining would were universally known, but with an accent that Amelie had been taught to avoid.

"I have seldom slept better," Seeley replied; this being a fact that had been surprise rather than pleasure to him, for he had lain with resolve to rise again at a later hour and make explorations during the night.

He would have been conscious of more self-reproach on wakening had not the voice which roused him given him the opportunity of meeting Herr Richter to which he had now come. But after his experiences of the last day, and with such anticipations of the next as its events and his own purpose would be likely to give, it was surprising and disconcerting that he should have passed at once to a sleep that was deep and long, and he had wondered, while he had dressed, whether he had not undertaken something which he was inadequate to perform, even when opportunity came, almost miraculously, to his feet.

But all contemplated action was confused by developments which appeared fantastic. Either Herr Richter knew that he was Seeley Whitcombe, and was playing with him accordingly, or the invitation that brought him there was as mad as a dream could be.

Men in the position of Herr Richter did not invite casual strangers to personal interviews to ascertain that their credentials were good. Still less did they invite such men to breakfast with them alone. (And at such a crisis as this!) But was it to be alone? Or was the invitation part of a derisive proceeding which was to expose the incognito in which he came?

He set out for the breakfast-room not knowing what to expect, but with the thought of the dead man in his room at the Hotel Central warning him that, even if events were moving with an inexplicable smoothness in the direction he would have them go, his time must be short, and taking some comfort from the automatic his pocket held. At the worst, a bullet might put an end to the man who had devised the attack which was threatened against the welfare of his own peoples. And, if he were dead, could that attack be made at all? There was some reason for doubt.

And if it were not made, what would the position be? The Treaty for the Regulation of Wars, throughout its 297 pages of legal jargon, had not dealt with the position which would arise should one belligerent threaten that upon which they would be unable even to begin. Could they give notice of the substitution of another form of attack? There was no such provision.

Presumably, nothing could happen for three months, and then it would be the turn of the English-Speaking Commonwealth to aggress. If that were so, was it not possible that the European Federation might call off the war?

But it was hard to think of its meek acceptance of such a position, especially since it would have arisen through a member of the opposing government assassinating a member of theirs.

But would that be known? His mind moved in a sea of doubt. He thought again of the fear he had had that such an act of violence as he was now contemplating, even though it should occur before the actual outbreak of hostilities, could be held to be a violation of treaty restrictions, with all its consequences.

But there would be the evidence that he had been detained in Herr Richter's house! How would that be explained? What different interpretations might be put upon Colonel Wagram's death! (But when he remembered that the man had been struck from behind, and that he was now wearing his uniform, he had a reasonable doubt of whether there would be much asset in that.)

Anyway—and it was the one conclusive argument in a confusion of possibilities of consequence which baffled forecast—there was no doubt that the European Federation would keep the terms of the treaty as long as they thought it to be to their advantage to do so, and not a second longer, pretext or none, and whoever might be living or dead. As his thoughts came to this point, the guiding light had stopped over the breakfast-room door.

XVI. RICHTER WILL RUN NO RISKS

"YOU WILL have visited Havana?" Herr Richter asked. "I suppose most Americans do."

"Yes. I have been there."

"Perhaps recently?"

"Yes. It is a fine city. You may say it is the whole island now."

"Perhaps you will have met Lord Whitcombe there?"

Seeley was literal in his reply: "No. I can't say that I have."

"Or your premier?"

"I have seen Mr. Long. He is a man who makes himself accessible to all."

"So I have heard. I suppose that, for those who depend for power upon the votes that the mob can give, there is advantage in that. But you have found Lord Whitcombe less easy to see?"

"I cannot say that I ever tried."

"But he is a man you admire?"

"Not without qualifications"

"Naturally not. But, Mr. Bulldozer, you can speak to me without reserve. Our countries may be near to war, but you may still have statesmen we can admire. That he is called Silly Whitcombe by some—"

"That is no more than a pun on his name. It suggests itself."

"That was what I was about to say. But I can see what your feeling is by the quickness of your retort. I was about to add that he is one for whom we have a special regard, as we know that he was opposed to the provocation which is bringing the world so close to the edge of war."

As he heard this, Seeley had a new doubt. He saw the possibility that, though his coming might have been betrayed, it might not be regarded as hostile, or even unwelcome. Might it not be that he was so greatly opposed to war, or so doubtful of his federation's ability to wage it successfully, that he had made this secret visit in the hope of finding some compromise by which peace could be secured at its last hour? If that were what Herr Richter had guessed, and if it disposed him to exploration of the possibilities of a peaceful settlement, should not he be met in a corresponding spirit? Might there not be a better outcome to this wild adventure than any that precarious violence was likely to yield?

But he was still puzzled. There was still a baffling sense of in-adequacy, of *wrongness*, to all solutions he could propose to the enigma of how he came to be seated at breakfast with Herr Richter in his private room, and alone except for the dark-eyed girl who had been so ready to talk last night and was silent now, and who was al-most as enigmatic as all else in an adventure which had more of the quality of dreams than of waking day.

There is one thing which all politicians learn: to be cautious when in a doubt, to move slowly when they cannot see far ahead. Now that Rex Bulldozer's denture and personality were no more, the natural character of Seeley Whitcombe had a firmer hand on the reins.

It was a blue-lit room. That was something to the good, but not much. It excluded the idea of what may be described as photo-graphic assault, which would otherwise have been possible in varied and sinister forms.

It did not preclude the probability that a record was being taken of all he said. It was not inconsistent with Herr Richter being able to take action or call assistance more swiftly than he could draw out the automatic that he could feel resting against his side. In particu-lar, it did not exclude the possibility that he might be electrocuted where he sat, at any moment that his host might decide.

Improbable? Perhaps. But was it probable that he should be seated there?

"I beg your pardon," he said. "I am afraid I did not catch what you said."

"I asked you to tell me without reserve what your knowledge, and what your opinion, of Lord Whitcombe are."

The two men looked at one another in equal, though different doubt. Neither had a clue to that which puzzled the other's mind.

Seeley thought again of the room in the Hotel Central, and what it held. Anything was better than further delay. He must bring a cri-sis of some kind, and seek the most advantage for himself that the position allowed. Nor must he forget that it was a magician with whom he sat.

"There are things I could say," he replied, "if I were sure that we were entirely alone, and that no record could be preserved."

Herr Richter looked at him intently with his pale, cold, rather prominent eyes, over which no eyebrows showed. It was a gaze so chilling in its merciless probing quality that Seeley found it difficult to sustain with a casual manner. He anticipated further queries to which it might be difficult, still feeling himself to be in the dark as he did, to give wise replies. But after a brief pause Herr Richter said:

"Very well. We will talk on my own lawn. There will be no listening there. You can go now, and I will follow when I have dealt with some matters which cannot wait."

Seeley's breakfast had not been much, but he made no trouble of that. He rose at once.

"A green light will guide you," Herr Richter said, and turned his eyes to the conclusion of his own meal.

As Seeley left the room, he heard Amelie already giving instructions to the unseen service to guide him towards the lawn, and he looked up to the corridor ceiling to see a thin line of green light appearing, and lengthening forward by the way that he was to go.

The development was one which should be satisfactory to him. He was presumably to talk alone to the man whom he had supposed it would be so difficult to approach, where they would not be overheard, nor, perhaps, seen. But he would have had more satisfaction had the matter been differently arranged. He felt, with a sound instinct, that even Herr Richter, boor though he was reputed to be, would not have dismissed him from the breakfast-table in that cavalier manner had he really thought him to be Seeley Whitcombe, with whatever purpose he might be supposed to have come. His reactions might differ widely, according to his own disposition for peace or war, but they would have led him to different conduct from *that*. And if that were not the explanation for this surprising contact, it gave Seeley a feeling of inexplicable happenings in which he was being drawn blindly forward to such an issue as might confound his own purpose, already of sufficient desperation, or where, through his own violent intervention, he might obstruct the natural development of some unpredictable event which might otherwise be beneficent in its results.

With these thoughts, he came to the wide, smooth-mown lawn on which Herr Richter and Baron Gluck had conferred during the previous morning. It was here that he had his first glimpse of any living creature in that huge establishment other than Herr Richter and his secretary. A man in white close-fitting livery disappeared through a door in the farther wall as he gained the lawn. He observed that three very comfortable chairs had been placed under the awning in the midst of the green expanse, from which he concluded that the inseparable secretary was to be with them again.

The high surrounding walls were unbroken by any window, and had no doors other than the one through which the man had gone, and the one through which he had come. The passage he had traversed had not been at right-angles to the boundary of the lawn. It had approached it at a slant, so that, even had the two doors which closed it been open, no one approaching could have seen the place where the chairs were set until he had himself become visible. And those doors of sliding metal had not been open. The first had slid backward as it was approached by the guiding, and had closed after he had gone through, before the second had opened to allow him further advance. Now the second had closed behind him. He moved out on to the lawn, and looked round the straight, unbroken lines of walls that contained it. There was a cold implacable quality about those white, smooth, concrete walls, symbolic of the civilization which had produced them, and inimical to all tender and gracious things.

Even the green close-cropped grass on which he trod seemed to be not merely tamed but jailed by their constricting height.

He considered (finding no pleasure in the thought) how entirely he was isolated and imprisoned there, and how impossible escape through those double doors might become if there should be such a development as would leave him dependent for safety on sudden flight. It was a matter on which he had sufficient time to reflect thoroughly, for it was to be a long while before anyone else appeared.

Herr Richter had said to Amelie, even as the door had closed: "There is something more here than appears. It may be no more than the impudence that these ungoverned Americans have, but I should make a better guess that he had matters of importance to tell. You must come with me, and be alert to remember all that is said."

He followed this by giving her various instructions to transmit to those whom they concerned; and a direct conversation with one of the chief-assistants at the laboratories; and then said: "I will hear what news there may be before we go out, and of any messages from Berlin," on which Amelie moved to the wall, and her fingers tested the responses of many wavelengths from the radio which it contained.

For all matters of current information and communication, the radio had, at this period, entirely superseded the printed word. That it had not done so during the earlier part of the century was mainly due to its own limitations at that time, supported by much timidity and lack of imagination on the part of those who controlled it.

It is well authenticated though almost incredible fact that, during the period of the second world war, the British radio service, which nationally controlled, and had access to larger funds than it could easily spend, after allocating no more than ten minutes to the morning distribution of both international and domestic news, would often find that short time more than sufficient for the information it had to give, and listeners would be told that a musical record would be substituted to occupy the four or five remaining minutes. Naturally, newspapers flourished.

But the primary cause of the failure of oral news in competition the slower production and distribution of the printed word was that it was only obtainable from the radio at fixed times, and in a settled order. To gain information on one point of interest, it was necessary to listen for an uncertain period to a recitation of other matters, with no assurance that the desired item would not be entirely ignored.

It was inevitable that people would rely mainly upon newspapers to which they could refer at their own times, and where they could turn at once to the news of their own choice, which would be given in much fuller detail.

This position was radically changed when improvements were made which enabled programmes to be received and stored, so that they could be switched on at any time, and at any desired point; and this advantage, added to the difficulties and complexities entailed in maintaining a complete censorship of a variety of newspapers, of the necessity for which the Government of the United States of Europe had been particularly aware (in the English-Speaking Union, the fallacious hope that freedom of action could be surrendered and freedom of speech remain had not yet been entirely lost), had resulted in the absolute substitution of the newer medium for informing and instructing the general public.

It is true that there were still great libraries of the books of more primitive generations, specimens of which, even including some of doubtful political wisdom, or setting forth the old superstitions of an unseen world, the liberality of the European Government had allowed to survive; but access to these was reasonably restricted to such as were able to assess them at their true worth.

Periodical literature, other than fiction of some approved and regulated types, had been entirely suppressed.

The control over radio transmission and reception had become so absolute that it was now the preferred medium for official communications, even of the most secret or personal character.

Now Amelie ran rapidly over headlines of news, including *Brutal Murder of Police Chief*, at which Herr Richter felt no inclination to have fuller details. It may be doubted whether he heard it at all. Contemplating, as he did, the destruction of the great majority of the human race, the incidental murder of one individual could be of little importance to his ears. There lay the trouble which reduced the practical advantages that the improvements of science gave. Human limitations remained. The great mass of recorded news would not come to his—some of it would not come to any—ears. It would be recorded for a few hours on the reception discs of a hundred thousand licensed receivers, and would then fade, as their surfaces smoothed themselves to take the news of another day. Even the daily newspapers had been less ephemeral.

Herr Richter said: "Never mind any more of that. I will take Berlin."

She switched on to a wavelength which only seven sets in the whole of Europe were allowed to operate, and they listened for a few minutes to reports of reactions throughout the world to the menace of coming war.

Herr Richter rose. "We will go now," he said, "and hear what Mr. Bulldozer has to say. I'm not sure that Wagram has got me exactly the man I want. I told him that a child would have some advantages. I am of a disposition to let him go."

He stopped as there came the sound of the low musical *pip...pip...pip* which was the signal that his attention was required by those who served him within the house. It was a sound seldom heard in that room, for Herr Richter was impatient of such interruption.

With a gesture of irritation, he switched on the voice. They heard:

"We have had a message from the police office that they have just had information that the man who murdered Colonel Wagram, and left the hotel in his uniform, drove the colonel's car here. They say that they hesitate to proceed further without having instructions from you."

"You say that Colonel Wagram has been murdered?"

"Yes. It was in this morning's news. He was killed in a room in the Hotel Central."

"When was that?"

"Yesterday morning."

"And the car was driven here?"

"It is outside the annexe now."

"And the murderer left in the colonel's uniform? I suppose that his name was Bulldozer?"

"Yes."

"In fact, the man who is on the lawn now?"

"So we suppose."

"Tell the police that they were right to let me know. It was by order of Major Heinz? Tell him he will be promoted to Colonel Wagram's office. He will do nothing in the matter till he hears further from me."

Herr Richter took two steps towards the door, and then paused in doubt.

"I told you," he said, "that there was more in this than appears. He might have killed Wagram to get access here. Yet there is little sense in that, for Wagram would have brought him. He might not have known that. We will see what he has to say, for which murder is not too great a price. He will know that he could not escape. There would be little risk. Yet why should I? He killed Wagram, which, I should say, would not be easily done. I will run no risk. Amelie, you shall tell him that we know of Wagram's death, and ask him to say what it was he would have me know. There is no need to look frightened at that. He will do no harm to you. He is not a criminal type. And he will know he could not escape. Do you think I would allow you to run risk, being of such value to me?"

"No," Amelie agreed, though her natural colour was still missing, "I can see that. What am I to find out?"

"Everything he can tell. He must explain, and you can say that it will be bad for him if his explanation be less than true. I should have examined his papers last night, and whatever else his pockets held, which may include weapons he should not have. But time was short for that which had to be done, and I gave no thought to what would then have appeared to have no importance at all."

Herr Richter yawned as he spoke, for he had reminded himself that his hours of rest had been few, and his discoveries had not included a drug which would abolish the need for sleep; and Amelie, who had slept well, rose with the lazy gracefulness that her habit was, and went to meet Seeley upon the lawn.

XVII. SEELEY IS OUTSIDE THE DOOR

HAVING WAITED A long while, with more self-control than most men would have been able to exercise, and with a hardening determination to end the baffling ambiguity of the position into which he had fallen by his own folly, or fate's caprice, Seeley found, as he had done before, that his purpose was eluded by events which did not move in the expected direction.

Frankness with Herr Richter might have been foolish or wise. Threats might have gained or lost. Violence might have had incalculable consequences. But such intentions became equally vain when Amelie advanced alone over the lawn.

"Herr Richter," she said, "has become very closely engaged, but he thinks it will be well for us to have a further talk, now that we know more than we did yesterday."

She took one of the chairs, and he asked: "Does it matter which I have?"

"No. How should it?"

He sat down without answering. She had, at least, told him that there had been no sinister difference between his own and Herr Richter's chair.

He had a feeling of confidence, as though dealing with a situation which he controlled.

He had no fear of this girl, though he saw her to be so closely in the confidence and under the direction of his immediate foe. He asked boldly: "What did you not know yesterday that you know today?"

"We know that Colonel Wagram is dead."

"Which you attribute to me?"

"It is his uniform you have on, and he was killed in your room."

"It is a reasonable conclusion to draw. But his death is a small matter beside that which has brought me here."

"If you could make Herr Richter see that!"

"So I can. You are not unfriendly to me?"

"No. But I must report all that you say."

"That is what I shall wish you to do. But you have told me what I hoped and believed."

Their eyes met, saying more than words, and something which she would not be required to report. But hers changed to a look of trouble, such as they had seldom shown during recent years. Seeing it, he asked: "Are we really alone?"

"We are alone, and unobserved. Even from the sky we could not be seen, which is one reason for this awning. While the doors are closed, there is nowhere in the world where it could be more certainly and completely true. Nor will there be any record of ourselves, or of what we say. Herr Richter intended to have privacy here, and what he does, he does well."

"So I believe. But if we are so completely isolated, how could you get the door to be opened for us when we have done?"

"We could not do it from here."

"Well, I should not have asked! So all we say will be lost, except that it will be remembered and reported by you?"

"Yes. I shall remember. That is why I am here."

There was a note of bitterness in her voice, strange to herself and inexplicable to him, but he did not probe its cause, or he might have learnt much. He asked: "Do you want this war?"

"No. Who does?"

"Does Herr Richter?"

She delayed to reply, looking at him with doubt in her eyes. She remembered hearing Richter say that he wished it could have been postponed. But that was somewhat different from desiring peace. And she knew that he was contemplating a slaughter of his own kind beside which the operations of legal war would be trivial in their results. But—for the moment at least—had he not said that it was inopportune for him? And was he not showing increasing irritation with every succeeding hour?

"I am sure," she said, "that he would be glad if a peaceful solution could be reached which would be satisfactory both to us and to you."

"We might arrange for a truce of a few months, during which a satisfactory formula might be found."

"But how could you secure—? Are you able to speak for—?"

"I could satisfy him of that. But could Herr Richter speak for Berlin?"

"That is a question for him, not for me. I expect he could. But I must tell him more of who you are, and how you come to be here. And of why Colonel Wagram was killed. So far," she concluded with a smile, "I have asked little, and been told less. You have asked questions of me."

"And you have told me much which it is essential to know."

He became silent. He would have liked to confide in her without reserve, but he was less than sure that it would be wise to disclose his identity to Herr Richter, especially before that gentleman had come to speak to him face to face. To tell her confidentially might be safe or unsafe. But if it should be safe for him, it must imply danger to her. He judged rightly that Richter would have no mercy on one who should fail in loyalty, or to give efficient service to him. And though he had no key to the enigma of Amelie's inseparable presence with an otherwise solitary man, he saw clearly enough that it was a position of service into which no friendship entered, and without intimacy of mind in the sense in which it is commonly understood.

"I don't think," he said, "that I can tell you more. You can tell Herr Richter—it is what I shall say—that you have pressed me to be franker with you, but that I have replied that I have that to say which is for his ears alone."

She looked disturbed and doubtful. "He will not see you without me," she said. "I am always with him. I remember what has been said."

"Yes, of course you would. I have no objection to that. But I cannot speak to him by way of message. I will wait till he has leisure."

"He may be annoyed. Surely there should be something said to explain Colonel's Wagram's death? I cannot tell what he may do."

"You can tell him that what I have to say is of such importance that the policeman's death does not matter at all."

They had both risen, but she stood troubled and hesitant.

"So I will. I cannot tell what he will say. You had better stay here. If he does not come, he may send to you to come to him."

She looked as though she had more to say, so that he stood waiting in silence to hear what it might be. Her thought was that Herr Richter would not venture to this carefully isolated lawn to meet the man who admitted that he was responsible for Colonel Wagram's death, which, indeed, he had already declined. She thought it to be quite as likely that he would refuse to see him again, and resume the experiments of the previous night, in the light of what had been learnt since. Those had had no apparent effect upon their victim, but she did not suppose that their continuation would be equally harmless. She had heard a whispered word of what became of the subjects of Herr Zweigler's experiments, both human and animal, and it had not been pleasant. But this thought sharpened the fear (which had been continually before her mind) that anything she said might be recorded on Seeley's brain, and so come to Herr Richter's knowledge. If that should be so, a word of warning, which might be of little avail to the one to whom it would be addressed, might be fatal to her.

It was an act of courage on the part of one whose capacity for courage had been little tested before, and of a significance in other ways which Seeley would be unable to understand, when she said, in her clear, slow, drawling voice, and (with no logical reason) in a tone lower than her usual conversational pitch: "Herr Richter may come, or I may return. Or there may be a messenger. The guiding light would go on. There would be a side passage." (Her hand moved to the right.) "No one would see."

She turned, and left him, crossing the lawn to the door by which they had entered. He could not observe that she made any signal, or that there was delay before it opened to let her through. Then it closed, and he was alone to ponder on what she had said.

It had been a clear warning, and he did not doubt that it had been honestly given. Its brevity and its ambiguity added to its significance so he thought—beyond the fact, having no clue to the fear she had felt even in that solitary place. He understood that if neither Herr Richter nor Amelie should come back, it might be of sinister portent for him, and, in that case, he must be alert to observe a turning to the right where salvation lay. But he hoped she would come again.

Ten minutes later, his hope went. A man dressed in Herr Richter's red-brown skin-tight livery came from the farther door and approached him across the lawn.

"Mr. Bulldozer," he said, in good English, and with a deferential manner which the glint of cruel speculation in his eyes belied, "Herr Richter requests your presence. A yellow light will guide you immediately that you have passed through the second door."

He bowed and withdrew, and Seeley saw that the door through, which he had entered was already sliding open. He crossed towards it, pausing for a short space beneath the heat of the June sun, which was near its noon. He looked up to a sky of blue, in which the regency of the sun was challenged only by one large, white, slow-moving cumulus cloud, and wondered whether he would be destined to see it again. Then he passed through the sheet-steel doors, and saw the golden ceiling-light for which he had been instructed to look.

It lengthened forward in the familiar manner, leading him backward along the corridor by which he had come, which curved to the right, but, for a distance of about fifty yards, had only two side passages, both of which were on the left. After that, there came one on the right, short, straight, and broad, which ended at a massive door.

He stood for a brief moment in hesitation, while the golden line in the ceiling lengthened before him unfollowed, and then turned to explore the short passage. If there were nothing there but a door which would not yield, he could return and go the way that the light led, but he must first know what the girl had meant: what it was that she had advised him to do.

He walked quickly to the door, and saw it to have a metal knob, very small and light in proportion to its own weight and size, besides which there was no evidence of bolt or fastening of any kind. He laid his hand on the knob, which seemed inadequate to the control of such a door, and found that it obeyed his hand without effort. The door moved open as easily as though it were a mere paper screen, confronting him with the bright light of the outer day.

Blinking in the sudden glare, he stepped out. His eyes, as they, adjusted themselves, looked round on a clear space of downward-sloping ground, with the high, white, unwindowed outer wall of Herr Richter's residence stretching away on the left, and the approach to the annexe in view not far away on his right.

His first consciousness was a glad sense of freedom, of escape, as he felt the movement of summer wind, and looked away to the farther hills. But after that he had a thought of contempt for his own weakness. Was he to fly from a battle he had not lost? Was his wild adventure to end in voluntary retreat from a house the entrance to which had once seemed to be the most difficult obstacle to the fantastic purpose on which he came? It would be to show his unfitness for that which he had never been asked to do. He should have left it for Silver Long, if he could do no better than this, even when fortune had befriended him in a way which he was still unable to understand.

Well, he had done no more than to probe the meaning of a hint which had been given him by one who had the mien of a friend. Now he knew her to be all that she appeared. She had meant that he should escape. It was something to know. And there must be a further implication that there would be acute danger in following the guidance of that ribbon of yellow light. It was some advantage to be warned of that. Certainly, he would go back.

And as he came to this resolution, he saw that wisdom and honour pointed the same way. In a hostile land, clothed in Colonel Wagram's uniform, how long would his liberty be likely to last? How far would he be likely to go?

The dangers which would have beset him, the difficulties of hiding and of securing food, would not have been the same as would have confronted a fugitive of fifty years earlier, but they would not have been less. And by flight he would have confessed guilt, and destroyed his own assertion that his dominant purpose had been to meet Herr Richter, and that he had matters of supreme importance to lay before him. This realization, that the bolder course was the only one that held any hope of ultimate safety, whatever perils it might provide, came so quickly upon the resolution to return that he would always remain in doubt as to the motive which had prompted that momentous decision; whether it had been courage or prudence that urged him on.

He turned back to the door from which he had not advanced more than a yard, and which was still wide open behind him. As he did so, he lifted a foot which had remained upon the stone slab immediately before it.

Gently, but inexorably, and far too swiftly for him to have slipped through it, the door closed.

He looked up at a blank wall. There was no bell, no key-hole, no knob. The door fitted so closely that it was difficult to detect any sign of its existence. Had he not known it, he would not have supposed that a door was there.

He looked at it for a moment in baffled exasperation, and then turned resolutely away.

XVIII. AMELIE SHOULD NOT THINK

AMELIE WENT BACK to Herr Richter, who was unoccupied, and somewhat restlessly waiting for her report. Like Seeley, though from different causes, he had an impatient feeling that events were not moving in explicable, natural directions. It gave him a sense of frustration, very inopportune at a time when Europe was depending upon him to confound her foes, and he himself was contemplating the control of a more devastating catastrophe. But so it was; and his condition was aggravated by lack of sleep, which his constitution did not allow him to disregard with impunity. He was particularly irritated by the thought that it might be expedient to keep Zweigler alive, for he was one whom he hated and feared, and for whom he had intended an early death, even if he should not have decided that the time had come when he must operate on a larger scale.

His mood inclined him to drastic actions, such as would shorten difficulties, and assert his power to the satisfaction of his mind. He would cut the knot, without scruple that he was wasting the string.

He asked sharply: "Well, what does the fellow say? Does he admit that he killed a better man than himself? And what excuse has he got for that?"

Amelie was precise in memory, and in the form of her reply: "He didn't exactly admit that he killed Colonel Wagram, but he said that it was a reasonable conclusion from the fact that he was wearing his uniform. I don't think he would say that he had killed a better man than himself. Anyhow, he says that a policeman is of very little importance beside the matter on which he wishes to see you, and that you will agree about that when you hear what it is."

"I will judge of that. What is it?"

"He would not tell me, beyond that it is something about postponing the war. He implied that he has authority to negotiate with you, and was anxious to know whether you could speak for

"The insolent fool! And it is absurd. Who does he claim to be?"

"He would tell me no more than I have said. He wants you to go to him on the lawn."

Herr Richter became silent, reviewing in his mind what he knew of this man, and how the event had been brought about. As he did so, his mouth set into hard lines of cruelty which Amelie was accustomed to see, though she observed them now as she had not done before. He said: "I shall not go to the lawn, nor will I risk you a second time. I told Wagram that it was a stranger I should prefer, but of a madman I had not thought. It is a homicidal lunatic that he chose. One, I should say, who had become insane at the thought of the coming war…and now he has the thought in an addled pate that to come to see me was his own idea. That is simple to understand. As to the contents of his brain, I have better hope than I had before. It misled me, because it is playing a madman's pranks. We may learn much if we follow it in its maniac ways. You need not keep Zweigler's name on the list. Not unless I tell you again. You can tell Heinz that I have caught Wagram's murderer, and am dealing with him so that he will be no more trouble to him. And give instructions that Bulldozer is to be guided back to his own room."

"I don't really think he is mad. He talked sanely enough. And he said he had things to tell you which it is most important for you to know."

Herr Richter stared at her as though he had heard something beyond belief: *"Think?"* he asked grimly. "When did I engage you to do that for me? Madmen will often talk in a sane way." He checked himself, and when he spoke again his voice was almost apologetic.

"You meant nothing wrong, and you must not think I am angry with you. You are one I trust, as I need not say. But you must not think. You must leave that to me."

She took this in a passive way, leaving him disturbed in mind at his own outburst. He depended so much on this girl, whose loyalty to him he had never had cause to doubt. Was there anyone (if not she) in the whole world who was loyal to him, beyond his own interest, or his own fear? It was a most reasonable doubt for him to have.

"I will rest," he said, "for a time. Till I return, you will answer any calls that come in. You must let Matza know that I shall not be at the wine-tasting tonight, nor at tomorrow's contest of colours and sounds, nor at the wrestling final on Monday. He will say I am too busy, which will cause no surprise. I may see them all on the radio here, if I have leisure. You may go tomorrow, if I can spare you so long, but you must not fret for some pleasures missed. You will have more at a better time. (I hope Gluck will not have lost sight of how essential entertainers are. But I can trust him for that.) Let Adolf know that I shall be at the laboratories tomorrow by, or before, noon. In the next ten days there will be much to be done. Do not disturb me, unless for a matter which will not wait."

Having said this, he withdrew to an adjoining room, where he would often rest during the day; for his occupations would keep him awake in the night hours, either because he was engaged on experiments which must be watched, or would mature, at such times, or because of the secret nature of what he did.

It followed that Amelie was alone when a query concerning Mr. Bulldozer came to her ears, and she was able to answer it without reference or giving report to him. But all she said was: "Yes, of course. You already have Herr Richter's instructions for that."

But though she had said this in the lazily drawling voice which those who applied for instructions in that household were accustomed to hear, she had looked both surprised and alarmed, as might have been recorded against her had she not been under the protection of a blue-lit room.

XIX. FEAR IN BERLIN

"You think he could do that?" The harsh voice of Air-Marshal Hirchel was incredulous. His upper lip lifted in a sneer which showed large regular teeth for which there was ample room in his heavy jaws.

"Yes," Baron Gluck answered, in a tone which ignored the Air-Marshal's manner. "I have reason to think he can."

"Herr Richter," the President said, with a quiet gravity, "is particularly dangerous in the direction of his scientific researches. He would not have proposed such a plan without having a well-grounded belief that he has the power which it requires."

Hirchel, a gross, overbearing man, set his jaw firmly. "He'll find we're able to deal with him."

"Baron Gluck," the President said, in the same quiet voice as before, "is entirely of that opinion."

Baron Gluck looked his surprise. "I am sure I did not say that. I asked what you advised. But my thought was to put your names on the list, where they have the first right to be. And to enlist your help in the selection of others, which I find to be beyond my single capacity to decide."

"My dear Gluck," the President replied with unaltered suavity, "may I say that, if you really think you had that intention, you are deceiving yourself? You cannot suppose that it would be of any avail to put our names on the list, for Richter would not regard such a recommendation, even from you. And if he should treat you in a better way, I am not one who can guess well. You have come to us for help, because he has put that upon you, which you, from whatever cause, are unwilling to do."

"Of course," Baron Gluck allowed, "if you can see a way—"

"See a way!" The Air-Marshal was amazed. "I should say we can see scores. We could put him to sit and burn in the acid of his own vats. We could skin him slowly till he said he had had enough, and would let us know what this secret is."

"There are two things you may overlook when you say that," Gluck replied. "And there is a third, which I have not told you yet, which is worst of all.

"First, we are relying upon him for the operation of war which we cannot otherwise execute, and by default of which we shall become the mockery of our foes, and the subject of their counter attack. It would be better to make peace at once. Having made the threat we have, you may say that to lose Richter is to lose the war."

"We could make him dance on hot bricks till all was done that he has undertaken to us."

"Perhaps we could. But there is the second point, that he might not be easy to reach. His house is strong, and protected in cunning ways, of some of which we may not be aware; but I can tell you that its doors (excepting only those of an annexe through which there is one well-guarded approach) are so charged that, though one can leave with safety and ease, to enter but one step, unless by consent of those who are within, is to be electrocuted at once. And suppose he should offer life to those of his own household and *werke*, while the rest of us should be destroyed; might they not become loyal to him—perhaps to put this deadly power into operation against us with a celerity which might be greater than ours?"

"I suppose," the president said, in the voice that no one had heard him raise during the long years of intrigue and crime which had established him in his present power, "that he could not hope to destroy the whole world in the same day. We could force him to produce the antidote or immunizing substance that he will be certain to have."

"But there is still," Baron Gluck went on, "the thing which I have not told, which is worst of all. He said that he can see no sufficient reason for the human race to continue if he should die, and in case he be unable to find some means of defeating death (of which I should say that his hope is not much), he has so arranged that the race shall perish, after his own decease, by a universal plague which they will be unable to stay."

"And you believe anything that he says?" Hirchel's voice held contempt, though the mottling of his high-coloured face revealed the fear which the president may have shared, but was more capable to conceal.

Baron Gluck replied: "I am inclined to think it is true."

"Then you should leave it to us, and we will deal with this rat in a way which will make every scientist tremble for what may be coming to him in the next week. If we had drowned them all, as I urged ten years ago, we might now be having a clean fight, and my planes would not be idle while they make war in their dirty ways."

"It might be said to that," the baron answered, "that it is to science you owe all that the plane can do for the prosecution of war. And it might be said, beyond that, that science has not been only disastrous but has been actually beneficial to man. Suppose we should not be guided in what we eat by the test of the drop of blood which is taken each month from behind our ears?"

"Well, I could endure that."

"But you cannot deny that our diets for the next month would be badly arranged."

The President's quiet voice interposed in a conversation which was becoming too discursive for him: "There is the fact that he eliminated foot-and-mouth disease throughout the entire world by a method he did not disclose and that his rivals have been unable to understand. We must not overlook that. My dear Gluck, you had better go ahead with the list, and the Air Marshal and I will be your debtors if you will think of good reasons why our names should not be removed."

"You mean we must accept this danger for ourselves, and sentence of death on most of our fellow men, as something that we cannot avert?"

"There are times, my dear Gluck, when we think many things which we do not say."

As though desiring to close the conversation with this statement of abstract fact, the president left his seat and walked over to the broad, flat-fronted window from which he would look far down no the wide levels of fertile land, and the covered sewer which was the Spree.

For there was nothing left of the bomb-flattened Berlin of a half-century before, or of the partial rebuilding which had been permitted by the generosity of its victorious foes.

All had gone; and had been replaced by one huge building, of which the towering, seldom-windowed walls must be measured in miles rather than yards.

Massive, white, and cold, it rose squarely into the skies. It was said to be of an impregnable strength.

It had one great entrance—an entrance designed for State occasions that never came—where two hundred steps swept upwards and inwards beneath the unbroken curve of the concrete arch which was surely the greatest ever fashioned by human hands; and over its façade, in letters of fifty feet, which their height diminished to those who gazed at them from below, were the words:

THE UNITED STATES OF EUROPE
CENTRAL ADMINISTRATION

Within those walls, in that one huge building, Berlin was wholly contained. Within lived its four hundred thousand officials and their Servants, and such families and mediums of relaxation as it was etiquette for them to have.

The cargo-planes which settled smoothly, hour by hour, on the runway rails of the airport upon its roof, brought them all that they could require, or the world could yield. Many of them, though they might take flights in the air, would never put foot to ground outside its walls from their births to their dying days.

And as Berlin was held to be of an impregnable strength, so the bureaucracy which it contained had thought themselves to be rulers whom none could shake. And it had come to this, that Stuttgart made them afraid… *Stuttgart*!

With no change of manner, no sign of the anger that stirred his mind, the president gazed out through the great sheet of flawless, unbreakable glass which was the outer side of the room, over the peaceful, unified, uninhabited land below. "The Russians," he thought, "saw the danger that armies are. They had commissars. They abolished them, with consequences which— Why did we not control the scientists in the same way? Why should we suppose that those who are cunning to break the atom apart, or ruthless to tear the flesh of the living dog, would always be simple to use their knowledge, not for themselves, but their fellows, or tender lest they do a hurt to those who may have done nothing for them? Yet I should say this Richter is a half-wit, for all his craft."

"Gentlemen," he turned round to say, "you will do me the honour of dining with me tonight? I will arrange that your own cooks shall provide the vitamins which you most require."

XX. SEELEY WILL NOT ESCAPE

SEELEY looked at the closed door. It was clear that there was no means of opening it, or of signalling for it to be opened from the inside. It was a door of exit; not intended for the use of strangers who might apply for admittance. It seemed that his bold intention of re-entering that strange and hostile house had been rebuffed in a manner to which there was no reply. If he had made an error when he had turned from the guiding light, it seemed that it had become beyond his power to undo.

But he was not one who would lightly accept defeat. When the way was open before him, hesitation might delay action. Where were several ways among which to choose, he might pause between them, so that, for a time, he would not advance at all. But if circumstance showed a disposition to bar his way, or to thrust him back, his spirit rose at the challenge, and he would become aggressive to gain his will.

Now he lost no time, and there was no sign of indecision in his quick walk to the annexe entrance. He had decided to return, and would not be turned aside by a closing door. He noticed that Colonel Wagram's car was still standing where he had left it, and there seemed confirmation in that of the wisdom of what he did. Even the police did not interfere where Herr Richter was concerned! If there could be security anywhere in Stuttgart for the man who had struck Colonel Wagram down, it was within these walls, and by Herr Richter's decision.

He entered the annexe boldly, and demanded admittance, as a guest who had wandered inadvertently from the house where he stays must surely be entitled to do. He was prepared for questions, and to give such explanations as the position allowed, invoking appeal to Miss Latour, or, as a last resort, to Herr Richter himself, who, whatever he might think of how he came to be outside, would hardly be likely to refuse him admission.

But there was nothing asked. Only a short delay—in fact, the time which it had taken to make the report to which Amelie had replied—and then the steel door slid open. A voice said: "Follow the light with care. It is an extreme danger to turn aside."

But he had no disposition to do so again. He would face this out, as he had resolved to do from the first. Amelie had meant well, but the position was not one which permitted a thought of flight. He followed the guiding ribbon until it paused before the door of the room where he had spent the previous night. He had scarcely entered when the low *pip...pip...pip* of polite enquiry led him to switch on the connection, and to take a query as to what refreshments or other comforts he might require. He answered briefly, having greater matters upon his mind, and added: "Will you be good enough to enquire when Herr Richter will see me, and add that it is of great importance that our meeting should not be longer deferred?"

There was an instant's pause before another voice answered, politely enough, but with a distinguishing absence of deference in its tone: "Herr Richter will be informed of what you have said."

Well, he must wait with what patience he had, or take the hazard of leaving the room without guidance, which would have been dangerous in most of the larger establishments of that period; and must, he knew, be acutely so in that of Herr Richter, and by one who was other than a welcomed guest.

He would do that if he must, but he resolved that he would wait till the night hours. If he were ignored until then, it would surely mean that there would be no better method of attempting the purpose for which he came.

The resolution reminded him that he had intended the same thing on the previous night, and then passed into heavy and what he believed to be dreamless sleep. For the first time he wondered whether the coffee he had taken had been drugged. It seemed improbable, as he was not aware that he had been disturbed, or his room entered; but it was possible, and might have been no more than a routine precaution against any night activity on the part of one who had been admitted within those well-guarded walls in a trustless way.

He resolved that he would order coffee again that night, but would dispose of it otherwise than down his own throat.

After that, he moved to the radio wall and spent some time in investigation of what it could yield, with a profit he had not expected to get.

He had not supposed that he would obtain access to the more secret wavelengths which the bureaucracy confined to its own uses, but he knew that, in such a house as that, there would be facilities available far beyond those which the general public would be permitted to use.

So he found it to be. After a brief search through the local news, by which he learnt that:

> *It has been ascertained that the death of Colonel*
> *Wagram was the work of a homicidal lunatic of un-*

*certain nationality who has been handed over to Herr
Richter for research purposes, Frau Wagram having
signed the usual certificate of discharge.*

—the full significance of which was not easy to guess. He made a
brief reference to the television section, where he was able to get a
sight of his hotel room as it had appeared while Wagram's body was
being removed, and then turned to the foreign stations, and was surprised and pleased to find that the House of Representatives in Havana was in session, and was being addressed by Mr. Silver Long,
whose confident words he was able to hear.

"...may prove," he heard, "to be a transforming fact. The discovery is so new, so secret, and of such a nature, that we have no
fear that it may have been treasonably communicated to a foreign
government, as more than one of our major scientific secrets certainly have, nor should we greatly fear such a contingency, for there
would be no antidote that could avail.

"Indeed, it is our intention to communicate its nature, and what
would be its certain results, to the Ambassador of the United States
of Europe in the course of tomorrow, so that his federation may have
time to consider whether they will not withdraw an ultimatum
which, after the passage of three short months, would bring such
overwhelming catastrophe on their own heads.

"They may destroy the cattle—they may even destroy the entire
fauna of our own lands—but it would be they, in the following
months, who would have empty fields, for they would be glad indeed to buy peace at the cost of handing their livestock over to us.
They would buy peace, as I do not doubt, at any price which the
terms of the treaty entitle us to require.

"For to that treaty, as I have told them already, and as it is needless to say to you, we shall most strictly adhere.

"The new weapon, deadly and surprising as it will prove to be,
does not transgress it in any way. It does not threaten the lives either
of beast or man. With the warning which we shall give, it will be
simple to provide for the safety even of the household cat. Only
vermin, outside control, if any such remain in the civilized European
or North African lands, will be endangered by what we propose to
do. But I have said enough, or too much."

If is voice if he would have said more, was drowned in a burst
of cheering such as it was good for Seeley to hear, but when he re-
sumed it was to give even sharper attention to words which, though
spoken in that world-wide publicity, were actually meant for himself.

"As to rumours concerning Lord Whitcombe to which the honourable member for Tennessee University has made allusion, they are such as are bound to arise at such times as these, and are rightly assessed by sensible men; but I anticipate that he will be among—"

The voice ceased abruptly.

Seeley's fingers moved quickly among the studs, trying every device he knew to recover the transmission during the brief remaining seconds that it would be of value to him. But he was always met by the obstruction of an educational programme which was explaining, with great lucidity, the wasteful blunders of evolution, before it had the good fortune to come under scientific control. "This demonstrable lack of anything comparable to human intelligence in the functioning of Creative Force…," he heard, and it was no satisfactory substitute, in spite of the importance of the matter with which it dealt.

"Oh, well," he thought, giving up the attempt to obtain that which was more vital to him, but no less cutting off the programme which had been imposed upon it, "the Creative Force needn't go blundering on any longer. It's got Richter now." And then saw that his own sarcasm had a double edge, for if the Creative Force never blundered, what of its production of Richter himself?

But he had no inclination for further reflection upon the nature of reality, which is a subject for leisure hours, and he saw that a playwright's purpose cannot be easily read before the curtain has risen for the last act. *Before?* But suppose that curtain were rising now?

It was possible; but he still had a better hope. The words of Silver Long had been confident, and their content had been beyond anything that he could have expected to hear. He supposed that the reference to himself had been deliberate, and guessed that the complete statement would have been such as would have given him a hint to return in unmistakable words.

As it was, he thought he had heard enough. Could he not now reveal his identity to Herr Richter, and use it to negotiate conditions of peace? Might he not go to Berlin and be welcomed there?

If they knew who he was, they would, at the worst, be unlikely to do anything hostile to him before tomorrow, when the nature of this new weapon would be communicated to Herr Bocker in Havana, and doubtless transmitted to Berlin without a minute's delay. The only weak point in what had come to look like an easy programme (though making mockery of the purpose of his disguise and tragedy of the homicide that was on his hands) was that the day passed, and Richter did not send for him.

He remained in idle waiting during the long remaining hours, and this leisure, with a mind somewhat relieved as to what the cause of his own race (if not of all mankind) might require him to do, gave him time to turn his thoughts where inclination would have them go, which was to recall the form of one who had the grace of a goddess of fabled days, and (which should have been more to him) who had the eyes of a friend.

Besides that, he had leisure to give a close inspection to the room in which he was left so long, and he saw one thing which he did not like. He saw a faint line in the wall, which, on close inspection, was evidently that of a door—a door that would open only from the farther side.

There would have been less menace in that if he had not been certain that it had not been equally visible on the previous day, when, on first occupying the room, he had made inspection of the walls, as prudence required.

He concluded that a door, which had been made to fit so closely that it should not be observed, had not been opened for a time, so that its existence had not been apparent yesterday, unless to a more minute examination than he had given, but that it had been used since, so that it had become somewhat more visible, though still easy to overlook.

Then someone must have been here while he slept. But he had suffered no harm. His possessions had not been taken. Even Colonel Wagram's gun.... It was a puzzle he could not solve. But he would drink no coffee tonight; and anyone who should come would encounter a watchful man.

XXI. GESTAPO WILL TAKE A HAND

SEELEY WAS STILL waiting in a solitude which became increasingly hard to endure with patience at the evening hour at which the president received his guests in Berlin.

They joined him in his private dining-room, which was small but appointed with every luxury that the earth of 1990 could yield for the service of man, and which a sound hygiene did not condemn.

They entered together, and as they crossed the lizard-skin carpet, which was smooth-surfaced to baffle the dust that still intruded its rebellious elements into the fabric of a half-tamed world (and yet as soft as any carpet could ever be), the dining-table moved smoothly forward through the service wall, which closed behind it in a manner of some ingenious complexity, but to which they were too accustomed to give any regard. As it did so, the president said: "You will observe, gentlemen, that four diners are here. I have asked Gestapo to join us, for he is a man of action, and I am inclined to think that his view of this matter will be interesting to hear, and may even be beneficial to us. He has to come from Prague, where he has gone to put a wreath on the monument to one whom he would call a greater man than himself—Heydrich, as it is needless to say—but he should be with us in a few minutes now."

The Air Marshal said that that was a good move to have made. He added that if Gestapo couldn't bell the cat there'd be few vermin that could, and then checked himself to say that he hadn't meant to call Gestapo a mouse, which would be absurd. So it would have been. Nor had he. He had meant to call him a rat. But walls have ears, even among friends in a blue-lit room. And Gestapo was a dangerous man.

Baron Gluck took no notice of what he said. He was annoyed and alarmed that the president should have added Gestapo to the circle of those who knew.

"Can you trust him?" he asked dubiously. "If it should reach Richter's ears that I have—"

"Trust him?" the president echoed in surprise. "I should say that no one has done so since he could talk, or perhaps sooner than that. But we can be sure that he will do that which is best for himself, and we must see that we are in the same boat, as we always are. But I will tell you this, I have changed my mind since I heard what Long had to say this afternoon (which was morning to him), and I am now resolved to bring this thing to a quick head; for it appears that Richter is a menace to all mankind, and we must be united to draw his sting."

Baron Gluck made no answer to this, for he was one who would prefer to ponder a new idea before making reply, and they sat down without waiting for Gestapo to come, as the etiquette of the occasion allowed, and each of them proceeded to regulate the heat of his self-warming dishes to that which his physician prescribed.

There was separate provision for each, for no host of that day would have committed the crude offence against the health of his guests implied in the provision of a common dish. For how could they be scientifically fed without regard to their ages and weights, their blood-pressures and bile-secretions, the ingredients, quantities, and times, of their last meals, and a hundred other factors which could not be the same by a millionth chance?

But they had scarcely seated themselves, and declined each other's courteous offers to erect the little screens which would conceal foods for which your neighbour might long, but which it would not be scientific for him to have, when Gestapo Schmidt came into the room.

He was a small, thin-featured man of about fifty, having been born in Munich during the earlier period of the Second World War, and had been named Gestapo by a father who was enthusiastic in admiration for the German political police of that day.

Names so bestowed are rarely found to be appropriate in later years to the characters and circumstances of those upon whom they have been thrust; but young Gestapo gloried in his, and the ideals which it gave him had done much to bring him to where he sat. Beside his methods, there was straightforwardness in a snake's coils, mercy in a boar's tusks.

His look was sharply alert, and his small black eyes glittered with animation as he listened to the tale that the president told in his level voice; but he showed no sign of fear, and little of concern, at the nature of what he heard.

"This," he said, "is good news for Zweigler—better news than he'll ever know it to be." He smiled at his own thought as he said this, his lips moving into crueller lines than when they were at rest, as will those of men who are actively evil in what they do and enjoy.

"Zweigler?" he was asked. "Who is he?"

"Zweigler is one of his chemists. He's been double-crossing him for some time. He's in Betz's pay. I've known this for some time, but I only got proof yesterday, and I was going to let Richter know tomorrow. I thought Richter was being more use to us than Betz is ever likely to be, and we'd better play it that way. I thought he'd make Zweigler jump!" (The smile came again at the amusement of that idea.) "But it looks as though it's got to be the other way now."

"Richter," Baron Gluck said, "Is not to be lightly regarded. The facts which we have told you show that an error in dealing with him may have disastrous consequences for ourselves, and even for the whole of the human race."

Gestapo looked at the baron without respect, or any evidence of being impressed by the warning he had received. "I wouldn't call Richter such a big song," he replied. "He's only got local police, and the Chief of them's just let himself be trapped in a hotel room, and got knocked on the head."

"It's not," the president said quietly, "exactly a matter to be judged on such grounds as those. Richter claims that he has so arranged that his own death will be followed by an outbreak of universal plague which there will be no means to control. He has shown before now that he can do remarkable things in the control of viruses, either to cause or cure."

"That's how I understand it to be," Gestapo answered easily, though with more respect for the president than he had shown for the Minister of Education. "We've just got to call his bluff. We'll tell him we'll run the curtain down with a bang unless he thinks of something better than that."

"Your difficulty appears to be," the president replied, "that he may commit suicide if he be pressed too hard, or have no hope of his position being maintained."

"We've got to risk something," Herr Schmidt argued reasonably, but not in the tone of a man who intended to lose any sleep, "but I wouldn't call him that sort. And we've got to get him where he can't kill himself except in our way. You can leave that to me. This is where Zweigler'll come in useful to us. But if that's all you've got to say, I'll be getting back to my own room. There's a bit of trouble in Oslo I want to deal with before it gets worse than it is now. But, if I am to let the air out of Richter, how'll you get on with the war?"

"We are seriously considering calling it off," the president replied. "But we shall not finally determine that till we have Bocker's report tomorrow."

"You won't want to call it off any less when you hear that;" Herr Schmidt replied, with the assurance of one who knew, as in fact he did. He had known what the threat was to be before Silver Long had made public announcement that morning, but it was not his habit to boast of knowledge, or to give it away unless there were a purpose in such disclosure. Let Bocker make his report tomorrow. But he would help, if required. He added, as he got up: "If you tip the scale to go on, you'll have to ask me to put Conroy to sleep, and to do it quick. He's the bird with the sharp beak in that nest."

"We cannot," the president replied, "do anything which could be held to violate the terms of the treaty. The attitude of the Latin-American Federation is too uncertain to be ignored."

"Yes," Gestapo Schmidt allowed, with the first sign of regarding any danger seriously that he had yet shown, "there's Mendoza. You need to steer wide of him. But you can leave Richter to me."

With this assurance he went, leaving the three statesmen together, of whom Baron Gluck was the first to speak. "I hope," he said, "we've done right. Richter's a dangerous man."

"Oh, Gestapo'll find some way that'll make him dance," the Air Marshal said, with satisfaction. "But he's a man who always makes me feel a bit sick."

The president ignored that. He had never been known to express an adverse opinion upon any man, living or dead; being one whose words were discreet, and spoken with direct purpose, which such opinions would not assist. He said: "You will observe that Gestapo knows much. This Zweigler—he is a man of whom I had not heard—what he knows of him may be decisive to save our race."

XXII. AMELIE COMES IN THE NIGHT

SEELEY tasted the coffee, and could detect no warning flavour. He hesitated, but caution prevailed. There was a small hollow recess in the service wall, as there was in all houses of the better sort in that period, where clear water constantly flowed, and where anything in liquid form or of small size could be washed away. He stood there for a moment, and had a doubt of whether the coffee might be observed as it flowed, and it become known that he had not drunk it; and so, in an excess of needless caution, he did not pour it out, but put the full cup aside, to be disposed of at some later hour.

He resolved that he would not leave the room until the third hour after midnight, by which time men are said to be in their deepest sleep; but, if he had not himself been disturbed by that time, he would go to see Herr Richter during the night, taking him perhaps at some advantage of surprise and occasion, and justifying himself (if it should become needful to do so) by disclosing his identity, and pleading the urgency of the peace mission on which he would let it appear that he had come.

After what he had heard on the radio that afternoon, the thought of violent action against Herr Richter must be delayed, if not put permanently aside. But for his own rashness in assaulting Wagram, and its fatal result, he supposed that he would be free to go as he would, either in his own name, or as the Bulldozer that he had professed to be. As it was, he saw that revelation of his identity, and profession of a secret mission of conciliation, might be the only road of escape from the consequences of what he had done. But what did Herr Richter intend that consequence to be? What was his purpose in keeping him here? He could see no sufficient answer to that.

While he thought thus, he sat on the side of an unused bed, watching the door which he believed to have been opened during the previous night, with Wagram's gun in his hand.

He was prepared to watch this for hours, but he found that a shorter time was enough. It was scarcely midnight when he saw the door begin to move noiselessly inward, and his fingers tightened upon the weapon.

But they relaxed when he saw who his midnight visitor was. Amelie stood in the dark frame of the door, which remained open behind her. Her eyes fell on the full cup. She said: "So I am in time. I would have come earlier if I could."

"You mean it is drugged?"

"Yes."

"Why should Herr Richter do that?"

"Because he thinks you are mad."

"Why should he think that?"

"He thinks you confuse yourself with Lord Whitcombe. He had a means of taking some of your thoughts during last night."

Seeley stared at this, as he well might, though he did not doubt the truth or the friendly purpose of what she said. Still, there was a flaw. He said: "During the night? But he must have drugged me before that."

"He drugged you to read your thoughts, and he says that he was confused in that way. But he is content now that he is sure that you are insane."

"You believe that?"

"No, but you must convince him. It is the one chance that you have."

"Chance of what?"

"Chance of life. They will be here in two hours expecting to find you drugged. They intend to photograph all the convolutions of your brain while it is alive, but to do that they—they would do that which you could not survive, as they would not mean you to do. I have been told that Herr Zweigler has kept a dog's brain alive for four days after its body was gone—so that it could remember, or continue to feel or dream—I did not understand how it could be, or what horror it might mean, but I have to warn you while there is time."

"It is what I shall never forget, nor can I hope to repay. Herr Zweigler seems to have some unpleasant ways. But when he comes— *They*, you said. How many do you suppose there will be?"

"There will be—but, if I tell you, he will never forgive."

"You may be sure he will never know."

"But he will. He will read your brain. I have come only to ask if you are sane. I have said nothing else, and have gone away. You must think that—*only* that, if you cannot put me wholly out of your thoughts."

"But I shall not wait for these gentlemen, be they many or few, so you need have no fear about that. When they come I shall not be here.

"How do you think you can get away?"

"By the door of which you told me before."

"But you cannot! Not at this hour. From midnight until an hour after the dawn it would be death to enter or leave. There is live current around the house, which is set loose by an opening door."

"Still, they shall not take me alive, so you need not fear that. Nor shall I leave them a brain that will be useful to them. You can see I am armed. And I will keep a bullet for that. So you can tell me with how many I have to deal."

"There will be Herr Richter and Zweigler, and two men to do what they are told. But perhaps, if you can make them believe you are sane, they will proceed in a different way."

"I will make them believe that, and they will be well advised to alter their plans. You see, I *am* Lord Whitcombe, and when Herr Richter knows that—"

"Mr. Bulldozer," Amelie interrupted, with an earnestness that Seeley found it pleasant to hear, though he was less content with the substance of what she said, "you must put that idea out of your mind. Lord Whitcombe is a great man, whom you may do well to admire; but he is not you, and you are not he. How could it be, when he is in Havana, and you are in Stuttgart now? You must use the judgment which you do not lack upon other things."

"Then you do think I am mad?"

"Not at all. I think you are inclined to make a mistake, which you must correct."

"It is most politely expressed. But I am sane enough to give it a plain name, and sure enough that I am Seeley Whitcombe not to mind what you say. Except that I cannot endure that you should have that opinion of me, which I must find arguments to remove. You did not happen to hear the speech that Silver Long made in Havana today?"

"Yes. I had to hear it to report it to Herr Richter."

"Then you may possibly recall that lie alluded to rumours concerning Lord Whitcombe's absence from Havana?"

"Yes. I remember." (There was a bitterness in her voice which he had heard before, but which had no meaning for him.) "But that was not quite what he said."

"Perhaps not. I did not hear it completely. But the rumours he mentioned must have been of that nature, because I left Havana very secretly some days ago."

"Why should Lord Whitcombe have done that?"

"To see Richter, and do something to stop this war."

"But—it is not sense. Herr Richter does not know who you are. I am certain of that. And it was Colonel Wagram's action that brought you here."

"I understand that no better than you."

"But I can partly explain. It was Herr Richter's instructions to Colonel Wagram to bring someone of no account here, or a, stranger, if he could be found, for the experiment he is intending to make. You mean you would have come here apart from that?"

"That is what I should have endeavoured to do. Could you get a radio sent to Havana for me?"

"I might. It might be the last thing I should do."

"Then I will think of something better than that. There will be many more things for you to do when you have come back to Havana with me, as I shall ask you at the right time."

For a moment there was a light of joy in her eyes which he did not miss, but it died quickly. "That," she said, "would be vain to hope. I am in a net which you could not break."

"You do not know what I can do. But hope is the right word. I will remember that you have said that."

"You may think it to have meant more than it did," she retorted, with a lightness in her drawled tone which there had not been in the quicker words she, had used before, but he was not deceived. She went on: "What was the radio you would have asked me to send?"

"It would have been no more than to say that I am a guest here, and shall soon be back."

"You would have sent it to Mr. Long?"

"It could not have been better directed."

"It would have been useless. It would have been stopped. There would have been enquiry here."

"That is what I supposed."

"Yes. I see. But...I had better go. I have stayed too long. You must make Herr Richter believe. He has no mercy in what he does."

"He is a devil you should not serve. God protect you till better days!

"God?" she echoed vaguely. "But I forget. You have the beliefs of another land. We are far apart."

She remembered, though not with joy, that she was of the premier race which had put superstitions aside, and he was one of those of whom Herr Richter would scientifically purge the world, with—perhaps—many millions of his own, though there seemed to be some confusion about that part of the plan. Actually, she was not of

Germanic blood, her parents having been of the Latin lands. But she saw no difference there, for it was a matter they had preferred to put out of sight, as most of such Europeans would.

She went, with little hope in her heart either for that night or beyond, debating with herself whether she should accept the peril of telling Herr Richter what she had done, and that she was sure that it was Lord Whitcombe whom he was intending to kill.

She thought, in the strange new mood which was upon her, she might even have had courage for that, but she saw that it would involve disclosing that the drugged coffee had not been drunk, and Seeley might have little cause to thank her.

She got back to her own room none too soon, for Herr Richter had issued an urgent call for her, having summoned her already without reply.

XXIII. ZWEIGLER THINKS DIFFERENTLY

WHILE AMELIE TALKED to Seeley for a longer time than she had meant or than it had been prudent for her to do, Emil Zweigler sat opposite to Herr Richter in the comfort of a cunningly-padded pneumatic chair which fitted itself exactly to his support, whatever movement he might make, and listened to the account of their victim's behaviour during the day, and of the murder which he did not deny.

The comfort of the chair was nothing to him, for all he asked of physical life was that it should be so conducted that it would not disturb his work with any protest of heat or hunger, of cold or pain.

Positively, he desired no sensation at all, whether pleasant or hot, for they could not fail to disturb his work.

He worshipped knowledge alone, which is no ignoble deity, but his sacrifices at his chosen shrine were such as even the god he served would not approve. To discover facts (which he would have called truths, lacking precision of language as scientists often do), there was nothing he would not do or omit, providing only that its consequences would not retard him in further research.

He sat opposite Herr Richter, whose success he envied, whose ambitions he despised, and whose personality he contemned, a very tall, thin, angular man with lank black hair, a sallow skin, and a mouth that was a straight tight-shut slit in a cadaverous face.

"There is no doubt," Richter said, "that he is insane."

"There is a good deal to support that conclusion," Zweigler more cautiously allowed.

Richter was not satisfied with that measured support. "Had you heard the conversations—" he said. "But Miss Latour shall tell you herself. She will do so with greater accuracy, than I could repeat what she reported to me."

It was at that point that he had telephoned for Amelie's attendance, and been surprised by the absence of response from her own room, and more so by Greta's inability to locate her promptly. But the interval before she replied to the continuous query that was to be heard in her own room was not beyond ordinary explanation, and he received her presence without enquiry as to why it had been delayed, but with an immediate demand that she should repeat the conversations she had had with Seeley both during that day and the one before.

She gave them with the detailed accuracy which was easy to her, and Zweigler listened with the concentrated attention which was equally normal to him.

He heard her without interruption or comment, and then asked: "You thought his manner to be that of an insane man?"

She saw the opening which Herr Richter had given by requiring this recitation from her, but she knew also that was not the kind of question to which she was expected to give an independent reply. "Herr Richter has explained to me," she said, "that those who are insane will often talk in a sane way."

There was nothing to give her away in the drawled indifference of the reply, and it was one which Herr Richter could not fail to approve; but it no less told Zweigler that which he had particularly wished to know, and he was persistent in his further query: "Then I must understand that he appeared sane in every respect in these conversations with you?"

"Yes," she said, but still as though she answered questions that were indifferent to her; "he gave me no reason for doubting that."

Richter interposed sharply: "Not when he talked of having some secret of importance for me?"

"No," she said. "If he were Lord Whitcombe, that was what you would expect him to say."

"Which," Herr Richter replied, "it would be absurd to suppose."

"But are we sure of that?" Zweigler queried. "Are we quite sure? You heard what Silver Long said today about Whitcombe's rumoured absence?"

Herr Richter said that he had not heard. He had been occupied in more urgent ways. He had heard of the threat of a new weapon, which he did not seriously regard. (As, with the purpose that filled his mind, it was unlikely he would.) He had heard nothing of less important events.

Zweigler turned to Amelie again.

"There was nothing he said or did which was inconsistent with his being Lord Whitcombe?"

"No, nothing at all: that is who I suppose he is."

She said it in her most casual way, and, even so, in some uncertainty of how Herr Richter would receive such an opinion from her. But he did not demur, and she saw that he had himself been brought to a strong doubt.

He said: "Well, if it be so, he will have proof to give. He will have credentials to show."

Zweigler asked: "What did the police find in his room?"

"I have heard nothing of that. Heinz would not proceed further in the matter without instructions from me. Doubtless, whatever was found will be in custody, and will be secret to him."

"There may be much to be learned. But I should say that it is Lord Whitcombe, and it is a great fortune for us."

Amelie thought that much had been gained seeing that Zweigler put the thought of madness aside in favour of that of concealed identity, and that Richter was evidently inclining to the same view. She assumed that Lord Whitcombe would be free from the peril in which Mr. Bulldozer would have lain. But next moment she had reason to doubt of that.

"It is great fortune?" Richter echoed dubiously; and Zweigler replied: "Surely so. For his will be a brain which it will be in every way profitable to explore."

"So it should be." Herr Richter considered the matter from an angle which he had previously ignored, but he gave no further indication of what he thought, beyond the fact that he required Stefan and Yung to meet him in the operating room, as he had done on the previous night.

He left Amelie in doubt as to what he would have been likely to do should he have found his victim unconscious, as he expected, and in a further anxiety as to what would occur when he and his followers should be met by one who was wakeful and warned and armed.

She had a bold thought that she would follow, to see what would occur, or even interfere to influence the event. She had had no word of dismissal from Herr Richter. She might say that she had supposed he meant her to come. There would be little likelihood that he would make trouble of that alone, and what she might do further must depend upon what she found, and what wisdom or courage she might be able to show.

But then she had a new thought, at which she stood in a fresh doubt, neither having resolution to put it into action, nor to thrust it out of her mind, so that time was lost; but, in the end, courage prevailed, so that she did what she had thought, though in a great fear, and then, in the mood of one who had started upon a path that she could not leave, she went to see what was happening in Seeley's room.

XXIV. MAINLY CONCERNING A CUP OF COFFEE

THE INFORMATION which Amelie had given had not merely warned Seeley of the intrusion which he would have to face, it had given him the true cause of his detention in Richter's house, so that, for the first time since he had been visited by Colonel Wagram, he was relieved from the atmosphere of nightmare improbability which had confused his mind, and may have restrained him from decisive action at an earlier hour.

There were now three dominant facts which he must regard:

First, the public announcement of Silver Long had released him from the wild purpose on which he came. To pursue it further might be actually against his Government's policy and the best interests of the Federation he served.

Second, there remained the awkward fact that he was guilty of the manslaughter, if not the murder, of Colonel Wagram; and the motives on which he had acted, of whatever urgency or importance, were not such as would constitute legal defence, or gain the sympathy of those who might judge the case. In the social order of that day, men like Richter might ignore such laws, either to commit or condone, but they could also invoke them if it would serve their purpose to do so.

Third, Herr Richter, while knowing nothing of who he was, or why he came, or of the crime which he had committed, had purposed to use him for some scientific experiment which might involve torture, insanity, or death to himself, and which was of a clear criminality, which even that magic adjective "scientific" could not legally overset. But was he in a position to protect himself or invoke the law? He saw little ground for satisfaction in this direction, apart from observing that, though he had been absolutely ignorant of the purpose of Colonel Wagram's visit, the sinister intention against himself which the policeman had certainly had might be useful to confuse the issue in a remarkable manner. That might be a good card to play if he should be put on trial for Wagram's death. At present he was—or was he?—in Richter's power, and fate was concerned with a different deal. He watched the door, his hand tightening on the pistol it held. He would be no subject for Richter's experiments. A bullet—or perhaps four—should be final to answer that. And he knew that he could shoot well. But after that, as the minutes passed, cooler counsels prevailed.

He saw the position in which he was placed as one from which violence was unlikely to give him more than temporary relief. He had had a persistent doubt during the past day of the wisdom of the blow that had ended Colonel Wagram's life, and it was a warning against repetition of that impulsive error. He was inclined to condemn himself on the ground that he had acted rather in accordance with what he had understood to be the approved methods of those who engage in international intrigue, than a logical estimate of probable consequences, and it was a blunder which must not be duplicated. Surely the wiser way would be to insist on his own identity—to persuade Richter to make the enquiry which would establish it beyond doubt. He made the same miscalculation as Amelie when he assumed that by proving himself to be the Interfederal Secretary of the English-Speaking Commonwealth he would escape further danger of becoming the subject of Richter's experiments.

So he pondered and resolved, until the moment came when the door in the wall moved backward, and Stefan and Yung entered the room.

They had entered quietly, but otherwise with even less precaution than they had used on the previous night, when they had been told that their task would be to carry a drugged man on to the observation table in the next room. So it had been, and so they had no doubt it would be again.

They saw one who was sitting back easily in the only really comfortable chair that the room held, and the fact that a hand was in his jacket pocket suggested no menace to them. But they were men of muscle rather than brain, accustomed to obedience rather than thought. They saw that something had gone wrong, and for a moment they stood still, hesitating what to do.

For the same moment Seeley was disconcerted by the fact that Richter had not come. He judged by the brutal faces of those men that they were mere tools, with whom negotiations, such as were in his mind, would be impossible, and whom it would be of no final importance to capture, even should that be in his power.

But he was of no mind to fall into their muscular clutches, and when, after that moment of mutual adjustment to the unexpected, they advanced upon him, he said sharply: "Stand back!" at which they halted, though not before he had drawn the pistol, which he had not intended to show.

Stefan did more than stand back, he moved behind Yung, and towards the door, evidently intending to withdraw, which Seeley might have been unwise to allow, but the intention was blocked by the entrance of Richter, with the taller Zweigler looking over his head.

Richter was no fool, or he would not have come to the eminent position he held. His defects were of character. He was crafty, ruthless, covetous, and cowardly—a combination which had brought him to this crisis of his own life, and of a world which had allowed men to pursue knowledge of natural forces which could be used to their own destruction. He looked round the room, and saw everything, including the full cup of coffee, that it could show. He decided instantly what course he should take, and probably acted with more resolution because Zweigler was there. He had a resentful knowledge that Zweigler despised him, and he was one before whom he could not allow himself to show timidity or irresolution.

He said instantly: "You had better remain within call in the next room. I will speak to this gentleman alone. Zweigler, you will stay with us."

As the two men withdrew, he went on: "You can put that pistol away now, Lord Whitcombe. I am glad that we came in time."

Seeley asked: "So you know who I am?"

"There is a report that Lord Whitcombe left Havana some days ago."

"So I did. I should be interested to hear what those men were intending to do to me."

"If the Secretary for Interfederal Affairs of the English-Speaking Commonwealth wishes to murder one of our police, he would do better to apply to us in his own name, so that the matter might be diplomatically arranged."

"I should also be interested to know what Colonel Wagram intended to do to me."

"Then you would have done better to keep him alive. Dead men cannot be expected to talk."

"I heard all that he was of a disposition to say."

"Then you may know more than I."

"I suppose not. I came to talk of more important matters. Are you willing to deal with them here—I mean of interfederal affairs—or to leave them until we are in a more private and suitable place?"

"You claim to be Lord Whitcombe. I do not say you are wrong. But can you prove that?"

"You can radio Silver Long by your embassy code."

"We will assume it for the time. What is it you wish to say? I have no secrets from Herr Zweigler in such matters as these."

"Then I shall be pleased for Herr Zweigler to hear. I would urge you to abandon this war which you cannot win, whatever loss, in the first period, you may occasion to us. You will have heard what Mr. Long said, which he will confirm to Herr Bocker today."

"You mean you knew of this new weapon before you came?"

"You must judge of that by the fact of my being here."

"Then you had better tell me what it is, so that I may judge what we have to fear."

"You must see the impropriety of my doing that."

"But Mr. Long has said that he will communicate it to us."

"I meant the diplomatic impropriety of informing you before your ambassador has been told."

"It can be entirely private to us."

"How could you assure me of that? I would prefer to discuss the matter on other grounds."

"Which it would be useless to do."

The eyes of the two scientists met as these last exchanges were made. Hatred and treachery might divide them, but there was common ground on which understandings were swift to come.

Seeley's refusal to admit or deny knowledge of this new weapon, of which Silver Long had made his boast to the world, had put the same thought into both their minds. If he knew—as was a most probable thing—he might know much more than would be told to Herr Bocker. Torture might force confession, but it might be untrue, or essentially incomplete. But if they could acquire and explore the brain in which that secret knowledge was stored—!

Seeley saw that glance of understanding. of exultant anticipation, and guessed its meaning as they could not have expected, they having no suspicion of Amelie's warning to him. But that glance had brought a sudden knowledge of deadly peril to him, and his mind moved swiftly to face it.

He could shoot the two—he supposed that he could shoot them more quickly than they could do anything which would be a menace to him. But how should he proceed after that to win release from that hostile house, and from a country that might have been roused, with all its deadly scientific resources, pursuant and lethal, to hunt him down?

He saw that they might still be less menace to him alive than dead, if they were under control. But he could not hope to control two. One he might.

"I know what is in your minds," he said, "and if you move an inch, except as I tell you, I will shoot you both for the dogs you are."

There was a hard threat in his tone which held a warning they could not miss. They became still, as though frozen.

"Herr Richter," he said, "you will move over to the table, pick up that cup of coffee, and drink it. If either of you make a movement I do not like, or calls out, or if the cup of coffee be spilt, I shall shoot that moment, and shoot to kill."

Herr Richter was not one whose brain ceased to function because he feared. He remembered that the narcotic the cup contained was harmless, however strong; and—equally essential now—that it did not act until half an hour after it was drunk. And he could mix a complete antidote, if he could get back to his own rooms within that time. He saw it to be a risk he must take, and he hoped to allay Seeley's suspicions by doing it in a willing way.

"You have no cause," he said, "to be suspicious of us. It is not we who murder Chiefs of Police when they call upon us. If you wish to make peace for your country, you seem to be going about it in a strange way. But if you think that coffee is poisoned, I can assure you that it is outside my knowledge, and, to prove it, I will drink it myself, as you desire, if that will make you understand that you owe us some apology before we part for the night."

"Don't waste words. Drink it."

Herr Richter moved to the table, he took up the cup, and drank it, spilling nothing, and turning it upside down for Seeley's satisfaction.

"And now," he said, "perhaps you will not mind if we retire."

He turned towards the door as he spoke, and saw it silently shut.

XXV. GESTAPO IS IN CONTROL

HERR SCHMIDT WORKED late. Hours of day or night had little difference in the huge building that was Berlin; and the area of his control, which stretched from the Urals to Dover Straits, had its own differences of daylight hours. His work was done through hundreds of chief controlled, each of whom was responsible for the good conduct and docility of his own district, over the resident of officials of which he had entire authority, subject only to Herr Schmidt, to whom he reported direct, and to the checking activities of certain roaming inspectors, and informations or complaints from other departments, which also went direct to Herr Schmidt's bureau of report.

Now he sat alone. The crudity of the physical presence of sub-ordinate secretaries belonged to the earlier half of the century. Typed reports slid smoothly before him. Oral reports were received as he pressed the controlling studs. He dictated for Dictaphone record or radio transmission; he spoke readily to any of the eight hundred chief officials whom he controlled.

On a slab at his desk-side, eight hundred tiny discs were pearl-white, except when one or more would glow with a colour which would indicate the urgency with which the official it represented wished to obtain instruction or make report.

Long habit made Gestapo Schmidt quickly aware of any changes of colour upon the slab, even when his attention appeared to be directed elsewhere. Now he glanced at it, and saw that two studs had turned to rose-red, which he ignored, but one was an intense violet, indicating a matter which should not wait.

He pressed it, and next moment heard the reporting voice: "Württemberg 5 reporting. Radio for Silver Long, Premier, Havana, Cuba, issued from Stuttgart by Herr Édouard Richter has wording: 'I am in conference with Herr Richter at his residence, and propose to return tomorrow. It is signed Lord Seeley Whitcombe.' Shall it go forward?"

Gestapo answered sharply:

"Not yet. But all concerned must stand in readiness for further instructions. There is no doubt that it came from Herr Richter's house?"

"None."

"Could it have been sent without his knowledge?"

"It is difficult to believe."

"But it is an evident forgery."

"Yes. The signature—"

"Exactly. By whom precisely was it transmitted? Have you learned that?"

"By Herr Richter's personal secretary."

"The Latour girl?"

"Yes. That is the name."

"I know. Hold yourself in readiness for further instructions, and warn Stuttgart to do the same."

He cut off, and sat for a few moments in thought. It was something he had not anticipated, and which was difficult to fit to the facts he knew, which yet must be quickly done. It was his capacity to deduce accurately which had brought him from triumph to triumph to where he sat—the most feared, the most hated, and (he believed himself to be) the most powerful man in the United States of Europe and their North African extensions.

What did he certainly know?

It had not been sent by the man whose name it gave, for he would not have signed himself by his title. Someone had worded it who had blundered in that particular. But it did not certainly follow that it had not been on Lord Whitcombe's instructions, or at his desire.

It had been sent at an hour which was normally one of rest. This, while of no certain significance, was suggestive of secrecy in its despatch, or (more remotely) of a faint hope that it might go through without high official observation.

In opposition to that was the possibility that such observation might be welcomed, or even be the primary object of its despatch. He considered this possibility the more seriously because it was after the pattern of his own mind. There were few things he did that were direct in method or aim, and (as all men will) he supposed that others tended to resemble himself.

But against that assumption there was the fact that the radio had been despatched by Herr Richter's personal secretary, and the particularity of Gestapo's knowledge included the detail that this was an almost certain indication that it had been by his direction.

Many radios might be issued from his residence in a day's length, despatched by any of its considerable staff, but those which originated from himself would be dictated to, and despatched by, her.

He considered and dismissed the possibility that she might have sent it against his wish, or without his knowledge. It was immensely improbable in itself, and there was nothing to suggest such an interpretation.

He came to the question: was it true? And though he recognized an extreme improbability, he had no difficulty in arriving at an affirmative conclusion.

If it were improbable in itself, it was almost equally so that Herr Richter should despatch such a radio which was untrue. It would be a senseless jest from a man who could be satiric at times, but from whom laughter was never heard. There was confirmation also in the rumour of Lord Whitcombe's disappearance, of which he was previously aware.

If it were true, it raised questions of how, and for what purpose, had Whitcombe made this extraordinary and secret journey? He recalled the death of Colonel Wagram, of which he already knew enough to recognize the advantage of knowing more. He called

Württemberg 5, and was soon sufficiently conversant with what had occurred to decide that Lord Whitcombe and Mr. Bulldozer were one, and that the death of the police chief, by whomever it had been inflicted, had been condoned, and most probably ordered, by Herr Richter himself.

Probably he had been used as an intermediary in some preliminary negotiations, and then eliminated because he had learned more than it was convenient for him to know.

In this conjecture, Gestapo, for all his shrewdness, was widely wrong; but he was bewildered, as Seeley had been before, by ignorance of the sinister motive which had led Herr Richter to desire that a stranger should be brought into his house. It was an irrelevant, unguessable fact which acted like a joker among the pack.

He came to the question: should he report this occurrence to the Government? It held possibilities of fundamental importance, and it was his elementary duty to acquaint them with it without delay. But it was a course which he was instinctively reluctant to take. He always hated to part with knowledge, which he would hoard, often uselessly, as a miser will gather gold. And he had the matter of supreme importance, that of Herr Richter's treachery to his race, already upon his hands. It made anything that Lord Whitcombe might do or agree of little value, or even none, except that it might be used against one who had become the common enemy of mankind. He decided to act alone till he had fulfilled his promise to the president to deal with Herr Richter in a satisfactory manner; and if he should then, as a supplementary flourish, produce the English-Speaking Commonwealth's Interfederal Secretary like a rabbit out of a hat, it would enhance a reputation which he had previously supposed to be at its maximum height.

There remained now only the question of how this knowledge could be applied to the major operation he had in hand. He had been considering getting in touch with Zweigler during the night before he had been diverted by this report. He would certainly do so now, for Zweigler might give him essential information as to what had already occurred, and perhaps be of active assistance also.

But first he would be prepared in another way. He contacted Württemberg 5 again, and issued an order to his secret agents in Stuttgart. It went out on the carefully isolated wavelength which was issued by himself, and receivable only by his most trusted agents. Herr Richter might control the Stuttgart police, but Gestapo Schmidt controlled force which was more powerful than they.

It read:

> *Watch Édouard Richter's residence on all sides. Inform me and maintain surveillance of any who may enter or leave.*
>
> *Be ready on the receipt of further instructions to effect the arrest of Richter on a charge of the murder of Wagram or of being an accomplice thereto. It will be necessary for the arrest to be made in such a way that an opportunity for self-destruction will not occur.*
>
> *Inform Major Heinz that you are guarding the house owing to rumours that our enemies have designs on Herr Richter's life.*

He had no doubt that these orders would be obeyed with exactness, and that secrecy would be maintained, for all who were enlisted into his well-paid ranks knew—and had signed a declaration that they understood—that though other breaches of discipline might be forgiven, failures in obedience or secrecy would be punished with death, and with no hope of mercy at all.

The pretext for Richter's arrest was not without reason, and, though he cared little about that aspect of the matter, Herr Schmidt was inclined to believe that he would be charging a guilty man, for here again the joker confused the count. His excellent intelligence service had been able to tell him that Wagram had called at Herr Richter's residence, and that he had then driven to his own offices, and, after a short time there, during which his car stood at the door, he had gone on to the Hotel Central and required an interview with Mr. Bulldozer. Subsequently, Bulldozer had appeared in Wagram's uniform and entered the car, which had been driven back to Herr Richter's residence, where it and Mr. Bulldozer had remained.

It was a reasonable deduction, however erroneous, that Richter had known that Bulldozer was Lord Whitcombe, and had employed Wagram to make contact wit him, and that Wagram's death had either followed some violation of instructions, or insubordinate action, or had been a mere precaution against possible disclosure (perhaps to members of the Government unfriendly to Richter?) of what he knew.

It was possible (though the evidence did not confirm it) that Richter had been present at the fatal interview in Lord Whitcombe's room. It was even probable that he had been in the car, for, if Lord Whitcombe had found it empty, how had he been driven to Richter's residence? It was not impossible that he would have found the policeman's car, been able to drive it, and found the place he sought, without guidance, or enquiring of anyone; but there were evident improbabilities. Herr Schmidt decided that either Richter himself, or someone acting on his instructions, had been in the car, and that that person was either a principal or an accomplice in Wagram's death.

His instruction that Major Heinz should be informed of the watch upon Richter's house was in accordance with his regular practice of conciliating local police authorities with apparent frankness, which was often the surest protection to the secrecy of what he actually did.

Having taken these precautionary steps, he turned his thoughts to Zweigler, on whom he mainly relied. Zweigler had been given a private code and a secret wavelength by which he could (and often did) communicate with Betz during the night.

By betraying Richter's most cherished secrets to Betz, Zweigler aimed at revenge on a man he had come to hate, and, as a reward, a position of independent power in the Hanover laboratories.

He had found his difficulty to be that Betz demanded more than he could supply. He had been largely foiled by Richter's secrecy, by his habit of withholding some essential detail, even when he appeared to be confidentially enlisting his subordinate's aid, and, most of all, by the fact that Richter committed so little to written record, and relied so largely on his inseparable secretary's retentive mind.

"It would be foolish to come away till you have learned more," Betz had said, and, while maintaining this attitude to Zweigler, had informed Herr Schmidt of what was going on, for he was a cautious man, and would do nothing of which the secret police did not know and approve.

Herr Schmidt had said: "Go ahead, draw him out, learn all you can, you will find it will be at no cost to you," at which Betz had been pleased, and Herr Schmidt had thought to please Richter also by exposing his subordinate's treachery, so that he would have increased his popularity with both these powerful and dangerous men, but now he saw that it must be handled another way.

He gave instructions that Zweigler should be called up on the Betz wavelength, and then connected with him.

XXVI. Liveliness in the Night

AMELIE, STANDING SILENTLY at the door, unnoticed in the tension of a moment at which the antagonists had had their attentions concentrated upon one another, had heard the latter part of their conversation, and seen Herr Richter drink the drugged coffee, with a purpose which was not hard to guess.

Her own mind was in a state of confusion and doubt, as it gradually realized what the full consequences of her unauthorized action in sending the radio in Lord Whitcombe's name would be likely to be.

Herr Richter had judged her to be incapable of thought, which, though an extreme, was not an absolutely wrong diagnosis. Abstract and particularly analytic thought did not often engage her mind. But economy of thought is consistent with lively feelings, which will more easily rule an unreflective mind.

Realization of the full horror of Herr Richter's intentions had come gradually, as they had been exposed to a mind which was at first in a state of incredulity merging into bewilderment, and which had been accustomed to regard the employer with whom she was in so exceptional a relationship as beyond criticism in the wisdom of all he did.

This growing realization, changing from a stunned horror to more lively revulsion, had been reinforced (she would never ask herself to what extent) by the peril of a man to whom she was drawn by a waking passion which bewildered her in another way.

These combined feelings, roused by the crisis of the night, had led her to the despatch of the radio which Seeley had proposed, without a clear reckoning of what its consequences must be. But, having done it, the instinct of self-preservation spurred her sharply, as it will always be potent to do.

Had Seeley turned his eyes toward her, he would have seen the difference, in alerter movements and livelier eyes, which had transformed her from what she was. She herself felt as though she waked from sleep which had long held her in a dream which she had been unable to break.

As Herr Richter drank, she saw instantly the advantage that would lie in closing the door.

Had he not been under Seeley's control, it would have been of no lasting avail, for he would have been able to call help in a way which would have been volcanic in its results. But now it would give her time—it would put him to sleep—and the radio, whether it would go through or be held up by the watchful police, would be calling for outer intervention with a far-reaching voice—a voice which might be sufficient for Seeley's rescue, rather than for her own safety. But she was not fearful of that. She felt that she had entered into an alliance he would not leave.

As she sent the radio, she had not seen all it implied for her. Vaguely, but positively, she had known that she was incurring the great danger of Richter's discovery and punishment. Her thoughts had not gone beyond a resolution to take the risk. But, having done it, she became conscious that she had broken with her employer forever. She was in no mood to wait for discovery to come and penalty to follow. She had engaged in an active war.

Stefan and Yung were still waiting near, almost within sight of that softly closing door. She went to them and said: "Herr Richter will not want you again tonight. He says you can go off duty till the usual hour tomorrow. You will say nothing of what you have seen."

They went at once, with no suspicion that anything was wrong. They were not thinking men, and they were accustomed to take Herr Richter's orders through her. They did not doubt that their master and Zweigler had been equal to dealing with the trouble that their victim had made. Miss Latour's approach to the room, and her return with that order, was conclusive to them.

She went back to Herr Richter's room, which was the centre of all control. She called up that in which the three men were now confined, as she was able to do without the possibility of being overheard by others.

After a repeated effort, Seeley replied. She asked: "Do you wish to have the door opened?"

"There's no hurry about that. Perhaps if you'd ask me again in an hour from now."

"Yes. Or less. He'll be asleep in half that time, more likely than not. I suppose that's what you mean?"

"Precisely."

"You won't be afraid of letting Herr Zweigler out?"

"Well, we needn't unless we like."

She cut off at that. She had not failed to observe the discretion of his replies, which did not disclose to those who would be with him the nature of what she had asked, or even to whom he spoke. But it was needless to her. She had started on a path from which she had no thought of retreat, and it was with more satisfaction that she heard the "we" of his last reply.

She waited for half an hour in a house in which the night silence was unbroken, no one in it but herself, and the three men in Seeley's room, having any suspicion that it had become the scene of abnormal events, and then called him again.

He spoke now with less reserve than before. "I suppose," he asked, "those two men who were here before are not lurking outside?"

"No, I sent them off. There'll be no trouble, if you've got Herr Zweigler under control."

"Then I don't mind how soon I get out of here."

She returned to a room in which Herr Richter now lay on Seeley's bed in a heavy sleep. Seeley and Zweigler sat opposite one another. The pistol was still in Seeley's hand, and his eyes were alert to watch any movement that his companion might make, but Zweigler showed no sign of hostility to his captor or of perturbation at his own position. He looked speculatively at Amelie as she entered the room. "It would have saved a lot of trouble," he said, "If you'd let me know before now."

"Let you know what?" she asked, with no friendliness in her voice.

"That you'd let Richter down."

She looked at him without replying, but Seeley saw the loathing in her eyes. She might have abandoned her allegiance to Richter, for which she had more cause than he yet knew, but her feeling for her employer was still confused between old loyalty, recent repulsion, and present fear. For Zweigler she had never had anything but antipathy, which Richter's expressions of similar feeling had not reduced.

"Never mind, Amelie," Seeley said. "You can leave this to me."

Zweigler, looked from one to the other. He said easily: "You think you're on top now, but you'll find it won't last unless you play ball with me. I thought I'd made you understand that."

So, perhaps, he had: much had been said in that room in the interval between Amelie closing the door and opening it again, from after which Herr Richter had acted as though its closing had been an obvious accident, equally annoying to all, and had made repeated efforts to reach the communication studs, argument and persuasion having persisted, even after the barrel of Seeley's pistol had been thrust forward to stop his advance.

After that, he had counted minutes, and, playing against time, he had tried to lead the conversation to a point of agreement which would prevail on Seeley to let him summon help to open the door, and had been frustrated of any possibility there might have been (which was not much), by the enigmatic attitude of Zweigler, who gave no support even to arguments which were sound. For Richter had pointed out that if Seeley should dispose of himself and Zweigler, by whatever method, his difficulties would only have begun. He would be alone in a hostile house, so guarded that it was dangerous for a stranger to move without guidance even from room to room in the night, and no better than a fugitive alien criminal of uncertain identity if he should escape alive through its deadly electri-fied doors—one whose death at the hands of the pursuing forces of order would not be hard to defend, and who, if his identity should afterwards be revealed, might be supposed to have perished in a lawless effort to destroy the man on whose genius the United States of Europe relied for success in the coming war.

Seeley listened, and was unmoved. He could not say that he re-lied upon the help, and was resolved on the rescue, of Herr Richter's confidential secretary, for, should he come to some swift disaster, what might the consequences be to her? He did not know of the ra-dio she had sent in his name, and though he had supposed, from the moment the door closed, that she was responsible for that vital help, and had known it certainly since she had called him up, there might be nothing in that for which she might not be able to make such ex-cuse as would have an innocent sound.

Zweigler steered his own course as cautiously between rival risks. If he were to find himself at Seeley's mercy after Richter had lapsed into unconsciousness, he would prefer that he should be con-sidered a friend of the wakeful man rather than of him who slept, and he was disposed to think that a moment had come at which he could profitably throw off the mask of allegiance to one whom he was already betraying. But if Richter should find some last moment means of restoring his position (and his cunning was enough to make this a dangerous possibility), to have disclosed such an atti-tude might bring retribution too swift to avoid.

So he temporized, till Richter talked with a wagging head, and the light went from his frightened, malignant eyes. But when he slumped in his chair and his breathing changed, Zweigler spoke as one who was in a joint conspiracy against him: "There's no sham-ming there. We can just hoist him on to the bed. He'll wake in about eight hours. If we put him in his own room, it might give him a headache to make out whether it hadn't all been a bad dream."

"I've no time for that. You can lift him on to the bed. He may sleep longer there."

Seeley's tone was curt, but Zweigler took no notice of that. He lifted the drugged man with an ease that showed the strength of his lean frame, and went on: "He needn't wake in eight hours, if you don't want. I can give him something to make it a lot longer than that."

"Or to wake him up?" Seeley asked cynically.

Zweigler, giving no sign of having heard, sat down in the chair from which he had lifted the unconscious man. He said: "Now we can have a real talk, and you'll know where you stand."

Seeley looked at him with a repulsion he had little inclination to hide.

"I'm listening," he said. Let the man talk! Till Amelie should open the door, how could he occupy his time better than in learning what Zweigler would like to have him believe?

Zweigler said: "I daren't talk till I was sure you'd be more than equal to him. He'd kill me as quick as a wink if he knew how I feel to him. That is, if he had the power. But, for you and me—that is, if we go by the same road—I should say that his day's done. You don't know whether to trust me, of course; but you soon will. Ever heard of Betz?"

"Yes. Everyone has."

"Then if you'll come to my room—we couldn't do it from here—you shall talk to him, and you'll understand a lot more than you do now."

"How should I know I were talking to him?"

"Trust Miss Latour? Suppose you ask her to check it up? After what she did just now—"

"I might. I'll see what she has to say."

"If she's broken with Richter over this business—and that's how it looks, though it's not an easy thing to believe—you'll find she'll say the right thing for me. She'll want to get out of here herself before he wakes up—if he ever does."

"If he ever does?"

"I mean, if we let him."

"I don't—" Seeley began, and stopped abruptly. Why should he tell this man what he would, or he would not, do? To trust him would be absurd. His whole attitude now might be a pose, with no further objects than to gain momentary security for himself, and sufficient freedom to enable him to give the alarm in a house which would immediately wake to active hostility, sinister in its methods, and likely to be fatal in its effects.

Yet he judged that there was genuine hatred between these two crafty and powerful men, associated in devilish practices such as, however they might attempt to disguise their nature by calling them scientific—as though the stamping of the word on the basest metal would mint a good coin—yet must expose themselves to each other for what they were. This development, utterly unexpected though it must have been, might seem to give Zweigler a chance which he would be reluctant to miss. At least, there was little doubt that he would sacrifice Richter for his own safety, if he saw, or could be brought to see, that he could win advantage therefrom.

Seeley resolved to say no more till Amelie should come, as, almost at once, she did.

She heard the suggestion that they should "play ball" with Zweigler with a frown that gave no welcome to the idea; but she said nothing, looking at Seeley for a lead as to what the position was.

He said: "Herr Zweigler assures me that Herr Richter will not wake till morning. Whether he should or not, we can shut him in here. Can this room be isolated, so that he could give no signal for his release?"

She considered this, and gave an affirmative reply. "If I issue instructions for that, in his name—yes, that could be done. But it should not be from this room."

"Probably from his?"

"Yes."

"Then we will go there. After that we will hear what Herr Zweigler has to say. You had better go first, and he will go next to you. We shall not be likely to meet anyone?"

"No. That is certain. Wandering is not allowed in the night."

They went through long corridors, dimly lit with diffused light that was faintly blue, Amelie leading the way, and Zweigler following with Seeley's pistol too near his ribs for any trouble to be likely to come from him. It was evident that she was not taking the most direct way, but one which was known to her to be free of tho deadly snares that that house held in the night for unwary feet.

Having come to Herr Richter's room, which she opened without effort, though it might be slow to yield to a stranger's hand, she called up the control room and gave instructions in Herr Richter's name that the one in which Mr. Bulldozer was lodged should be isolated completely, both for outward and inward calls, until he should himself order differently.

There was no doubt that those instruction us would be exactly obeyed. Almost all his orders were issued through her, and discipline in that house was not such that its servants would ask for explanations of what they were told to do.

Seeley had a new doubt. "Frau Richter?" he asked, "You have not forgotten her. If she should become alarmed, and enquire?"

Zweigler answered that, his eyes meeting those of Amelie in what was evident agreement as to there being nothing to fear from that direction: "Frau Richter does what she is told. She does not leave her own rooms during the night."

XXVII. Later in the Night

"IS IT FAR," Seeley asked, "to Herr Zweigler's room?"

Amelie said, "No." She could lead them a near way. But at that Zweigler demurred. He would take no risks. Let them go back the way they had come, to the room that had been Seeley's—that being a way that Richter had kept open, and the safety of which they had proved, and from there they could go to his own room by the way that was known to him. He would risk no short cuts in the night.

Amelie made no difficulty of this. "It's a long way round, but it is really the safer," she agreed.

Seeley looked at her questioningly. "You know of no reason that we shouldn't go to his room?"

"No. It depends upon what you're meaning to do."

"Herr Zweigler says that he can speak to Herr Betz from there, who will satisfy you that we can trust him to help us get away."

Amelie showed no pleasure at this suggestion. "We could manage that without help from him," she said definitely.

"So I supposed."

"And I have sent out the radio for which you asked."

"Then, in any event, I should soon be free."

So it might be. But what of her? Would she be allowed to leave the country with him? Or could he save her otherwise from the vengeance of her employer, when he should be released?

It seemed that, for the brief hours of the night, she held control of that house, to order whatever she would. Did her authority extend beyond, to order a plane in Herr Richter's name which might have them far on the road to safety before morning should come?

His knowledge of the procedure involved was enough to see difficulties, if not for himself, certainly for her. It was probable that she could give such an instruction as would secure his own prompt release to the swift freedom of the air, if she should herself remain in Herr Richter's room to deal with any confirmations that might be required. That they could go together was of a more doubtful complexion. And the danger of obstruction would not be for him, but for her, "I think," he said, "we'll hear what Herr Betz may have to say."

So they went to Herr Zweigler's room, and, as they reached it, Zweigler said: "We shall have to wait about twenty minutes. That is, till it is half-past two. That is when they signal that reception is clear, and then if I have anything to say I plug in."

"You can't get through to them until they do that?"

"No. The wavelength is used in other ways, which they wouldn't be likely to wish me to hear."

"It must have been very dangerous to you to have such a reception,"

"Not at all. No one comes in here. They know it is too well guarded."

Seeley said reluctantly: "Well, we'll wait." He knew that his chance of safety lay in his use of the night hours. Even Amelie might be unable to explain Richter's disappearance, and maintain authority, when the house waked to the normal activities of the day. Indeed, to admit his absence would destroy her control, which rested solely on the assumption that he was issuing orders through her. But, all the same, the time must be lost. He would not change his plans now.

And then—almost at once—the signal came.

Zweigler looked a genuinely surprised, even alarmed, man. "I don't know what it means," he said. "I never knew that happen before"

Seeley, alert for any treachery, looked at Amelie with sharp suspicion, but she had no suggestion to make. He had another thought. Zweigler had expected to spend the night in a different place. He said: "You didn't expect to be here at two-thirty."

"No. They give the signal, and keep the line open for three minutes. It doesn't matter if I'm not here. I don't talk unless I've got something to say."

"Amelie," Seeley said, "you'd better take it."

Zweigler looked worried. "If they hear a woman's voice—"

"She won't speak. She'll only listen. There must be a reception signal that she can make?"

"Yes. Two red, three blue."

"Go ahead, Amelie."

"They'll hear anything we say after—"

"Amelie understands that." Amelie made the connection. She looked puzzled. She slid the insulator and said: "It's not Hanover. It's the High Police from Berlin. Someone must answer quickly."

Zweigler's face expressed amazement, if not incredulity, real or assumed.

Seeley asked sharply:

"Haven't you got an amplifier?"

Zweigler said: "Yes. There." Amelie's eyes followed his pointing hand. Under her expert touch the voice broke into the room, clearly enough, though not so loud that it would penetrate through wall or door.

"Are you there, Herr Zweigler? Why don't you reply?" The voice was impatient, and almost minatory in tone. Seeley knew that his German was good, and he must hope that the speaker was not familiar with Zweigler's voice.

He said: "This is Zweigler speaking. I was engaged upon something I could not instantly leave. You do not usually call at this hour."

"Never mind that. This isn't Hanover. This is the High Police, Central Bureau, Berlin. Herr Schmidt speaking. I am aware of your betrayal of Herr Richter, concerning which our attitude will depend entirely upon your following our instructions now. You are listening?"

"*Ja*. I listen," Seeley replied, motioning Zweigler to silence. But as Zweigler heard these words he had the look of a satisfied man. There was evidence enough in them of his disloyalty to Richter, in which it was his immediate object to make Seeley believe, and the High Police, whom he might have no less reason to fear, were plainly offering to make a bargain with him. He had no desire to interrupt. He wished only to hear.

The voice went on: "Herr Richter is a traitor to the state, who must be liquidated, which will be entrusted to you. He is planning not only the controlled mammalian plague which is to afflict enemy lands, but a human plague which will destroy the race, excepting only such as he will preserve for his own comfort and use; and you would not be likely to be among them if Herr Betz should communicate to him what he has learnt from you in the past month.

"Prompt action against Richter would doubtless avert this danger. But there is another. Richter asserts that he has made arrangements that this plague shall break out uncontrollably at any time following his own death, so that the human race shall not survive longer. He must be compelled to disclose the method of that operation, and to nullify it before his elimination can be undertaken with safety. Can you arrange that? And what help, if any, shall you require?"

Zweigler did not wait for Seeley to reply. He said quickly: "I can do that. I shall need no help, if it can be so arranged that the servants here will take their orders from me."

"That must be assured. There is another matter, of less importance, but it must have attention. There is a Mr. Bulldozer in the house?"

Seeley gave Zweigler an emphatic signal not to interfere further. He said: "Yes. He is."

"He is Lord Whitcombe, the Interfederal Secretary of the English-Speaking Union, who has come here in disguise. He must neither be harmed nor allowed to go. He may be required as a witness of the murder of Colonel Wagram, or charged as an accessory thereto.

"At present Herr Richter is charged with that murder; there being substantial evidence against him, though it is not beyond doubt. There is a warrant issued for his arrest, which will not be executed unless that course should appear wise in support of your own plans. It will be done at once, if you call up Badenstrasse, 37, Stuttgart, on DXM 43.2, giving the password *expedition*, and saying how the house shall be entered.

"I suppose that you will have the remaining hours of the night in which you can prepare your plans, and decide the time and nature of any help you will need from us. I will call you up in an hour from now, to ascertain what you propose.

"You will understand that this is a matter which cannot be bungled, and any errors on your part would be followed by your arrest for the crime of betraying the confidence of your employer, which I need not remind you is a capital offence under our law. On the other hand, success will be rewarded with liberality."

Seeley said: "You need not wait for an hour. If you will call up again in fifteen minutes—"

He was interrupted curtly: "I said an hour. Do you give directions to me?"

The ill-mannered tone may have provoked him to say impulsively that on which he had intended to reflect. He answered: "But there are matters which you should know. It is Lord Whitcombe who is speaking now. Herr Zweigler is with me. Herr Richter is in a drugged sleep. His confidential secretary, Miss Latour, is also with me, and can issue orders in his name, which will be obeyed. The house is quiet, no one but ourselves knowing what has occurred. It is necessary that Herr Zweigler and I should have a short talk, but after that it may be essential to act quickly. If you will be available in fifteen minutes—"

"It is only essential that the instructions to Herr Zweigler should be exactly obeyed. I must ask you, Lord Whitcombe, to assist him, or stand aside. Who drugged Richter?"

"I forced him to drink a cup of coffee which had been intended for me."

"Why should he have wished to drug you?"

"I was lured here, Richter not knowing who I was, as you evidently do, as a stranger whom he could use for experiment on the human brain, in which Herr Zweigler was assisting him."

"But you say Zweigler is with you now?"

"I had brought him here at a pistol's point to hear him speak to Hanover, that I might be convinced of his disloyalty to Richter."

"You know how Wagram was killed?"

"Yes. But it would not be an opportune moment for its discussion."

"Herr Zweigler, you are there? You admit the accuracy of what has been said so far as it is known to you?"

"*Ja*," Zweigler replied, in a voice which could be distinguished from Seeley's, leaving beyond doubt that two men were there. "That is how it is."

"And you are there, Miss Latour? You agree?"

"Yes," she said. "What you have been told is all true."

"In ten minutes time I will come through again."

Seeley thought: "An efficient man. I should say Richter would have had a poor chance with him, even if I had not prepared the way." He recognized the probing quality of the three brief questions which had gone to the root of all that had occurred since he had entered that house, and the acceptance of what must have been the surprising substance of his replies without further words. But he had no leisure to spend in admiration of the Chief of the High Police of Berlin. He looked to Amelie to ask: "Would the servants here obey the Government—the police—against Richter?"

"I don't know," she said doubtfully. "It's hard to imagine—"

"I can tell you," Zweigler interposed with decision. "They wouldn't. Richter *is* the law in Württemberg. And the police. If Schmidt's men were actually in the house, I wouldn't say what would happen. But they wouldn't go against him at a word from Berlin. They'd wait for him to come round, and then ask what they should do."

"Then I think the best course will be—"

Zweigler interrupted him without ceremony. "The best thing you can do now is to leave this to me. You're safe enough, but you've got to stand back. You can't threaten me with that pistol now."

"So long as Miss Latour and I are safe, I don't want to threaten anyone. But I think you misapprehend the position. Apart from Miss Latour's assistance, I should say that both you and I are very far from safe in this house. And she's only safe as long as they don't guess what she's helped us to do."

Amelie added a word of confirmation to this, which Seeley did not understand, but he saw that it reminded Zweigler of something he did not like, and could not dispute. She said: "Reske wouldn't listen to you."

Reske was the engineer who controlled the electric defences of the house. A touch of one of his switches would turn any doorway or corridor into a deadly snare. Twice members of the staff had died after quarrels with him; and, though it appeared in each case that their own carelessness could be blamed, it was a coincidence which made him feared. And Zweigler knew himself to be one whom Reske did not approve. No less, there was shrewd perception of the strength of his present position in his reply: "I've nothing to fear from anyone in this house. I've done nothing. I've been forced here by that pistol of yours, and listened to what's come from Berlin, as we all have.

"Suppose I called up Reske now, and asked his opinion as what's best to be done, he couldn't fall out with me for that. But if you get in my way, you'll have Herr Schmidt on to you, and I'm sorry for any man in this continent whom he means to have."

"We are talking," Seeley said, recognizing more force in the argument to which he listened than he was willing to show, "about questions that don't arise. What you've got to think about is how you propose dealing with Richter, which you'll get asked in about four minutes from now. I'm going to let you do the talking next time."

After that Zweigler became silent, nor did he appear to give attention to some low-voiced conversation which followed between Seeley and Amelie, which was not surprising, for he had no small problem to solve.

XXVIII. THE PROBLEM OF HERR RICHTER

THE RECEPTION SIGNAL came punctually, in response to which Amelie plugged in, and adjusted the amplifier.

"You there, Lord Whitcombe?" Herr Schmidt's voice enquired.

"Yes; but I'll leave Zweigler to talk to you this time."

"What is Miss Latour's attitude in this matter?"

"She had already learnt or suspected enough of Richter's designs to have decided that she could not continue in his service. You can rely on her absolutely."

"Very well. I will hear Herr Zweigler now."

Zweigler said: "There are three methods of persuasion that can be tried. We can have Richter tied when he wakes, so that he can hurt no one, including himself, and we can then proceed by torture, or fear, or hope. We can threaten or bribe. But there is a surer way than any of these. I can inject that which will change his will."

"Change his will? In what way?"

"In such a way that he will become weak of purpose, and do anything that is asked. He will become like a spaniel dog."

"You are sure you can do that? It would be an experiment in which it would be your peril to fail."

"It has been done before, and I may be able to make some advance on what past experiments have achieved. But, if it should not succeed, there will be no loss. Other methods can still be tried."

"So that you succeed, I can promise you a most rich reward. I have spoken to the president, who says that there would be few things you could ask which you should not have."

"I would ask but two things. I would have Herr Richter's place in control of the laboratories here, and I would have Herr Richter without reserve for my own use."

"They are rewards which should be granted with ease. At what hour do you propose that this experiment should be made?"

"The injection will require about five hours to prepare. It will be about 8:00 A.M."

"You will work at it in your own rooms?"

"Yes. In the one adjoining this."

"At seven-thirty, if not before, I will call you again. Lord Whitcombe, you will have access to Herr Richter's room?"

"I propose to return there with Miss Latour now."

"That is well. I will speak to you there on Herr Richter's wavelength, which Miss Latour will know, on matters pertaining to your own countries."

With these words, Herr Schmidt cut off. Leaning back, in his Berlin office, he remained in thought while he allowed sufficient time for Seeley to reach Richter's room. He had the look of a satisfied but serious man. Once he muttered: "We must destroy them. They will become a danger to us," but his tone was that of one who considered something which he had no doubt that he would be able to do. Then he called up Herr Richter's room.

He asked: "Are you satisfied, Lord Whitcombe, that Zweigler will play straight with us?"

"He is not," Seeley replied, "a man whose word you could trust, nor one who would hesitate to commit any crime for his own advantage, or to satisfy his curiosity, but—"

"To do what?"

"To satisfy his curiosity. Richter and he would have murdered me for the sake of some experiments on the brain, if I had not objected in a decisive manner."

"'Scientific experiment,' they would have called it."

"That's what I said: to satisfy his curiosity. But Zweigler hates Richter. That's genuine. He'll do whatever he thinks to be to be his own advantage. I should say you've bought him. All the motives that would be likely to move him are on your side. Hatred of Richter, and greed, and fear."

"It is on those I rely. Lord Whitcombe, when you put Richter to sleep you were of service to us, and for that reason we are disposed to make no trouble for you. But can you tell me how Wagram died?"

"I can only say that you will be wrong if you charge Richter with that."

"Then we will ask no more. As matters are going, the question of his arrest may not arise. But you will recognize that in what he is proposing to do he is the enemy of his whole race, and that you are helping your own peoples as much as us."

"That is how I see it. I hope that there may be developments which will turn aside the threat of war."

"I cannot discuss that. It is the president's matter, not mine. But you may call this a war, though there is one man only against us. If he had got started, he might have been more than enough. I want to ask you one thing. Will you try to act the formula for the injection that Zweigler is making, or, if that should be impossible, some of the injection itself? It may be something of which we should know more."

"I will do that if I can, though it may not be a simple matter."

"Are you satisfied that all will go quietly—that there will be no attempt to revive Richter, or make trouble for you—before the morning comes?"

"I was about to mention that. People are accustomed to leave their rooms here, it they have occasion to do so, at seven, when clocks which are centrally controlled give a signal in every room. Some of the electric guards are taken off at that hour, but the annexe remains the only safe approach to the house, and that safety depends upon the goodwill of those who guide visitors after they have been allowed to enter. I suggest that you should send men, who should not be less than ten, soon after seven, and that they should act as a guard upon the room where Richter will be while the experiment is being made; but that cannot be safely done unless the electrical engineer here does not interpose. I have been discussing the matter with Miss Latour, and I am disposed to send for him, and to tell him the whole tale, if you approve."

"It is a risk of which I cannot judge."

"It may be a less one than to leave him in ignorance. He will report to Herr Richter, to take instructions for the day, at seven-fifteen. If he gets no satisfactory reply, he may be alarmed, and if your men come after that, or appear before any peaceful dispositions are made—"

"You must use your own judgment, or consult that of Miss Latour, on that; but I will make enquiry in an hour from now, and if you do not reply, I shall assume that matters have gone wrong, and become active in other ways."

Herr Schmidt cut the connection when he had said this, but he did not cease direction of his campaign. Sitting, as he did now, at his Berlin desk, he was accustomed to watch and control his operations with a particularity which left very little latitude for the operations of chance, or the discretion of subordinates, on which he did not choose to rely.

Now he called up Herr Zweigler, and after reiterating promises and threats, and probing further into the probable effects of the drug which was in course of preparation, he came to the real object of his call, which was to warn Zweigler against obtaining information regarding the antidote to the proposed mammalian plague in the hearing of Lord Whitcombe, by whom it might be used to the frustration of the European attack.

"You will," he added, "have also in mind that Miss Latour knows something of these matters, which may enable you to check the probable accuracy of anything that Richter may be persuaded to say. But you will also question her with a purpose which you must not disclose—that is, to ascertain how much she may have told to Lord Whitcombe, which it is important for us to know before deciding how we shall deal with them. And, as a matter of even greater urgency, you will discover where Herr Richter has his secret records, which no one hitherto has been able to trace."

After that he called up his Stuttgart agent; to whom he gave instructions to enter the house at seven-thirty next morning, adding: "You will watch Lord Whitcombe, whose purpose has no doubt been hostile to us, though he has been of some incidental use, and report all that he says and does, particularly in his relations with Miss Latour, who may have betrayed us to him." So he set each one to spy on others, as though each had a particular trust.

And meanwhile Amelie had summoned Reske, and told him all that had happened, and all of which Richter was accused, with the result that they found that there would be no trouble at all. The black eyes of the dark-skinned electrician, lithe as a panther in Herr Richter's close-fitting livery, glittered with animated amusement as he heard of the great scientist's most inopportune sleep. His sense of Latin humour was stirred to mirth at the thought of the man, who had plotted to destroy most of his kind so that he might rule over a weakling remnant as unquestioned king, lying in untimely repose while his intended victims discussed his fate.

"I have always thought," he said, "that it would end something like this." He agreed to cut off at once all the currents that threatened unwary lives in that evil house. Only, he hinted, if one should be required for Herr Richter at any time—it seemed that a friend of the great scientist might not be easy to find.

Reske heard of Zweigler's important part in dealing with the drugged man with no sign of dissatisfaction, though Zweigler was known to be one whom he did not like. "He will learn matters of great secrecy," he remarked; "and if he does all that is required, I suppose they will give him a great reward." He smiled again as he said that, as one who enjoys a joke that he must not share.

And meanwhile Herr Zweigler, busy with test-tube and retort and minute weighing of subtle drugs that must be mixed at an exact relative heat, plotted in a mind stimulated and excited by far-reaching plans, beyond anything he had hoped to reach. Should he not have Richter for his reward? Would not the apparatus in that sinister room into which Seeley had been carried during the previous night—the apparatus which Richter considered his, but which he himself had done so much to design—become wholly his, of which no other would even know? No other, unless it were Miss Latour and Lord Whitcombe, for whom it might not yet be beyond possibility to devise some snare which would bring them into his power.

He would have Richter—and Richter's brain. From Richter's brain he had confidence that he could abstract all its secret stores—far more than it would be necessary or possible to make him reveal as a living man. It would give him a double power. Himself and Richter in one. It would enable him, should he wish, to do, in an efficient manner, that which Richter was bungling now. But he was not sure that he would try that. He had sufficient shrewdness to see how complicated—how incalculable—its results for himself must be.

But he would have Richter's brain! And, less certainly, but regarded with an even more covetous determination—he would have that of Miss Latour. He did not actually *know*—she had been too reticent, and Richter too discreet, to allow of that—but he had made a confident guess at the truth—that it was there, even more than in his own consciousness, that Richter's secrets could be clearly and comprehensively found.

As he sat patiently waiting for the blue glow to change to purple in the retort, his mind pursued imaginations in which he probed the secrets of many brains, living, or moribund to his control. He gave little thought to any practical advantages which might follow, for, unlike Richter, who would ask himself, with every fresh discovery that he made, how it could be used in pursuit of profit or power, he regarded knowledge as an end in itself, so that he looked for no further reward.

And meanwhile Seeley and Amelie had returned to the room where Richter lay, and had found him still in the oblivion of his drugged sleep.

They had bound him, both hands and feet, without breaking that drugged repose, and sat watching for the hour when he should wake, in case it should be earlier than that at which Zweigler would be ready. He lay rather awkwardly now, and snoring in an unattractive manner—Édouard Richter, who, with his brother scientists, had dismissed God, and now, at his own decease, had planned to abolish man.

XXIX. THE ATTITUDE OF HERR RICHTER

MORE THAN ONCE Herr Richter had seemed likely to wake. He had moved, and jerked uneasily at the cords, but he had subsided again, and it was nearly seven when he opened his bewildered eyes, which turned to a look of anger and fright as he grew aware of his bonds, and of the two who were seated beside his bed.

These two, having found happiness for themselves, were of a mood to be kind to others. Love may seem to have been a small thing amidst events which must shake the world, but it is of a persistence which will not cease, and of a potency which removes obstacles which appear to be of a greater strength, as a seed raises a stone. They had talked of many things in the long hours of the night, and had come to a closer intimacy than might have been gained so soon at a duller time. Now they looked at Herr Richter without goodwill, which they would be unlikely to feel, but wishing him no further evil if he would talk in the right way, and to such result as would enable them to board a trans-Atlantic plane, as they had been planning to do.

Herr Richter looked at the girl, from whom he had always received obedience. He said: "Amelie, loose these cords, and Lord Whitcombe and I will talk like sensible men."

Amelie looked at Seeley, who replied: "We cannot do that. We know too much of your plans."

"What do you think you know?"

"You have said that the human race will not long survive your own death."

"What of that, if I had? I am a young man, and without disease."

"All the same, it is not a programme which is likely to make you popular with your fellow men."

"But it is one that you cannot change, and it should incline you to guard my health with extreme care."

"Perhaps it will. Herr Zweigler is preparing an injection now which is unlikely to do you harm."

Herr Richter's face as he heard this became colourless with a great fear. He twice started to speak, and then checked himself, as though struggling for self-control. His expression was such that Seeley became alarmed as to the physical condition of one who had said no more than was sense when he had urged the importance of guarding his health with care.

"You have no need for alarm," he said. "I tell you again that Zweigler will do you no injury."

"How can you be sure of that?"

"Well, we think we are."

"You do not know Zweigler. He hates me too much to let such a chance go. He will use some devilish drug which, if it leaves me life, will take my reason away. I will give you—there is nothing I will not give—if you will keep Zweigler away."

His voice rose to a shriek, causing Seeley to doubt the wisdom of having told him so much. He said: "You can't expect much sympathy from me, considering what would have happened if I had drunk that coffee; but that should show you that I should not tell you that no injury is intended if it were not true."

"It was Zweigler's idea, not mine! Why should you not seek for revenge on him?"

"I am not seeking revenge on anyone. What is being done is for the sake of all the men whom you would destroy."

"Why should you say all? I had another idea. I would leave two alive. They would be a real Adam and Eve, such as have been invented before. They should be you two. If you loose me now, I will promise that. You will be lords of the whole world. And there is no other way. If you kill me, you will be killing yourselves."

"No one has any thought of killing you. And you can avoid anything being done at all by telling what your plans have been, and the antidotes which would make them vain."

"I do not say that could be done. But if you loose me, I swear that you two shall survive."

"It is a kind of bargain I could not make. There is only one way by which you may win freedom and peace. That is by reversing all you have plotted to do. If you would do that, I would use such influence as I have to arrange that you should be sent to some quiet place where the means of evil would be out of your hands."

"You would gain nothing by that. The pursuit of knowledge would never cease. It would be another, if not I."

"It is not knowledge, it is its evil application, which wrecks the world."

"Then you should engage such men to combat that which you have reason to fear. You should reward them with all that the would can give. That is how you should be bargaining now."

"Perhaps we should. But even then we might not have the wisdom to ask for the right things. In the end, it is on the Creator's wisdom we must rely, and on His will to save us from what we are."

Richter's whole body gave a movement of exasperation that strained his bonds. "It is hard to talk to one who believes in such myths as that. Even Zweigler may be better than you. He will use a language we both know."

Seeley had been provoked to affirmative assertion beyond his own normal attitude (for he had reflected much on the nature of Reality, without reaching a certain goal), and there was much more in his mind which he had the disposition to say, but he was interrupted at this point by the entrance of Zweigler, closely followed by a small man in a plain grey uniform, his rank being shown only by the red breast-badge of the three-headed eagle which Seeley knew that less than two dozen men in Europe were entitled to wear.

Reske came behind with the detached air of one who looks on at a performance he would be sorry to miss.

Seeley said: "Herr Gestapo Schmidt, I presume?" He gave the formal greeting that international courtesy required to one whose reputation had roused his past, and whose aspect now roused his present, antipathy.

"Yes. This appeared to be a matter to which I should personally attend."

Richter's anxious eyes moved rapidly from one to another, seeking what this interposition might mean. He chose to assume that Herr Schmidt's coming would be unwelcome to those who had bound him there.

"Schmidt," he said, "you are in time, but no more. If you will clear the room, and cut these ropes, I will tell you how matters stand."

"I can hear what you have to say without that."

"With Lord Whitcombe present to send it to Havana in the next hour? Do you know that he has just offered me any reward I ask if I will secretly give him the antidote to the plague with which I have undertaken to wage this war?"

Herr Schmidt's lively eyes turned quickly to Amelie. "Is that true?" he asked sharply.

"There is no truth in it. It was not mentioned at all."

Richter looked at her with a hatred which showed what kind of fate would be hers should he recover his power. Cunning mingled with the malignancy of his glance as he said: "You think she knows, but you will find you are wrong. I have been wiser than that."

Schmidt looked at Amelie with a new speculation in his eyes. What might be the meaning of that? But it confirmed an opinion at which he had already arrived that she had spoken truth, and that Richter had lied.

"Lord Whitcombe," he said, "understands the position too well to have attempted any bargain with you. You must confess everything if you wish to escape what we have come here to do."

"I have told you that I cannot talk freely till we are alone. Why do you not clear the room? You can leave me bound, so that you will have nothing to fear. You will find that I shall satisfy you in every way."

It was evident to all those in the room that Herr Schmidt hesitated over this proposition. There was a moment during which Richter thought that the game was won.

"He will offer you," Amelie said, "what he offered us. We were to be the new Adam and Eve in an empty world."

Herr Schmidt's eyes were fixed intently on her again. "He offered that? What did you say?"

"Lord Whitcombe said we would make no bargain with him."

Herr Schmidt missed nothing. He saw implications of intimacy between the two beyond anything that he had previously suspected, or which had appeared reasonable to presume.

Amelie added: "It would have made no difference. He would not have kept his word. Do you think I have been with him three years, and I do not know?"

She spoke with more vigour than had been her previous habit, but yet with some return to the old lazy inflections, as though, having been jolted out of the dreamy atmosphere of her old content, she were now settling back to another assurance in which she might dream again. But, if that were so, might it not be a dream of another and better kind?

Herr Schmidt's resolution was probably made before he heard the warning her words contained. The mere fact that he had had a solitary interview with Richter would make him suspect. He did not suppose that any member of the Government would credit him with the restraint of any moral scruple, if Richter should offer him a personally attractive deal. He would be suspected, even if no bargain should have been made, and, if it should, he would be in alliance with a most dangerous and untrustworthy man.

The astuteness which guarded him in the absence of higher principles of conduct, put the temptation firmly aside. Had the offer been secretly made, could the interview have been unsuspected, he might have resolved differently. Now he nodded to Zweigler: "You can try your own way."

Zweigler stepped forward. Richter shouted protests and pleas. He struggled to burst his bonds. Zweigler seized him in his long lean hands, rolling him over on to his face. With one knee on his back, his fingers pressed into his neck.

A scream rose to a high note, and stopped abruptly. Richter became quiet and limp.

Herr Schmidt asked: "He is not injured?"

"Not at all. But I must have him still for what has to be done."

Zweigler took from his pocket a hypodermic syringe with two tubes, which were about four inches apart at their base, and converged inwards. He applied it to the back of the neck of the unconscious man, so that its needles would penetrate at each side of the cervical vertebrae. He continued a steady pressure until the tubes were nearly empty of the brightly purple liquid they had contained.

He stepped back from the bed, with a sneer of gratified contempt slightly showing his teeth.

"When he becomes conscious again," he said, "he will be a different man."

Herr Schmidt stretched out a hand. His fingers closed on the syringe. "Allow me," he said. "I have not seen one of this pattern before."

Zweigler loosed it reluctantly. Herr Schmidt's curiosity appeared to be satisfied at a short glance, but after that he dropped it into his pocket.

Zweigler said anxiously: "I cannot part with that. It is not safe. A difference in the dosage—"

"It will be safe with me. Let us see its results, and then—"

He left the sentence unfinished. Zweigler controlled his anger and did not pursue a useless discussion. Seeley observed how deep were the antipathies, how extreme the distrusts, of these men who had discarded the faiths—who would say they had outgrown the superstitions—of earlier days.

Herr Schmidt asked: "How long will he lie like that?"

"It may be five hours or six, and after that he will be sick for a time, and only partly conscious of what he says. But he will quickly recover from that, and then he will be a quite different man."

Herr Schmidt looked round the room. Who should watch for the awaking? Who go? Whom, or what combination, could he trust? He said:

"We will all stay. The time will not be long." He turned to Seeley to ask: "You play chess? Then perhaps we may—"

Seeley said he should be pleased.

Herr Schmidt believed that he could learn much of a man's character at that game, and was indifferent that he should reveal his own.

Chess is a game of mathematical exactitudes, which are the same for all. But it is one of countless millions of possibilities, and no two men play it in the same way. A may usually defeat B, and B may defeat C, yet C may be more than equal to A.

Amidst innumerable differences there is a broad distinction between those who play with extreme soundness of defence, watching for the infinitesimal advantage which will be tenaciously held to the gradual certainty of success, and those who depend for their own protection upon speed and audacity of attack.

Herr Schmidt, playing a versatile and subtle game, which was yet not greatly concerned about gain or loss, observed a quality in his opponent's methods which he disliked; for he would play with the extreme care of the most orthodox tradition until he saw a weakening, however slight, in his adversary's array, when he would change to a concentration of fierce attack which risked all on its decisive success, and on it being such as would leave no moment for any counter activity on other parts of the arena of mimic war.

Herr Schmidt thought: "Shall I let him go alive from this land? I am unsure. It is a matter on which I must think well."

XXX. ANOTHER WEAPON OF WAR

MR. SILVER LONG received Herr Bocker it a breezy manner which that gentleman did not approve. He had anticipated bluff, even to a colossal extent, and had come prepared to accept a threat, of whatever nature, with a sceptical politeness which would put it aside in the casual manner which the occasion required. His experts had told him of three possible weapons of offence, all of which their own scientists could control. Even if it were something new, and of a genuine sort, the three months' notice which the Commonwealth was so generously giving should allow counter-measures to be prepared.

"The fact is," he thought, "that they are in so great a panic in the dread of what we shall be able to do to them that they have resorted to this desperate device of warning us of their own plans (or what they think we would not like them to be) before the date which the treaty requires. They must think we have simple minds."

But Herr Bocker was a very shrewd, though somewhat over-confident man, and he had an uneasy feeling, almost as he entered the room, that the high spirits of the premier were not assumed. If that were so, there was the more reason that he should be met in a way that would make them sink!

"I should say at once," he said, "that I have come to fulfil the courtesy which should be observed between federations which are not yet divided by war, however near it may be, rather than with expectation of hearing that which will be of moment to us. It is not only that we are assured that you have no weapon we cannot meet, but we conceive our own attack to be one which you will not endure.

"I would stake much," he added, in the tone of a reasonable man, and with the smile which the words required, "that it is a war that will not begin, and more, that should it do so, it will be over within week."

"Your Excellency," Mr. Long very cheerfully replied, "you have said what I expected to hear, and, being the man you are, you have said it well…and now I will show you this."

He turned to a table on which was a thin metal tray, of the colour of lead, but of a substance which Herr Bocker was unable to name. He touched it curiously, and drew his hand sharply back. He said: "It is of a great heat."

"It is not heat you feel. It is cold. But I must warn you not to touch, for these things must be handled with care. Not that the tray is of any account. Betz would tell you what that is, as would others of those on whom you depend. It is isolation only which it provides."

Mr. Long drew on gloves of some grey fabric which the ambassador was again unable to name. The premier said: "It is what is on the tray which will be of interest to you."

Herr Bocker had already observed a block of concrete, about as large as a child's head. He could name that. And a metal siphon about three inches in height. How they could be formidable in the United States of the Old World was not easy to guess.

Mr. Long took the siphon in a gloved hand. He said: "The concrete of which Berlin is built is many times harder than steel?"

"Incomparably so. Everyone knows that. I have heard that its resistance is 27.3 to that of the hardest steel that was ever made."

"I have a piece of concrete here which, I am assured, is of equal quality. You will observe that I squeeze upon it but one drop of the liquid which this siphon contains."

The drop of brimstone-coloured liquid fell silently on the concrete

Nothing happened. Herr Bocker was correctly polite in his query "Is it an experiment which had gone wrong?" His voice expressed concern, as at a friend's trouble, which he was powerless to help.

"I think not. If you will look closely, you will see that there is a change." Herr Bocker looked. He saw that the concrete immediately around the liquid had flattened and sunk. The process continued at an increasing rate, spreading through the block. In three minutes the lump of concrete had sunk into a spongy bun-shaped mass.

"If you would like to test its consistency," Mr. Long said cheerfully, "I will lend you a glove. You will find it to be much softer than white-hot lava, and as cold as the tray.

"If a drop of this liquid, however small, be applied to a block of concrete, however large, this is what will occur. It is a spreading process which will not stop."

"It is a weapon," the ambassador replied calmly, "which you could not use, so that we may spare debate as to whether it would be frightful to us."

"We could not use it, you say? What could withhold us from that?"

"It is treaty-barred. It is too nearly of the nature of high explosive to be allowed."

"Not at all. High explosive was barred because it was deadly to men, but this can be avoided with ease."

"It is a point on which you would find that Mendoza might not agree."

"But he does. It is an opinion for which we have already asked— he being, in a way, an umpire on what we do."

"An umpire who is friendly to you."

"He is friendly to peace, and to the hope that men will allow themselves to endure."

"We are changing words to no gain. I will report what I have seen."

"It is all I ask you to do." They parted with the courtesies that their functions required, and Herr Bocker went back to his embassy to make report to Berlin. "When you consider this," he concluded, "I suppose that you will agree that there is no choice between peace and a total war."

XXXI. Is It the Same Man?

THE DAY PASSED, and the man who had aspired to the dominion of a depleted world lay unconscious amid the little group which changed somewhat from hour to hour, but remained substantially the same.

He lay somewhat more comfortably than when Zweigler had stepped back from the bed, though he had made no movement of his own, for at mid-morning Frau Richter had entered the room.

Pale and quiet, she had taken no notice of the others there, but had stood gazing for one silent moment at the unattractive spectacle of the drugged man, and then said aloud, but not as addressing anyone present: "So it has come to this." Then she had stepped forward, and adjusted the pillow beneath his head.

Herr Schmidt watched her intently, but said nothing till she had left. Then he asked Reske: "She could tell us much?"

"Nothing at all. He would not confide to her."

It was evening when Richter's hands moved, and he began to mutter and then stir uneasily, as one oppressed by a dream which he could not break.

Zweigler said: "It would have been better had he been put to bed before the return of consciousness. And we should not be here. He should have time to adjust his mind."

Herr Schmidt looked antagonistic to this suggestion. He asked: "What should you propose?"

"He may feel unwell at first. He should have rest, and some food. Frau Richter might have arranged that."

Herr Schmidt said: "He must not be left." He looked round the little group. Was there one there he could trust? He spoke to Amelie. "You would wait?"

Amelie hesitated. How much did he mean her to do? How much responsibility to take? She asked: "Only to wait?"

"Yes. You could call up Frau Richter."

"Yes. Of course. Very well, I will do that."

Frau Richter replied at once. She would come. She could bring Greta?

Herr Schmidt agreed to that. He said: "We will wait in the next room. We must hope it will not be long. We must be called in as soon as he is ready to talk."

He did not think that there could be any risk in such a withdrawal while he kept Zweigler within sight. Even if the drug should have been a failure, it did not appear a contingency to be seriously considered that Richter would be in a hurry to commit suicide. But he said to Amelie: "You would call us at once if Richter should be awkward in any way?"

"Yes."

"Very well. We will go."

Herr Richter had opened his eyes by this time, though they appeared to be unconscious of what they saw. Frau Richter had come, bringing Greta with her. They were taking the ropes from his hands and feet, which it would have been more reasonable to have removed earlier.

He was groaning, as one whose physical condition was not good.

Seeley, Reske, Schmidt, and Zweigler withdrew to the next room

Frau Richter was a woman from whom life had washed out any colour she ever had. She looked at Amelie to ask in a flat voice: "What are they going to do with him now?"

"Nothing that I know of. They just want him to explain his plan for everybody else to die when he does, and get him to drop the idea."

"There's no sense in that. He never was sensible," the woman answered, in her flat voice.

"He was a very clever man," Amelie answered, old loyalty contending with new independence of thought. It was curious that they had both spoken of him in the past tense.

"Oh, yes. He was clever," the woman conceded readily. "That's what's brought him to this."

"This," under her indifferent ministration, consisted first of a good meal, which the reviving man was persuaded, though with some difficulty, to eat.

While he ate it he asked no questions, and showed no animation, but he thanked them for what they did in a tone his wife had been unaccustomed to hear. He showed neither curiosity nor alarm as to what had happened to him already, or might be preparing now. Amelie, looking on and seeing most of the game, observed that he would look down or aside, as though unwilling to meet the eyes of the woman who had the name of his wife.

The placidity of the scene was interrupted by Herr Schmidt's impatience. His enquiry as to whether he and his companions could return to the room was answered by Herr Richter himself. He said: "Yes, of course; let the gentlemen come in."

When they had entered, he spoke at once, without waiting to be questioned, and as though he were continuing a conversation which had been interrupted only for the requirements of sleep and food.

"It seems to me," he said, "that you have two grounds of complaint, both of which I can remove, with some ease to my own mind.

"The one is that I had discovered a means of hastening the decease of my fellow men, so that they would not greatly outlive my own, and I had so arranged that it should operate at my death, with a universality which there would, I think, have been no means to avoid.

"It is a programme which you naturally disapprove, and which you would prefer that I put aside, as you need have no doubt that I will.

"You may wish to go beyond that, and have proof of what my intentions are. I do not object to that, so far as I am concerned. I will explain what I had arranged, which was no more than to start, among those who should be round me in my last hours (as you are now, but my health is good) an epidemic of an uncheckable kind—actually very similar to that which I was considering operating at a more immediate day, which intention is the substance of your second complaint.

"The second project was already causing me much anxiety and doubt, and is one which I will abandon at once; but when you ask me to disclose what I had intended, and the means of immunity of which I am also aware, I do not refuse, but I wish you to know the nature, and to consider the possible consequences, of what you ask me to do.

"I shall be letting loose, to yourselves or others, knowledge that cannot be withdrawn, and that any of them may use at any future time, and against which the whole human race could not be immunized continually without enormous trouble of a recurrent kind.

"You will consider that there is in many of us a strong impulse to demonstrate by actual experiment that which is theoretically sound. It is a propensity, I confess, that has not been absent from my own mind, and that may have been the major causation of what I had done or had planned to do. But I have come to look on these matters differently, after mature thought. The impulse I had has died, and my judgment disapproves both the equity and the wisdom of such designs. You are safe with me. If I give the knowledge to others, you will be no more so with me. Will you be equally safe with them?"

"What we require," Herr Schmidt replied, "is conclusive evidence that these plans have been put aside, with a knowledge of antidotes to which resort could be made if there should ever be occasion to do so. We might require experiments to demonstrate that you had been frank with us."

"After which, Herr Schmidt, if I know your methods, I should have a short life. I do not know that I could fairly complain of that. But could not that idea be developed, so that you could have all the proof you desire, without peril to the future of men?

"Could not the president nominate a committee of yourselves or others—Herr Betz might be one—to whom I would explain these matters without reserve?—a committee in whom there would be absolute confidence, and who would agree to join me in self-destruction so soon as their report should have been approved?"

The black frown on Zweigler's face showed that this programme had no attraction for him. "You aren't being asked," he said, "to worry about us or the world. You've just got to tell us the tale, and we'll decide how far it's to go." He thought that, if there should be a full disclosure there, it was improbable that it would be completely understood by anyone but himself. Were not all the secret stores of Richter's brain to be added to his?

But Herr Schmidt preferred the singular pronoun. "I am here in the president's name," he said, "to decide what shall be done, concerning which I am disposed to return to Berlin to confer with him."

He looked at the four companions of his night's vigil with considering eyes. He had to ask himself again whom could he trust, and how far?

He turned to Seeley to ask: "Lord Whitcombe, will you be responsible for Herr Richter's safety and restraint until I return, with the assistance of our friends here, who, being of his household, may be somewhat less independent than you?"

It was subtly and inoffensively put, and won a certain affirmative from one whose abilities he was disposed to rate more highly than he had done when he entered the room.

"I am anxious," Seeley replied, "to return to Cuba as soon as possible, and I shall hope that there may be no objection to Miss Latour (whose service is finished here) returning with me; but I do not object to stay while I can be of assistance in a matter which concerns all nations alike."

Herr Schmidt said: "There should be no objection to that, and the matter may be concluded before tomorrow is done."

He understood that a bargain had been proposed, which he would keep if he should see no reason of self or national disadvantage in so doing, that being the high-water mark of honour to which be was accustomed to rise.

Seeley knew that. He saw the occasion to be critical for Amelie and himself, as it was for Richter (and Zweigler, unless he made a bad guess), and for the fate of mankind.

He knew that Herr Schmidt, having excellent and private means of communication with the president, would not return to Berlin without reason of particular weight.

He made a correct guess that he would not have done so had he been concerned with the Richter problem alone, unless it were merely a manœuvre of withdrawal, so that he should not be on the scene during developments on which he had already resolved.

Actually, Schmidt was influenced by his secret knowledge of the new weapon of war of which Silver Long, almost at this hour (the day dawning later in Havana than Stuttgart), was telling Herr Bocker, of which he judged that particulars would have reached Berlin before he should arrive. How would it affect the Government's policy? Would they decide to prosecute or abandon war? How important would it become, in the former case, to prevent Seeley's return? Certainly that of Miss Latour could not be allowed. Or, in the latter, might it not be essential that he should take no action which would affront the English-Speaking Commonwealth, or offend their Interfederal Secretary, whose goodwill would be of importance in future years?

There were questions here the solution of which went beyond his authority, and which, had it been more than it was, he could not have resolved without knowledge of the policy on which his Government would decide.

Had there been nothing to do beyond the discovery and frustration of Richter's schemes, or to decide, beyond his (and Zweigler's) subsequent fates, he would have taken counsel with none. But he saw that the position had become more complicated; and he was satisfied that he had brought matters in that room to a point at which they could be safely left for a few hours. Or was he? He caught a look in Zweigler's eyes which he did not like. He judged him to be sullen, resentful, suspicious. He thought that it was important that his absence should not be long. But he did not doubt that he was taking the right course, and that he would be equal to the control of anything that might occur.

XXXII. Zweigler Has Much to Say

HERR SCHMIDT HAD judged Zweigler's feelings correctly. He was one whom he might have bought absolutely at the price which Zweigler had plainly asked, and which he had promised.

For the control of Stuttgart, and the liberty to do what he would with Herr Richter's brain, there was probably nothing, consistent with his own safety, that Zweigler would not have been willing to do.

The trouble was that he did not trust Schmidt, and this distrust had been roused to an active fear by the retention of the syringe, which it is possible to regard as Herr Schmidt's greatest mistake. The fact was that each of these powerful and evil men was inclined to add to his natural antipathies a contempt for his opponent's methods, and a confidence in the superiority of his own, which increased his liability to be overcome.

Yet Herr Schmidt's error (if such it were) arose, not from this excess of confidence, but from an alarm that he could not entirely still. He had not gone so far as to doubt that scientists could be controlled, but he had come to see that this control was a matter which must be taken in hand.

Now Zweigler had introduced the idea of a drug which would produce an amiable disposition in ruthless men. Why should not this concoction be analysed, and, if its results should be equal to Zweigler's boasts, manufactured in wholesale quantities and injected into all scientific investigators? It might be made a preliminary condition of taking up a scientific career.

His observation of Richter, since he had been under its influence, had assured him of its value if it should be so used, and his mind had already gone further, to consider whether it might not be valuable for the transformation of all men who were politically troublesome, or even for the whole population, who might thus be brought to a regimented docility fascinating to the official mind.

There might, he foresaw, be some degree of popular resistance to such a proposal, but the idea that he might overcome this was not as foolish as it would have been half a century earlier.

Fifty years of controlled wireless and press propaganda had produced a generation which was supersensitive to such impulsions, and even at that distance of time the ideal of individual liberty had been a fading dream. Now, even in the English-Speaking Commonwealth, where freedom flickered, though it had ceased to burn, if it could be demonstrated that greater comfort or safety could be gained by a more rigid servitude, most people would regard the issue as resolved beyond further debate; and in the United States of Europe it had come to be assumed without thought that what bureaucracy dictated must be obeyed.

Herr Schmidt took a swift plane to Berlin, leaving some of his own men, and some of the local police, in and around a house which had become otherwise defenceless.

After Herr Schmidt had left, Richter asked, in a tone of good-humoured obsequiousness, whether there would be any objection to his returning to his own rooms. His attitude was rather that of a patient among nurses, than of a captured and thwarted man. He seemed conscious neither of resentment nor fear. Certainly it had been a potent drug, and whether he had been aware of what had been done was not easy to guess. If he were, he showed no resentment, even of that.

Seeley said: "I don't see why you shouldn't; but we shall have to guard you carefully. We mustn't forget that yours is a very valuable life, and that the house has become more accessible than it was, although we've got all the police protection we could require. What do you say, Herr Zweigler?" he added, a thought rising in his mind that Richter might have access to vital things in his own rooms that he could not otherwise get. *Suppose he were acting now*.

But Zweigler said shortly: "You should be the best judge of that. Herr Schmidt left it to you."

Seeley saw that Zweigler's attitude would not be to challenge his authority, but to leave it without support.

The whole party went with Richter to the room where Seeley had met him first, the room where he ate and worked, and where Amelie had been his constant companion during the last three years.

But he wanted to go on through that to the bedroom beyond. He wanted, he said, to rest. He would rest till Herr Schmidt's return, when he would be ready to arrange matters with him at any time.

Seeley made no objection to that. Frau Richter, who had come with them, her colourless presence almost unregarded, followed her husband. Whether affection or duty, or some less positive motive, controlled her would have been hard to tell.

Seeley said to Reske: "Perhaps you would stay with him first, and see that nothing happens we shouldn't wish? I will relieve you after a time."

Reske agreed readily, leaving Zweigler and Amelie, both of whom, from widely different motives, Seeley had wished to keep near him.

It was natural to distrust Zweigler, and his attitude raised a vague fear of what he might be planning to do. He must still have an ill-defined authority in that house, and probably in the *werke* beyond, now that Richter had become indifferent to its control. For every reason, it was best to keep him under observation as much as could be contrived.

Having no authority over his movements (though it was an easy guess that they would not be disregarded by Schmidt's police), Seeley tried what conversation would do to keep him. It is a hook which most men will take if it be baited with subjects that fill their minds.

"You have done a marvellous thing," Seeley said. "How long will Herr Richter continue like that?"

"While he lives. It is a permanent change."

"But one which you could doubtless neutralize by some other injection?"

"It is a question that only experiment would resolve. Other drugs are potent in other ways, which might be inconsistent with the condition you have observed. I could not go further than that."

"I must suppose that the necessary experiments have not been made?"

"How could they?" Zweigler replied bitterly. "How could they, with such laws as restrain us now? Most men have no thirst for knowledge. As you know, they are mere cattle, of no account. Yet would our Government—and yours would be worse, I know that— would they give me a mere hundred of normal children on whom experiments could have been made?

"Have I not asked, and implored, and was not the best offer I got that of a few, imbecile or diseased, which had to be brought from their asylum by night, as though there were evil in what I did?

"They would not listen, even when I pointed out that the extra children could be specially bred, which could have been disadvantage to none, and should have been at my own charge.

"Herr Richter, specializing in epidemic virus, and subjects akin to that, could get assistance for what he did, even though he has worked in most secret ways. But I, dealing with the greater, more difficult subject of the human brain, could get no sufficient support in what are supposed to be civilized, rational times!

"Even in what I have been able to do, I have had to lean upon Richter's aid."

He brought out Richter's name with a concentrated contempt which showed how bitterly he had resented having to disclose and share his experiments with the more influential scientist as a means of getting the human material which they required.

Seeley remembered how narrowly he had himself escaped contributing to the cause of knowledge, but he controlled the feelings the memory wakened. He said, with the sound of sincerity which the words allowed: "Yes, I see how you feel."

It was sufficient to cause the thwarted scientist to burst out again: "It is such things that make us despair of the human race, and even the purge which Richter designed an unimportant, if not advantageous, thing! We have chased superstition from the world, but prejudice and ignorance are more difficult and enduring foes."

Seeley tried to bring the conversation to a cooler level by asking: "If such a change as we have witnessed this afternoon can become permanent, the question arises: should the new man be held responsible for that which his predecessor did, owing to a character which is no longer his? Should he be held to be the same man, either for reward or penalty?"

But he found the subject to be one in which Zweigler took no more than a tepid interest. Consideration of judicial or social questions of an abstract character was of little attraction to him.

But he pointed out that it could be no more than an extension of the injustice which all punishment of anything so complex as the human body must be. You cannot hang a murderer without causing the death of every separate corpuscle in his blood, of which countless millions are doing their humble necessity work with the diligence, and no doubt with the conscious intelligence, that it requires, and surely without individual responsibility for the crime for which they will be made to suffer.

Seeley observed that he regarded the human body as containing, or consisting of, innumerable separate entities over whom their owner (if such he could be considered) exercised only muscular control, and that of a partial character.

It was a subject that he would have been glad to continue, but Zweigler rose, saying that he had work which he had left too long, and, with Lord Whitcombe's permission (this proviso being said in a tone that left it uncertain whether it had been seriously meant, or was mere courtesy, or even contempt), he would return to his own room.

Seeley was left with Amelie, who had been busy during the conversation in answering many calls for Herr Richter, which she had done in every instance by saying that he was unwell, but that everyone must do their best to carry on till they should hear further from him.

Now she ordered a meal, to which they sat down together cheerfully enough, in the enjoyment of their brief precarious peace, and listening to such news as Amelie had selected as likely to be of interest to Seeley, or of possible importance for him to know.

The perilous electric defences of the house had been cut off, but they felt little satisfaction in that. They felt themselves to be surrounded by dangers of equal deadliness and of the same invisible, unpredictable kind. To an observer it might seem that they had brought each other into a position of peril which neither would have encountered alone. Had Seeley not appealed on the scene, it may be supposed that occasion for Amelie to defy Herr Richter's authority would not have arisen; and, more surely, that an intention of leaving for the New World would not have entered her mind.

It is also clear that the path of freedom for Seeley would have been more readily opened had he not shown that he had reached a stage of intimacy with Richter's confidential secretary, and a desire to take her away, which was not likely to be regarded with favour at a time when war was threatened, in which Herr Richter's secret process was to be the first weapon of offence.

Having this opportunity of solitude, they said little, for Amelie was one who could be silent with ease; and Seeley, even with the substratum of satisfaction her presence gave, was preoccupied with speculations as to what developments might confront him, what obstacles bar the way to the freedom he was resolved that they should find together, or both should miss. He got as much satisfaction from thought as would a blindfolded man who must go forward with explosives about his path.

XXXIII. Zweigler Becomes Dangerous

ZWEIGLER RETURNED TO his own room to face a problem, the nature and complexity of which he was able to see, and upon the correct solution of which his freedom to continue his own work in his own way, and probably life itself, must depend.

There was one relevant fact—that of the new weapon of war which the Havana Government had threatened to use—of the importance of which he was not fully aware; but apart from that, he judged both danger and opportunity shrewdly enough, though that insight might not solve the problems which it disclosed.

He had the wit to see that there were alternative courses, both having their own perils between which he must choose, and that it would be worst of all to wobble between the two.

Either he must make his utmost endeavour to fulfil Herr Schmidt's instructions, relying upon his gratitude or good faith for the promised rewards, or he must act on the assumption that the Police Chief was hostile to him, and consider only his own protection, which he must secure by every means in his power.

The first alternative held the attraction that it was a path which it would be easy to tread, and offered rewards which it was his utmost ambition to win.

Against it was his fear that Schmidt held him both in dislike and contempt, and that he might not only miss reward, but be destroyed as soon as his use was done, as one who was trusted too little, and knew too much. He saw that, even if it should be considered necessary to arrange for this removal in a legal manner, Herr Schmidt's knowledge of his betrayal of his employer to Betz would provide all that the occasion would require.

He remembered, with natural resentment, the manner in which Herr Schmidt had taken the syringe. Putting resentment aside, it was an indication that he was regarded as no more than a distrusted tool. It is probable that this incident was decisive, but, apart from that, there could have been no real alliance or co-operation between two such men, each unrestrained by ordinary scruples, and each viewing all that the other represented in a mood that fluctuated between fear and contempt.

Having arrived at this point, Zweigler must ask himself: "What could he do?"

He had already served Schmidt's purpose by the injection which he had given to Richter, though his further assistance would almost certainly be needed in the interpretation and possibly in the neutralization of whatever Richter's confessions might disclose.

For that time he was probably safe, though even that was less than certain. He would be safe unless the Government had decided to take Betz, or one of the other two living European scientists of equal reputation, into their confidence, and give further charge of the investigation to them.

But even if that were a groundless fear, his use might be over in a few days, and his elimination appear to Schmidt to be a mere act of routine, to make a tidy end of the affair. How could he avoid that?

There was one obvious way: to liquidate Schmidt at an earlier hour. That, in itself, to one of his knowledge and resources, would not be difficult; but he saw that it must be done in such a way that it could not be attributed to him—if possible in the course of some development by which he would obtain praise as the saviour of all mankind.

And, after that, he would have peace and leisure and power for the pursuit of knowledge, which was his sole purpose in life, in which he had been so frequently thwarted by smaller men.

There was another possibility. He might lead Schmidt into some blunder by which he would discredit himself, and lose the confidence of the Government, and the position he held. But that appeared both more complicated to contrive, and more precarious in its results. He did not underrate his opponent's subtlety of resource, and such an attempt would be too much like fighting a duel with his adversary's own weapons, which were less familiar to him. No. It must be liquidation; and, as a subordinate aim, events must be so directed that Miss Latour, and (of less importance, but still having great attractions) Lord Whitcombe should end their lives on his laboratory table.

For nearly two hours he sat motionless, except for an occasional restless movement of his long fingers, which might have been thought to be unravelling knots from a tangled skein. So he would often sit as he patiently analysed the results of complicated experiments, and planned such as would utilize them for further gain.

The issue of his reflections may have been less satisfactory to himself than was usual on these occasions, for he was thinking against time, as he was not accustomed to do, and he observed factors concerning which his knowledge was partial or inexact. It was too much like compounding a substance from ingredients which had not been precisely weighed.

But he rose at last, signalled for food, which he took hurriedly, with little notice of what he ate, but well-founded confidence that his special vitamin requirements would have been exactly observed, and went back to Herr Richter's rooms.

XXXIV. The President Approves

HERR SCHMIDT, HAVING arrived at his Berlin office, called up the president, and was accepted immediately. He said: "Matters of urgency have arisen on which I wish to make report, and take instructions from you, before I return to Stuttgart, which I should not delay."

"Is Lord Whitcombe concerned in these matters in any way?" the president asked.

"Yes. He is."

"Then I will see you now. The password for you will be: *Carthage fell.*"

This was no more than a routine precaution imposed upon any, high or low, who should have occasion to enter the presidential quarters in Berlin. It had followed the assassination of a former president by a man who had been most cunningly disguised as one of his confidential secretaries. Herr Schmidt thought nothing of that, but it was a pleasant surprise that the interview should be so readily and promptly conceded, and that it should appear probable that it would be with the president alone. Was it possible that the news from Havana had not arrived?

In fact, the president had had Herr Bocker's report about ten minutes earlier, and he had already convened a meeting of his Inner Council, which would be held in half an hour, and be followed by that of the Committee of Public Safety, so soon as its members could reach Berlin—among whom Herr Richter would have been included but for the abnormal developments of the last two days.

The president while keeping an open mind for such wisdom from other lips as he might be destined to hear, had already forecast the course which it would be expedient to adopt, and had seen that the presence of Lord Whitcombe in Europe might be so handled as to be advantageous; and that it had become of great potential importance that he should be treated with a full measure of diplomatic courtesy until the issue of peace or war should be fully resolved.

This being the immediate consideration, it took precedence even over the vaguer menace of Herr Richter's contemplated treachery to his kind. It was welcome news that Schmidt had returned to Berlin—it was important to ascertain that Lord Whitcombe had received no cause of offence as yet, essential that the course of future events should be guided in the right way. He had a clear half-hour before the Council would meet. He would see Schmidt at once. How could it be used in a better way?

He received the Police Chief with his inscrutable but unfailing courtesy. For ten minutes he listened to a concise and lucid summary of the events which had followed Herr Schmidt's arrival at Stuttgart, and of what he had learned of the liveliness at Herr Richter's house during the previous night.

"You will see," Herr Schmidt concluded, "why I am here. I suppose that I can deal with Richter. I am disposed to think that there will be little trouble from him, owing to that devil's injection that Zweigler gave." (He did not mention that he had some of it in his own pocket. He always hated giving knowledge needlessly away.) "And I can deal with Zweigler later, as you will doubtless wish me to do, for he is too dangerous to continue to live.

"But Lord Whitcombe is a separate matter. He is an able man, and may be more dangerous than Zweigler, though in a different way. He had won over Richter's confidential secretary, even before they knew who he was, and while Richter was (if I am not wrong) intending to use him for some experiments on the brain that he was allowing Zweigler to make. He had turned the tables on Richter, and dosed him with a narcotic which had been meant for himself. He had Zweigler sitting facing the wrong end of a pistol barrel. I believe, though the details are still obscure, that he had killed Colonel Wagram before that. And his manners are as pleasant and mild as though he would be disturbed by the idea of killing a fly—"

"He is of English blood," the President interjected. "That is how they are. You can never tell what they may do next, though, if they are left alone, it is most likely to be nothing at all."

"I have no doubt you are right. Now he is watching Richter for me (and Zweigler, who needs it more), and I have promised that he can return to Havana, and take Miss Latour with him, without enquiry being too closely made into Wagram's death.

"But I do not know how much of Richter's secrets the girl has learned, and would betray (or may have done already, it is a probable guess), nor how much Whitcombe may hear from Richter of what is to be our first weapon of war, which, if I allow them to continue together, it may be impossible to avoid."

"Not by you, my dear Schmidt, not by you," the president replied "You have dealt with this delicate matter with a discretion that it is easy to praise; and so, I have no doubt at all, you will continue to do.

"You will treat Lord Whitcombe in every way with the consideration due to so distinguished and welcome a guest; and in regard to his return to Havana, you will say that we shall, of course, facilitate it in every way. But I could not permit the departure of so important a visitor without according him the interview due to his reputation and rank, so that you will invite him to come here, bringing with him the lady, whose departure shall have my personal *visa*, by which all other formalities are excused."

"By which," Herr Schmidt replied, "I may conclude that there is to be peace, at least for this time."

"Should Lord Whitcombe ask you concerning that," the president smiled his reply, "you will say with truth that you do not know."

XXXV. MORE FEAR IN BERLIN

"IT WAS AN optical illusion, or a chemical trick. We should be fools to be turned aside by such nonsense as that." The Air Marshal protruded a truculent jaw as he said this, though there was uneasiness in his voice.

"Herr Bocker," the president replied smoothly, "inclines to take a more serious view. He reports that Mr. Long offered him any further demonstrations he may desire, even—or so he hinted—to a possible disclosure of the formula itself."

"But that would be," Baron Gluck exclaimed, with a natural incredulity, "to put the weapon into our own hands."

"Which," the president replied, "Mr. Long hinted, they might not strongly object to do. It is not to wage war, so he said, but to prevent it, that they are most greatly concerned.

"And, beyond that, you will observe that this invention, if it can do all that is claimed, is more deadly to us than it would be to the New World. Even England would be less sharply concerned. For though they use concrete, it is not the only substance with which they build. They still use wood, which they propose to do to a larger extent when the slow growth of their new hardwood forests will allow. They use natural stone. But concrete is universal with us. It is the symbol of what we are."

The Minister of Construction spoke for the first time. He said briefly: "We have got to get out of this."

Another voice added bitterly: "There would only be Paris left." *Paris!* They looked at one another in silence. There was no more to be said.

They had a vision of the vast building in which they sat—the immense hollow block of concrete which was Berlin—sinking, lava-like, into one shapeless mass, which would contain all the treasures and furnitures of its collapsed rooms, and themselves, unless they should have been sufficiently active to flee—to flee to the roofless inhospitalities of the flattened lands, the monotonous straight-sided, league-long fields— No, it was a nightmare they could not think to endure.

"The members of the Committee of Public Safety," the president went on, with no abatement of his usual cheerful urbanity, "should join us within an hour, when we will hear what they may have to say. But, subject to that (which may not be much), I propose to give an interview to Lord Whitcombe, of whose curious visit to Europe some of you have already heard, and to propose conditions of peace, which will include his own safety, to him.

"I may also offer him a young woman, who has been confidential secretary to Herr Richter, and whom, I understand, he is most anxious to have."

The faces of his sombre colleagues brightened somewhat as he said this. He was one on whom they had learned to depend, and who showed no sign that he would be likely to fail them now. One who would always have a card up his sleeve, if those which had been dealt by impartial fate seemed unsuited to win the game.

XXXVI. Zweigler Becomes Active

ZWEIGLER SAID: "I have come back because it must be time that I should take a turn at watching Richter, though I should say myself that there is no occasion at all."

Seeley saw that he must be diplomatic in his reply. With no definite suspicion, he was yet resolved that the two scientists should not be alone together. Richter, in his present condition, might put old animosities aside, and be ready to answer any questions without reserve. Yet he could not reasonably deny Zweigler access to Richter's room.

And there was another limitation to what he planned. He was conscious that it would be easy to sleep; but wakefulness would become harder with every hour. There had been little but broken dozes possible to any who had shared in the vigil of the last night, and least of all for himself. Amelie's yawns in the last hour had been frequent and undisguised.

Youthful strength and excitement may combine to prolong wakefulness, but the need for sleep must prevail at last.

Only Zweigler, most accustomed to irregular rest and long spells of sleep or watchfulness, showed no present sign of the long tension of the last twenty-four hours.

Seeley thought: "I must allow that. It is certainly time that Reske should be relieved. But Amelie shall be with him, or I. We must get some sleep, one at a time, or we shall be unfit for whatever tomorrow brings."

"We were intending," he said, "to take the next turn, but you can do that if you will, and one of us will be able to rest. Perhaps you will tell Reske and Frau Richter that they are being relieved."

He brought the name of Richter's wife in, though they had no understanding with her, so that it might sound the more natural that two should relieve those who would be asked to retire. He proposed that Zweigler should go in advance of himself, so that he might have a word with Amelie which Zweigler would not hear.

Zweigler, making little reply, went on to the farther room. He looked on a peaceful scene, for its three occupants slept.

Zweigler's keen glace swept the three; decided that their slumbers were of a genuine kind; recalled a plan which he had previously discarded; saw a risk and a chance; and resolved instantly to test the opportunity which had come in so unexpected a manner.

He stepped quickly and quietly to where Reske sprawled in the case of his pneumatic chair; slipped his hand along its yielding surface; secured the bunch of keys which hung from Reske's belt, and from which he did not part either by night or day; and detached two of them with a smooth manipulation which a professional pickpocket might have regarded with awe.

Almost in the same moment, he was at the side of the sleeping woman, and his hand was on her shoulder.

"Frau Richter," he said, "would you not sleep more comfortably in your own room?"

When Reske waked in the next minute, at the sound of conversation around him, the woman was on her feet, and Seeley was entering the room. He had no reason to think that Frau Richter had slept, or to suspect the solitary chance that Zweigler had had. That he should count the keys on his belt was an improbability hardly deserving thought, though Zweigler had his course prepared for that, or even if he should have been disturbed in the act of theft.

Reske, looking somewhat shamefaced at having been found in that unconscious condition, and not yet completely awake, retired from the scene, doubtless to seek the solitude of his own apartment;

and he had scarcely gone when Zweigler said: "If you are resolved to watch, there can be little reason for me to stay. We are all needing our share of rest, but, if you do not see me before Herr Schmidt's return, you may be sure that I shall be ready for what he may then require to be done."

Seeley said: "You must do as you think best." He had no desire for Zweigler's company, nor had he any authority to control his movements, but he was vaguely uneasy, with a return of the old feeling that events were not moving in a natural way. Why should Zweigler have come at all if he did not intend to remain? Well, as to that, his explanation might be genuine that he would have done his share, but saw no need for a double watch. Or he might have come with no other purpose than to draw Reske away, that he might plot with him. Against that, there was the fact that two men were reputed to be unfriendly to each other.

It was most surprising of all that any of these men should be willing to leave him alone with Richter. Might not Richter, in his altered personality, be willing to disclose the formula of the war weapon which he was to place, in a week's time, in his country's hands? Or, potentially even more important, the antidote by which it could be made of no effect?

It seemed explicable only on the assumption that it was not intended that he should return to his own land. If his death were planned, as soon as his use for these short hours should be done, they might consider that there could be little importance in what he might learn. He felt as one who descends in darkness by steps which may have fallen away. It was inevitable that he should go on and down, but each time his foot might reach out to a firm stair or a headlong fall.

Reske went to his own bedroom, where he relaxed, with a mind at ease. He was still watchful of his keys, because a habit of years is not lost in an hour, and particularly not so when weariness has made action mechanical to its maximum possibility. But, even in regard to those keys, his feeling was one of relaxation, their deadly importance having ceased during recent hours. He undressed. He took the bath of regulated steam which it was his habit to do. He drank the refreshing draught which his dietetic physician had prescribed. He sank into the comfort of his pneumatic mattress with the keys reattached to the belt he wore, and with the consciousness that his door was secured in an effectual manner. He had not noticed that the eleven keys had become nine.

Half an hour later, Zweigler came along the passage and passed his door. He paused at the next one and inserted one of the keys into its lock. Here was his risk, though it was not much. If Reske should be on the other side of the door, he would have a difficult explanation to make.

But he entered an empty room, which he crossed, and unlocked a door on its farther side, where he must repeat his hazard.

The second room he entered was also empty. It was twice the size of the one through which he had come, lying behind both that one and the one in which Reske slept; and it had another door opening into that room, which was standing wide, so that Zweigler, looking cautiously in, had a sight of the sleeping man.

Along one side of the larger room were two great switchboards, for this was the control room both for the lighting, and the electric power, the disposition of which had made the house a fortress into which none could penetrate without guidance at less than a deadly risk.

With the second key Zweigler unlocked the smaller switchboard. He drew on rubber gloves, not being one who took avoidable risks, though he supposed that all current had been cut off. He manipulated wires. He worked quietly and swiftly, stopping twice to make pencilled calculations which he wiped from the surface of his pocket-tablet as soon as their use was done.

He closed the switchboard and locked it again. He paused in a natural hesitation. Having succeeded so far, should he risk all for a refinement of perfection, such as few would attempt? It may be called folly, but it was a point on which his training in scientific exactness prevailed. He entered the room in which Reske slept, and there, his long, supple fingers moving with a silent adroitness which gave no warning to the unconscious man, he put back the keys.

XXXVII. Amelie Is Not Sure

HERR RICHTER, BRIEFLY roused by the movements and voices around him, had dozed again.

Seeley, watching him, was vexed by doubt as to what it would be wiser to do. Beyond all probability, almost beyond belief, he had come to this solitary vigil with the man whom it had appeared futile to attempt to reach, and that man had been so changed that he might be docile to answer anything which might be asked, even though no intimidation should be employed. And now he hesitated as to whether he should take advantage of the incredible chance!

Yet he did hesitate. There was one thing he could not control. If Richter should be docile to answer him, he might be equally pliable to tell Herr Schmidt what he had done. And the consequences might be hard to guess with exactness, but it was a reasonable assumption that they would not be pleasant for the Interfederal Secretary of the English-Speaking Commonwealth. Should he hesitate for that? Surely not, but for— But for two things. There was Amelie. He knew that he ought not to consider her beside the larger issues on which the fate of the world might hang. And there was the fact that Silver Long had announced that there was a new weapon in his Federation's hand, and had given him a plain hint to return. There was surely more weight in that.

And there were two other cognate matters to be observed. The more important one was the larger threat to humanity to which Richter had confessed, and on which Seeley had agreed that he would cooperate against him. The second, arising out of the first, was that it raised a grave doubt as to whether Herr Richter's intended weapon would ever be put into operation, and whether, if it were not, Seeley might not make his presence instrumental to the cause of peace, as he would be less likely to be able to do if he should have incurred the antagonism of the European Government by filching the weapon which they had threatened to use.

Weighing all these considerations, he saw reluctantly that silence would be the course of prudence, though, when the tale should be told—to an end which it was still futile to guess—it would be likely to hold little honour for him. The wisdom of what he did might be clear to his own mind, but he saw that it must have the aspect of a man who was not equal to the occasion to which he came.

And while he considered thus, half despising himself for deciding on that which was at once hardest and wisest to do, Zweigler, now returned to his own room, was using the radio connections at his disposal to ascertain that Herr Schmidt's return would not be delayed, which it had become essential for him to know.

Having done that, he had a satisfied mind. Chance had enabled him to short-circuit and simplify elaborate plans, as he could not have anticipated that he would be able to do. It would be four hours before Herr Schmidt could arrive. He decided that he would rest for that time, preparing for a day which he saw would be decisive for his own future, but which he had now ceased to doubt that he could control to his own advantage.

It was still dark when Herr Schmidt returned to a house where few waked but those of the household staff and his own police, whose duty it was to remain alert during the night. But he came himself with no sign of fatigue, and in a mood to make quick disposal of the two matters which the president had had the wisdom to place in the hands of the one man competent to bring them to a good conclusion.

Following his usual practice, he interviewed separately each of those on whom he relied, taking those of less importance first, and giving to each the impression that he trusted him in a special way and expected him to be watchful of other necessary but less dependable men.

Having had the reports of his own police, which were of a negative kind, he saw Reske and Zweigler in their own rooms, the latter interview being the longer, and then Seeley and Amelie together, while Richter, now risen and more nearly of his normal demeanour, dressed in the adjoining room.

By the time that Herr Schmidt arrived at this last interview he had become a very thoughtful man. If all that he had heard were to be believed, there were more complications than he had anticipated, and the president's offer which he had been instructed to communicate to Lord Whitcombe was not likely to be performed. If it were not— But he gave no sign of his thoughts in the formal official courtesy with which he greeted Seeley, or in his subsequent words.

"All," he asked, "will have gone quietly while I have been away?"

"Yes. I think we have all taken what rest we could. Herr Richter has slept, or has appeared to do so, most of the time, so far as my own observation has gone."

"Which has been most of the time?"

"Except during the earlier portion when Reske and Frau Richter were with him."

"And Zweigler?"

"Zweigler came, but did not stay. He said that more than one was not required, and—though I did not say this—I was not satisfied of the wisdom of leaving them alone together."

"It was on your discretion that I relied. We will hear what Richter has to say now. But I have a message from the president which I may give you first, and which may be welcome to hear.

"He will facilitate your return to Havana, and further enquiry into the manner of Colonel Wagram's death is not considered a necessary prelude thereto. He only asks that you will wait upon him yourself, which can be arranged at an early hour, taking with you Miss Latour, in whom your interest is allowed, and the president will then give his own *visa* for her departure, by which all other formalities will be set aside."

Seeley heard this, and recognized that it had a fair sound, though he was too used to the language of diplomatic evasion to take it at more than its real worth. What he had been told was that neither Amelie or himself would be permitted to leave the country until the president had interviewed them.

"It will be an honour," he said, "which I should have been reluctant to miss. May I conclude that the prospect of peace improves?"

"It is a matter," Herr Schmidt replied, "on which you must not conclude that I know more than is public to all. But it is evident that it is one which your own Government can resolve in the right way."

It was at this moment that Herr Richter entered the room.

"I hope," he said with an amicable smile such as transformed his face from anything that Amelie had been accustomed to see, "that you have obtained our president's approval to the plans which I proposed?"

"If you mean," Herr Schmidt replied, "the one about scientists listening to you and then destroying themselves, I did not mention it, for two reasons: one being that it is a part of the matter which has already been entirely entrusted to me; and the other that I am convinced that your brother scientists would not consider it an acceptable plan."

"Perhaps if Zweigler and I were to offer—"

"It is a proposal with which Herr Zweigler told me, a few minutes ago, he would have nothing to do"

"But it would be for the safety of the whole world! Perhaps, if I should show him how great the peril would be if it should—"

"It would be waste of time. We must agree on a better way. But there is one question I would ask you first, concerning the records which you must have made during the years that you have had Stuttgart in your control."

"You mean you would ask to see them? But there are none have always avoided the written word."

"But—pardon me—in such work as yours—it is an incredible— I may say it is an impossible thing."

"But I have had the assistance of Miss Latour."

Herr Schmidt turned his eyes to Amelie. "You mean," he asked, "that your records have been in Miss Latour's care?"

"There are no written records. They are in Miss Latour's mind."

"Yes," Amelie replied to Herr Schmidt's questioning and sceptical eyes. "Herr Richter tells me, and I remember. I cannot forget."

Herr Schmidt considered the credibility of these statements, and their implications, if they were to be accepted as true. The fact that Amelie had broken with her employer made it less probable that she would be lying now. But if she were not—how much might she not have betrayed to Whitcombe already? Were the means of destruction which Richter had proposed to use against the enemies of Europe, and their antidote, already given away? And perhaps, beyond that, the more sinister powers with which he had proposed to make war on his own kind?

Perhaps, he thought, it would be best to first accept these statements as true, and probe what their consequences could be expected to be.

"Then," he said, "Miss Latour knows already all that we are asking you to explain to us?"

"Not at all. It has no meaning for her."

"I just remember," Amelie confirmed. "I couldn't possibly understand."

"But she might repeat to someone who could?"

"She could repeat to those who could understand much, but not all. There are matters I have retained. And there are arbitrary code signs which I am accustomed to use, which could have no meaning to them."

Herr Schmidt turned to Seeley. "Should you confirm that, Lord Whitcombe? Or do you find them easy to understand?"

Seeley controlled any resentment he may have felt at the implications this question held. "It is a matter," he said, "of which I know nothing. I was not aware that such information was in Miss Latour's possession in any form."

Herr Schmidt, having a shrewd though cynical mind, heard this without absolute disbelief, though to credit it was to reject the most obvious explanation of the attention which Lord Whitcombe paid to the girl.

"You could give me," he asked Herr Richter, "examples of this memorizing?" And, as he spoke, Herr Zweigler, and, shortly after him, Reske entered the room.

Herr Schmidt explained what had passed, and Herr Zweigler's eyes glittered as he heard. That was how he had half-believed and entirely hoped it would be. He looked at the glossy blackness of Amelie's head, with no æsthetic appreciation of what nature or art had done, but with a keen anticipatory lust of that which it must contain, and which he hoped would be spoil for him when he should be reading a pickled brain.

"That," Richter replied to the question which had been interrupted by Zweigler's entrance, "is easy to do. Amelie, will you repeat the formula MKZ, as I revised it a few weeks ago, for the fertilizing of certain Latvian lands? It can be checked in the laboratories, if Herr Zweigler will kindly undertake that trouble, for it has had no secrecy from those I trust in the department where it is made."

Amelie said: "Yes. I can give you that." She repeated a number of letters and figures, Latin words and abbreviations, which Herr Zweigler jotted on to his tablets with swift precision.

"There is no need to check that," he said, looking at it with critical and approving eyes. "It is clear that Miss Latour's memory is a marvellous thing."

There was a moment's pause, broken by Herr Richter, who, of the six that the room now held, had become, in his transformed personality, the one among them who was not actuated by a personal or separate aim, and whose sole desire was now to satisfy the wishes of those to whom he spoke. "Have you," he asked Herr Schmidt, "decided whether you wish me to disclose that which must be dangerous wherever it may be known, or to trust me that it shall not be used, on which you may entirely rely?"

Herr Schmidt answered in the tone of a man who had ceased to regard the question as of the importance which he had once attributed to it, or who had more urgent matters upon his mind: "The president does not doubt that we could trust you to do nothing to harm mankind. But will you tell me whether the formula which would have been used at this time for the destruction of the majority of mankind, or that which was to have that result after your own death—whether either or both of these are private to your own mind, or have been trusted to the memory of Miss Latour?"

"They have not," Herr Richter replied, "been entrusted in their entirety to Miss Latour, their supreme importance being too momentous for that, but there are some formulæ of processes which are intricate in themselves, and must be very exact, which, as a precaution against my own fallibility, I have entrusted to her. They would be without use, if not without meaning, to anyone who should lack other data which is exclusive to my own mind.

"And, though they would be of no use in themselves, I will tell you that I have become dependent upon them beyond what I had intended; for, as I have rested today, I have endeavoured to recall all that I should require to know, and I have been troubled to find how deficient my memory has become. I suppose that I have fallen into some degree of carelessness, having learnt that what is entrusted to Miss Latour is securely kept."

Herr Richter made this statement in the tone of one who has had no object beyond the exhibition of truth, and assumes that those who hear will accept it for what it is. But the eyes that regarded him were incredulous or puzzled on every side.

Zweigler was the first to give words to the difficulty which each had seen. "I don't know," he said bluntly, "what you can mean by that. You might have died any minute, and if you've arranged so that there's to be a following plague to kill us all off, you must have got everything fixed up now. You couldn't expect anyone to put it into action after you were dead, whether or not they understood what it was meant to do, even if they'd want to, which isn't sense. How could they, if some of it were in your mind, and some in Miss Latour's? You'll have to tell us something better than that."

"My dear Zweigler," Herr Richter replied, his placidity undisturbed by the offensive manner with which this was said, or the scepticism which it expressed, "of course I didn't mean that. The thing's in force now, as you might say. If I were to die tonight, there'd be millions dead by this time tomorrow, and the epidemic spreading faster than any plane could flee—or, at least as fast, for it would be sure to take it along.

"It's the antidote that I had in mind—the only means of destroying it that there is. Without that, if we should disturb it at all, we should only be disturbing that which we couldn't stop. What I was going to propose was that I should give you this antidote, and that it should be used in a way that I will direct, and that you should not ask me for more than that.

"It's the antidote that you want to use; not to publish that by which any man may destroy his kind."

"Perhaps," Herr Schmidt said, without committing himself to what further requests, if any, he might be thinking to make, "if Miss Latour will give us those parts entrusted to her, which Herr Zweigler can write down, we shall be getting ahead." He turned to the girl to ask: "I suppose there'll be no difficulty about that?"

"No," Amelie answered readily. "If Herr Richter will tell me what it is that he wants you to know."

"You had better," Herr Richter said, "give the KT formulæ."

The girl began, without any pause for recollection, to dictate a long and intricate formula, Herr Richter listening intently, and nodding, more than once in a satisfied way.

Herr Zweigler looked puzzled at first at what he heard and wrote, but, as it went on, a look of comprehending admiration came into his eyes, which Richter did not fail to observe.

"You are thinking," he said, as the dictation paused, "that the antidote gives you an indication of what the virus is. So it may; but it will still be useless to you. For there is one thing that it does not tell, and you will not guess."

Herr Schmidt took no notice of this remark. His eyes and thoughts were on Amelie. He looked as one who had a doubt where he must be sure. He asked her: "You could repeat that?"

"Yes, of course."

"Would you please do so?"

She went over the formula again, more rapidly than before, Herr Zweigler having no writing to do. But he followed closely, and when Herr Schmidt asked him: "Was it exact?" he replied: "Yes, precisely."

Herr Schmidt looked at Amelie. "I can see," he said, "that your memory is of an exceptional kind. Do you remember much in that way?"

"I have not finished," she said. "There is a second formula."

"You mean that would not be sufficient alone?"

Herr Richter explained: "The formula you have heard will delay the dissemination of the virus. It will bring it under temporary control. The second will be necessary for its destruction, without which it would be a continual menace."

"You can give Herr Zweigler the second formula, Miss Latour?"

"Yes, of course."

Herr Zweigler took up his tablets again, and Amelie recommenced dictation. For a minute or more she went on with her usual confidence, her voice taking on the drawling sound that was like the purr of an engine that ran smoothly within its power; but after that she hesitated, and a look of bewilderment, almost of fear, came to her eyes.

"I'm sorry," she said. "I'm not sure what comes— No; I can't remember at all."

XXXVIII. Zweigler Prefers a Full Net

TAKE IT QUIETLY," Herr Richter said. Don't try to hurry yourself. It will come back."

Amelie sat silent, conscious of the alert tension of her waiting audience. "It's no use," she said at last, in a despairing voice. "It's just gone."

"This never happened before?" Herr Schmidt asked.

"No, never. I've always remembered everything."

"It's a natural result of emotion," Herr Richter said—"of emotion and thought. I am afraid that Lord Whitcombe and I are about equally responsible." He spoke as one giving judgment upon others rather than himself. Perhaps his past self appeared to him in that way.

Herr Schmidt asked: "It is important?"

"It is essential. It is the latter part of this second formula of which I am most unsure."

"But it is your own work. What you have done once, you can do again?"

"So I should have to hope it would be. But research is not a path which can be left with certainty that it will be found for a second time. I have a more confident hope that Miss Latour's memory will return. She must be unworried and undisturbed."

"And if it could not be recovered?"

"It would be a disaster we must not anticipate. I must get back to the laboratory at once. What I have done it would be foolish to conclude that I could not do again."

Herr Schmidt looked at Herr Richter with speculative and suspecting eyes. Was he being fooled? It was hard to say. But he was inclined to think not. And there was a more urgent matter upon his mind. Still, this should not be ignored.

"I suppose," he said, "that it has become important that you should have all the help that the world provides. You may agree now that Betz and others should have full information, to enable their researches to be made on the same lines?"

"It is a matter," Seeley interpolated, "on which our own scientists will not decline to assist, if you will accept co-operation from them."

"It would involve," Herr Richter replied, "the disclosure of that which could not be sunk in oblivion again, and which I had hoped to destroy. But, if necessary, it must be done. Give me today; and tomorrow, if I am baffled, and Miss Latour's memory has not returned, we will talk of it again."

"Herr Zweigler," Schmidt asked abruptly, "what do you say to that?"

Zweigler had sat silent, with the look of one who has an alert but well-satisfied mind. In the last five minutes he had changed and simplified plans which had seemed simple enough before. To him there was no formula lost. He had no doubt that all he could wish to learn would be recorded both in the brains of Herr Richter and Miss Latour, and he was now resolved that they should be his to investigate beyond possibility of escape.

Herr Richter's position appeared strong today. Tomorrow, his own would be stronger far. It would be of an impregnable strength. He had meant to lead Herr Schmidt to a doom for which he could not be blamed—for which Reske's responsibility would be apparent to all. And, after that, he had thought that Richter and Amelie would be his in another way. But now, there was less to risk for a more absolute gain.

"I think," he said, "if you will all come to my room, I can show you a way by which this difficulty will be overcome."

Herr Schmidt looked surprised. When they had talked together, an hour before, in Herr Zweigler's room, there had been a proposal that he alone should return there to hear what Betz would have to say when the result of the examination should be communicated to him. But this was a different proposition. He asked: "All?"

"All, except Herr Reske. There will be no occasion for him to come."

Reske said: "But I think I will."

Zweigler made no answer to that. Did it matter, one way or other? He would find occasion to hold him back, and it would have the appearance of being the deliberate dallying of one who knew. He said: "As you like."

The six protagonists, who played this game for the fate of the human race, but of whom more than one were looking first for the advantage of their own hands, got up, and took their way through the vacant passages which led to Herr Zweigler's room.

They did not expect to meet anyone on the way. The household staff would use the service passages which ran parallel on the other side of the rooms—the sides from which the quiet, usually invisible service so efficiently, so unobtrusively, came.

Reske led the way, with Richter close at his side. Herr Schmidt, being a stranger to the house, was inclined, as was natural, to be led by them.

Amelie and Seeley were side by side, he endeavouring to console her with the expectation that that disconcerting hiatus of memory would return. "Tomorrow," he said, "when you wake, you may find that you will have no difficulty at all."

Her eyes thanked him, but the look of bewilderment and consternation returned. It was so strange a thing! It had never happened before. It had been as simple for her to remember as others found it to forget. And now, if the consequences should be— Herr Zweigler, slightly behind, called: "Herr Reske, there is some apparatus I may need to borrow from you."

Reske fell back, to learn what might be required. So they went on until they turned into the passage which led to Herr Zweigler's room, at which point Herr Schmidt paused, and called back.

"Herr Zweigler, will you guide us from here?"

"It is needless," Zweigler replied. "Herr Richter knows which it is."

Richter said: "Yes, of course," and would have moved on, but Schmidt laid a restraining hand on his arm. He said to Zweigler: "But you will have more than one room. We should prefer to be guided by you."

"It is the one which contains the transmission sets. The one in which you have been before."

"But you will not object to show us the way?"

Zweigler's uneasiness was not fully controlled as he gave an impatient answer: "There is no occasion at all. Herr Richter knows it as well as I."

They were all standing now in a little group at the entrance of the passage, Reske watching the exchange of invitation and excuse with a sneering enjoyment he did not attempt to hide, and the other three with no clue to what it might mean.

Herr Schmidt said, with the suavity of voice that he would use in his deadliest moods: "But there may be a reason which we both know. I shall ask you again, Herr Zweigler, to lead the way."

Zweigler had recovered his self-control with the certainty that there had been no discovery of his own design. They might suspect, he thought, but they could not know. He answered, with some astuteness, being cornered as he was: "There is some trap in this. There is no reason that you should press me thus."

"There may be a trap," Herr Schmidt allowed, "but it was not set by me. That you should have fallen back as you did, and now so strongly object, was the confirmation that I required."

"I know nothing of any trap. I objected to that which there was no occasion to do."

"When you took the keys from Herr Richter's bunch," Herr Schmidt asked, in his smoothly sneering tone, "will you tell us what good purpose you had?"

Zweigler saw that something was exactly known which it might be vain to deny. Yet deny he must, for what explanation could he invent that would have a plausible sound?

"I have no keys," he replied. "Nor do I know what you mean."

"When I saw Herr Reske before I came to your room he told me that he had been disturbed in his sleep, and had heard someone moving in the control room beyond, into which no one could enter except by his private key. He went quietly to the door and saw you manipulating the controls. He then returned to his chair and feigned to be still asleep to see what you would do. He felt you return the keys to his bunch, which you must have taken, as he supposes, a few minutes before; though, if you did that, the puzzle of how you entered his room is not explained.

"When you had gone he found that you had liberated current for the protection of your own room, so that it would commence to operate at this hour.

"When I left him, I saw you, and was invited to visit your room at about this time, with a purpose (if I had heard the truth) which I could not mistake.

"You had calculated, we must suppose, that Herr Reske's responsibility would appear to be beyond doubt, and that even he would not suspect that the deaths which would occur would have been occasioned by you.

"He would have had no explanation, and no defence, and the fact that he would have hung back, and escaped, as you were contriving would have been taken as proof of his knowledge, which would have been more difficult to believe had he perished, and you been the only one to survive."

"It is a most interesting invention," Herr Zweigler replied, "but there is no truth in it at all."

"Then we will not discuss it further. Will you be good enough, I Herr Zweigler, to lead the way?"

"Is it likely, after what you have said?"

"Which you have told me is untrue."

"But it may be true that Reske has charged the door."

"You knew that that could be done?"

"It is true of every door in this house, and is known to all. They can be electrified so that, if they be opened from the outside only, a fatal current will pass through all who may be standing on the outer stones, for a distance of several yards. The installations were made by Herr Reske, at Herr Richter's orders. They were for our protection during the night. Is it likely that I should so charge my own door when I am on the outer side?"

"You have told me that you did not. And I therefore ask you to lead the way."

"But you have told me that someone did."

"But do you assume that it has been left in that dangerous condition?"

"Do you assure me that it has not?"

"You have said that it was not done by you, and, if that be true, you will find that you are safe now."

Herr Zweigler found no satisfaction in the wording of this assurance. He made no motion to advance, until Herr Schmidt drew an automatic, and said: "You are in a doubt which is easy to understand, but you are a scientist, to whom knowledge is very dear. If you do not go ahead you will never know. Besides that, I will shoot you within two minutes from now, as one who has owned his guilt."

"You would do me a great wrong."

"I suppose not." The cynical amusement in Herr Schmidt's eyes changed to a sudden venomous anger, as he added: "You thought to plunder my brain when you had killed me there. Do you suppose I shall pardon that?"

"I had no such thought. I have never had," Zweigler protested, and so powerful this truth that, for the first time his tone had a convincing quality, which shook the certainty of more than one of the silent auditors who had not previously doubted his guilt.

For it was a fact that it had not crossed his mind that the brain of Herr Schmidt, stored with half the political secrets of Europe, and more than half its political crimes during the last thirty years, would be of any value to him.

It was a point of view which was not likely to occur to the Chief of the High Police, nor which would have pleased him to understand.

"Well," he said, with a recurrence of his earlier, almost bantering, style, "it is for you to choose. It is between certainty and a chance."

It appeared that Herr Zweigler regarded it in the same way. He saw Schmidt raising his pistol. He knew that the two minutes must be nearly over. He said: "I will not believe that you would commit such a crime against one who has been working with you." He showed courage of a kind, even under that compulsion, as he walked slowly forward. He paused in a natural terror as he came to the dividing line beyond which he knew that he might stand upon an invisible, dreadful death which would operate the instant that he should attempt to open the door.

But at Herr Schmidt's sharp: "There are three seconds left," he stepped forward and laid his hand on the knob.

XXXIX. WE MAY GUESS, BUT WE DO NOT KNOW

"I CAN SEE that you are a wise man," Herr Schmidt said, as he followed Zweigler through the open door. "Had you made the wrong choice you would be a dead one by now. But you will be wiser still if you can persuade me to keep you alive for another hour."

Herr Zweigler felt the relief of one who had survived a great fear. He was confident in his reply: "You are under a great mistake, which must be your excuse for that which would otherwise be most hard to forgive. But you will not forget that I have done so much for you that you may say I have saved the world; nor that you have promised me a reward which I am sure that neither you nor the president will be reluctant to pay."

"Oh, we shall pay! You need have no doubt about that," Herr Schmidt answered, in a voice which Zweigler did not find it pleasant to hear. "But as yet I am in doubt of how great the debt is likely to be. You brought us here because you can show a way by which the present difficulty may be overcome. You will tell us now what it is?"

The sudden question brought a blank look of enquiry to Zweigler's face, which changed to an instant of confusion as her realized how he had trapped himself. In a moment it was gone, and he had recovered an appearance of confidence and self-control, but it had been enough to condemn him in Herr Schmidt's eyes beyond hope of excuse or mercy.

The fact was that, when he had said that he could offer a means of overcoming the danger arising from Amelie's loss of memory if they would follow him to his room, it had been no more than a baseless pretext to induce them to come. As he had not intended that they should enter the room alive, he had seen no occasion for invention to go further than that, and the sudden question found him utterly unprepared.

Next moment he said: "It is with Herr Betz that I would speak, which I can do only from here," but it was a moment too late.

"That," Herr Schmidt replied, without further indication of what he thought, "is what I was proposing to do. Miss Latour, will you be good enough to make the contacts that I shall require?"

Amelie made no objection to that. She crossed the room to the radio studs and switches. It was work at which she was skilled, and which required considerable knowledge and exactness of touch, under the conditions of radio transmission that then prevailed. But Herr Schmidt's directions were clear, and it was not more than two minutes before the connection was established on the isolated wavelength that Betz was permitted to use, and, as she switched on the amplifier, his voice sounded into the room.

"Herr Zweigler," Herr Schmidt said smoothly, "is accustomed to talk to you. He shall do so now. He shall tell you all that has occurred."

So Zweigler did, any omissions he would have made giving way to the promptings of Herr Schmidt, who intended that the whole tale should be told. It even included an account of the apparatus for the exploration of living brains, and of the purpose for which Mr. Bulldozer had been invited. It included, under Herr Schmidt's prompting, an account of the inoculation which had made so radical a change in the character of Herr Richter; but the transformation had been so complete that its victim heard without resentment appearing, even for that outrage upon his identity.

When the whole tale was told, Herr Schmidt spoke: "I believe, Herr Betz, that you have had very useful information from Herr Zweigler for a considerable time, and that there has been talk of his transferring his services to your Frankfort laboratories. Should you still welcome him, if I should send him alone?"

"*Ja*," answered the guttural voice of the Frankfort scientist, "he would be most useful to me."

"Then he shall come. And as to these other matters of which you have heard, I shall give Herr Richter the day for which he asks, after which, if he should not have overcome his difficulty, there shall be full disclosure and consultation with you."

There was a moment's silence, which may have expressed Herr Betz's disappointment at the delay; but after that he only said: "That will be a most wise step. I will expect to hear from you again," and the conversation ceased.

Herr Schmidt said to Amelie: "Will you call the house service, to inform Major Gratz that I require his presence, with two attendants.

Zweigler's uneasiness was evident. He said. "The promised reward included control of the laboratories here. I may have asked to join Herr Betz, but that is no longer what I desire."

"The fact is," Herr Schmidt replied smoothly, "that you are so clever a man that I would prefer to have you some distance away. But you can be sure that you will be put to a full use."

The next moment Major Gratz, with his two men, entered the room. They were all in plain clothes, as was usual with the High Police, but their official aspect was easy to see.

Zweigler turned his gaze towards them, as Schmidt had anticipated that he would do. His glance was doubtful and apprehensive, for he had a disquieting guess that they had been summoned to set him on his way to Frankfort, for which he had no present desire. He must wait to see if this guess were right, after which he had an idea of how he might delay the proceeding until he could put it entirely aside. But his plan is of no importance, as it did not mature. Herr

Schmidt took advantage of that moment during which his eyes turned to the door. He struck him with his automatic on the back of the head. It was a blow from an expert hand, and Zweigler sank to the ground in a slack way, as though his backbone had been removed.

Herr Schmidt bent over him. He took his tablets, which he handed to Richter. "These," he said, "will be useful to you, particularly if Miss Latour's memory should have a further collapse.

"Gratz," he went on, "deliver this man to Frankfort to Herr Betz himself, but keep him unconscious until he is out of your hands, whether by violence or drugs, for if he have the use of his wits he is a most dangerous pest."

He turned to Reske to say: "Will you undertake to dismantle the apparatus by which the electric currents this house are generated and controlled? I would have it done at once, for it is productive of dangers I do not like. My own police will guard the house, and all who may remain here, till further arrangements be made.

"Herr Richter, you will have till tomorrow noon, without disturbance from us, to put right the evil that you have attempted to do. For that time Miss Latour will remain with you. If you should not require her aid after that, she may come with Lord Whitcombe to meet our president in Berlin, as has been already proposed.

"Lord Whitcombe, you will wish to remain here in the meantime? Then you will understand that the radio service is for your use as you will. I mention this because a message has been held up owing to a reasonable doubt of whether it had been issued by you."

He gave one more instruction: that the apparatus which Zweigler had constructed with such ingenuity for the exploration of the brains of his fellow men should be transported to Frankfort: "For it should not," he said, "be separated from him to whom its existence is due."

We may suppose that it was of interest to Herr Betz, and that Zweigler saw it again, but whether he was destined to use it upon the brains of others or to contribute his own, is a matter on which we may make a guess, but we do not know.

XL. But Should We Call It a War?

"SO YOU," THE president said, "are Miss Latour? When I see you, I understand that by which I was puzzled before."

It was neatly said, and had a sound of sincerity which may have been there. Looking at Amelie, that was easy to think.

She found it pleasant to hear, though she knew by the president's reputation that he would have sent her to death in the same suave and complimentary manner.

Seeley said: "Miss Latour has done me the honour to promise to come back with me, subject to your consent, which I have some confidence that you will not refuse."

He spoke in an atmosphere which gave some reason for the confidence which he expressed, for the major troubles which had threatened the world through the cunning perversities of Richter's genius had been put aside. Amelie's memory had returned after a night of uninterrupted rest, sufficiently to supply the data which Richter required; and he had been allowed to neutralize his previous sinister activities in his own way, as he should be the most competent, and, in his altered character, he could be trusted to do.

The question on which the future of civilization must still so largely depend—the question of peace or war—remained open, but Seeley was not without expectation that the president would be prepared to seek conditions of peace, to which he would not be slow to respond. It was an expectation which the president's next words did not reduce.

"I believe," he said, "that you were one of those whose policy would have avoided the brink of war on which we now stand."

Seeley, well aware of the subtlety of the man he met, was cautious in the wording of his reply: "I am always averse to war, for I believe that we must either abolish it, or it will destroy mankind."

"But it was to avert that danger that we agreed upon the system of limited war with which we are now faced."

"I have always been sceptical of the possibility of limited war. As you have decided to test its results, I must suppose it to be a point on which our opinions do not agree."

"Yet total war is no more than an invention of modern days. Before then, there were many wars into which nations put much less than their full strength, and which large numbers of their populations regarded as of little interest to themselves."

"There is the point. They were total wars to those whom they directly concerned, and who fought them with all the force that they could rally to their own aims."

"Holding these views, you will be glad if the present conflict can be composed?"

"You will agree that it has not been started by us. I will gladly listen to anything you propose."

"Not started, perhaps. But provoked would be a word less easy to set aside. Had we met earlier, I suppose that we should have maintained peace. As we are together now, we may discuss the possibilities which remain at a late hour."

The president said this in his friendliest manner, and Seeley replied in a similar tone, but with the reserve which he felt the occasion required: "I shall be glad to give most careful attention to what you say."

"I will say this. You have a potent weapon with which to annoy us when your turn should come. We have, as we think, one which will be more than you can endure, and which we shall use first, so that the question of what might follow would not arise. But I will allow that the thought of what you would have in reserve for us might incline you to endure much. They are both things to avoid, if we can do so without loss of honour, or more tangible things."

"I should not say that annoy is an adequate word. It would make shapeless ruins of every city, except Paris, from Amsterdam to Baku."

"We might find a defence which would render it harmless to us."

"Well, if it be a risk that you care to take!"

"I have said that peace will be better for both. If you can propose that which will be fair on both sides—"

"Your Excellency, you will have given thought to this matter, such as, during the last two days, I have had little leisure to do. You will doubtless have a proposal to make."

The president laughed in his most genial manner. "Lord Whitcombe," he said, "I have been told that you are an astute man, but less than justice has been done to the abilities that you have. That you are here at all—! But we will not go into that. I will offer this, which it will be to the world's advantage—which must include ours—for your Government to accept: we will withdraw the ultimatum which you have had, and consent to the increase in the temperature of the Antarctic Sea, if you will give us assurance that, if it should bring disaster to us, there shall be compensation in some equitable form, concerning which, if we should not agree, Mendoza shall arbitrate—and you may admit that he is not unfriendly to you.

"I will go beyond that, and accept the Asian settlement which you have desired, and to which we had not agreed, so that there may be no outstanding cause of dispute, and we may arrive at a basis of lasting peace."

"It is an offer," Seeley replied, "with which I shall be pleased to return, and which will have my support."

"Then it is one with which you may return, if you will, in the next hour; and with the satisfaction that you have brought an end to this war, besides that which you may derive from the companion whom you will take."

"They are satisfactions which it will be pleasant to have, and for both of which I must thank your consent, though it may be too much to say that I have brought an end to a war that has not begun."

"That has not begun?" the president exclaimed, with his disarming laugh. "Then should we say that Colonel Wagram's death had a peaceful cause?"

"It is an incident concerning which I must express my regret."

"It is a matter of no account amidst larger affairs. And the death of one man is not much for a modern war."

Seeley felt that he must agree upon that; and even if the total should be increased by a hundred per cent (for Zweigler's fate intrigued his mind with a great doubt), he felt that it was still low.

He parted from the president with the formalities that the occasion required, and with a mutual cordiality that may have been almost sincere.

At the last, the president turned to Amelie to say: "They are terms of peace by which, if they be agreed, we shall be losers by much more than our seals will show," being such a compliment as most women are pleased to have, without thought of whether it be more than a mere flourish of words.

But they were all in moods in which pleasure is lightly given or felt, the two men being aware that the shadow was near to lift which had threatened to wreck the civilization of which they were, and the girl with the prospect of a new life, which might be of no greater luxury than she had been accustomed to have, but would be fuller and freer than, even a week before, would have seemed more than a hopeless dream.

It was still true that the shadow remained, though it had lifted and moved somewhat away. It might be too much to hope that men would permanently withhold their news from using for their own destruction the physical forces which they had learnt to control; or that they would abandon the old attractive habit of war for the wisdom of Christian ways. But to ask now that would be is to ask no less than the final issue (if such there will ever be) of the war between evil and good—the long war that is always fought without being lost or won, the end of which may be forever hidden from mortal eyes.

* * * * * *

They did not return to Havana by the plebeian means of an airliner lumbering along at less than four hundred miles an hour, as Mr. Bulldozer had done, but with the lean speed of the president's private plane, which shot like a silver pencil across the clouds. They looked down on that shining pavement of cloud, and up to the cold vault of the moonlit sky, and they understood that there is not weakness, but quiet strength, in the long patience of God.

www.ingramcontent.com/pod-product-compliance
Lightning Source LLC
Chambersburg PA
CBHW050746250626
47155CB00005B/1943